MR. FIANCÉ

LAUREN LANDISH

Edited by
VALORIE CLIFTON

MR. FIANCÉ

BY LAUREN LANDISH

It's fake, but it feels so good.

Oliver Steele is supposed to be my knight in shining armor. He's tall, handsome, and as cocky as he is rich. With his good looks and charm, no one's going to suspect a thing. No one's going to believe our engagement is fake.

But he's taking this thing way too far. The way he wraps his arm around me like I'm his. The way he kisses me and presses his hard body up against mine. I almost believe that it's real. Almost.

He's doing it on purpose now, he loves that this is getting to me.

Two can play his game, I won't let him win. By the time our week together is done, I'll leave Oliver on his knees and begging.

But the minute we're alone in the bedroom, I know I'm in over way my head. When he undresses me with his eyes, I realize I lost before the game even started. It's only a matter of time before I lose myself in his touch and let him do whatever he wants to me.

I know what I want, but I can't tell what's real anymore

Want the FREE Extended Epilogue? Sign up to my mailing list to receive it as soon as it's ready. If you're already on my list, you'll get this automatically!

Irresistible Bachelor Series (Interconnecting standalones):
Anaconda || Mr. Fiance || Heartstopper
Stud Muffin || Mr. Fixit || Matchmaker
Motorhead || Baby Daddy

CHAPTER 1

MINDY

"Can we get some service over here?" yells a woman who's seated at one of the tables in the packed coffee house. "You girls are moving slow as molasses!"

I slap the lids down on a couple of cups and place them in a cup holder before taking them over to the counter. I pause for a moment to dab the sweat from my brow with my apron, sighing. My feet ache from running back and forth during the early morning rush and I need a damn break.

Jesus, I tell myself as I force a fraudulent smile on my face. This is the worst morning ever. It's a blistering hot day in July. The A/C's shoddy, it's like 100 degrees outside, and it feels like I'm working in the fiery pits of hell. And to make matters worse, it's a packed house and I'm running behind. I don't know how much more of this madness I can take.

"We'll be right with you, ma'am!" I call out, flashing her an easy smile and a playful wink that hides my irritation. I ring up the order for a man standing at the front of the line and then send him on his way with his two iced coffees. He's immediately replaced by another man, who spits out his order so fast I almost feel dizzy, barely catching it all. "We're just running a little behind schedule this morning."

"Bullshit!" the woman snaps, glowering at the line of people in front of me. She's a well-kept, middle-aged blonde with an immaculate short hairdo, garbed in fur-trimmed designer clothes that go along with her snobby attitude. "There's three of you back there, yet I've been waiting for over ten minutes for my frap." She shakes her head, practically frothing at the mouth. "It's ridiculous!"

A lump of anger forms in my throat. I quickly swallow it back, glancing to the sky. *Dear God, give me the strength!*

I grit my teeth, my eyes cutting off to the side where the equipment is. I see Cassie, one of my employees, taking her sweet ass time blending something. She's acting like we don't have customers piling up out the ass. Throwing her long, brown hair back, she takes in a deep yawn as if she's tired from working *so* hard. If she weren't new, I'd chew her out.

I shake my head.

At least she looks nice enough in our new uniform, a blue skirt that shows a lot of leg, with a white V-necked T-shirt with *Beangal's Den* printed over the chest. But looking cute and pretty doesn't mean shit to me if you're not getting work done.

Sighing, I look around for Sarah, my other employee, but she's nowhere to be seen.

Figures, I say to myself. *One disappears on me, and the other is moving slower than a snail. Why did I want to be the manager of this place again?*

"Ma'am," I say as politely as I can manage, turning my eyes back on her. I signal to the waiting customer that I'll be with him in a moment. "I understand your frustration with having to wait, but there's no need for that language. There are kids in here." I pause and add, "However, I promise that once you try our world-famous Tiger Caramel Frappuccino, you'll forget *all* about the wait. It's just *that* good." I flash her another smile and a wink, hoping to defuse the situation.

"Ha! We'll see! But if your service weren't so damn bad, we wouldn't have a problem," the woman hotly retorts, ignoring my peace-making attempt and looking as if she's ready for a fight.

I clench my hands, biting back a sharp response that instantly forms on my lips. Usually, I can handle even the most disgruntled customer with my charm, but this one seems immune to it. And she's testing my patience.

Taking a deep breath, I draw myself up, then speak in calm, even tones. "Ma'am, if you can't watch your language, I'm going to have to kindly ask that you leave."

Steeling myself, I wait for her to challenge me. But surprisingly, she just grumbles, muttering something nasty under her breath as she looks away.

I sigh in relief. I was half-expecting to have to call hotel security to deal with this one.

For the next five minutes, I go back to frantically taking and filling orders. I have to stop three times to tell Cassie to pick up the pace. It does little good. If anything, she moves slower, like she's silently protesting having to work hard.

Dammit. I just don't have the time to get on Cassie's ass right now. It wouldn't be so bad if Sarah weren't MIA.

It just so happens that as soon as the rush of customers is gone, Sarah reappears from the back.

"Where on earth have you been?" I gasp, setting down a tray I've brought over from an empty table on the counter. "We've been slammed out here! I'm doing three people's jobs!"

The twenty-year-old short brunette with dimples *normally* has a penchant for being overzealous about her job. She shakes her head as her eyes fall on Cassie. "I bet. She was probably up all night screwing Brad's brains out." I hold in a groan. Sarah loves to get digs in against Cassie whenever she can. I ignore responding to the bait as Sarah looks back to me. "I'm sorry, Mindy. I was just having a little trouble back there."

I frown with confusion. "What kind of trouble?"

Sarah tilts her head to the side, biting her lower lip. "Well, uh, my tampon—"

"TMI!" I say, cutting her off and looking around fearfully, hoping no one heard what she just said. "Jesus, Sarah," I hiss quietly, "what are you trying to do, scare our customers away?"

Sarah blushes, her cheeks turning a rosy red. "Sorry!"

I shake my head, gently grabbing her by the shoulders and guiding her toward the dining area. "Never mind that. I need your help.

There's like five tables that need to be cleaned off and wiped down, and I need a few supplies from the back."

Sarah nods dutifully, wiping her hands on her apron and making her way over to the messy tables. "On it, Boss!"

I sigh and shake my head as I watch her nearly run into a customer on her way. A pulsing ache runs down my side as I lean against the counter for support. I really don't know how I'm going to get through the rest of the day. The stress of running this place is getting to me lately. In fact, ever since I became the operating manager of Beangal's Den, I've been overworked and tired. Sure, I'm making more money than I ever have, but I'm beginning to wonder if it's even worth it.

I work so much now that I have no social life. The vibrant small-town girl who wouldn't hesitate to give a wild bull a run for his money has been replaced by an old maid. In fact, I can't even remember the last time I've been with a guy and let him do the . . .

A buzz at my side and a Taylor Swift ringtone of *We Are Never, Ever Getting Back Together* interrupt my thoughts. Grumbling, I pull my cell out of my pocket and glance around the cafe to make sure things aren't getting back out of hand before I answer it.

"Hello?"

"Mindy, my dear!" my mother's voice greets me in a singsong tone.

I hold in a groan. I love my mom dearly, but she's the last one I want to hear from right now. She always gives me a headache with her constant picking. "Mother," I reply cordially.

"My God, Mindy," she complains with a sniff, "we haven't talked in weeks. Can you sound any unhappier to hear from me?"

I knew I shouldn't have answered.

I try my best to keep my tone even. "Sorry, Mom. I'm just working right now. Can I call you back after my shift?"

"No," she replies flatly. "This is important."

I try not to sigh out loud. "Okay, Mom. You have two minutes before—"

A piercing shriek interrupts my words and I jump in surprise. I turn around to see Cassie wiping coffee off her chest at the counter. Luckily, she'd only gotten it on herself and not a customer. I swear, I don't know what I'm going to do with this chick.

"What the hell was that?" my mom demands on the other end of the line.

I pull away from the counter, shaking my head. Then I walk around, grab a towel from a shelf, and hand it over to Cassie. "Nothing," I reply. "Just the background noise of the cafe."

"It sounded like a dying cat."

Can't argue with that.

"There was something important you wanted to tell me," I remind her, getting back on point.

"I'm getting married next week," my mom announces, dropping the bomb on me without warning.

My jaw drops and my heart skips a beat at her words. While I've been expecting this, it still feels like a shock. After the heartbreak of Dad's sudden death during my senior year of high school, Mom swore on her grandmother's grave that she'd never marry again . . . until she met John Wentworth, a multi-millionaire businessman.

Unfortunately, I've heard more about John's status than anything else about him. During their courtship, it was almost all she talked about.

John has this, and John has that. John bought me this and John bought me that. And one of my favorites, 'Do I need to remind you how much John is worth?' It's a line she likes to pull out whenever I dare question the dynamics of her relationship. I swear, I think the only reason she's doing this is because he's loaded.

Still, despite my misgivings on the authenticity of their relationship, now is not the time to voice my displeasure or doubts. This is her happy moment, and whether I like it or not, I need to be supportive.

"Mom, that's wonderful!" I say in the most joyful tone I can manage.

"Isn't it?" Mom says proudly. "It's going to be absolutely gorgeous. He's already rented out the venue too. A grand ballroom that sits on the shore with breathtaking views of the ocean."

"Gee, Mom, that sounds great. I'm so happy for you!"

There's a short pause and my mother's voice drops a few octaves. "And I want you to come."

I pause, glancing around the busy cafe. Cassie's finally gotten most of the coffee off her shirt, although there is a giant stain on it, and is taking a man's order. Meanwhile, Sarah's busting her ass, bringing the sitting patrons their fraps. She's looking pretty worn-out herself.

"Mom . . . I don't know," I say slowly, not wanting to upset her. "This is a little out of the blue. With my work schedule and all, I don't know if . . ."

I hear her sharp intake of breath. "Are you kidding me right now, Mindy Isabella Price? I'm your mother, the most important person in your life and the one who gave birth to—"

"You're right!" I say quickly. If I don't head that off, I'll be here until next week listening to her tell me how she was in labor with me for thirty-seven hours and that I owe her the universe. "I don't know what I was thinking. Of course I'll be there."

"You need to take at least a week off," Mom adds.

"A week—" I began to protest. Dear God, with Cassie and Sarah running things? They'll burn the place down.

"Yes, a week! Everyone's going to be there. Your sister, your cousin, and your aunt. Your grandmother."

I open my mouth to argue but then shut it with a snap. It's a fool's errand. My mother has a head harder than granite sometimes. Shaking my head, I bite my lower lip, thinking. *Damn, she drives a hard bargain.*

But the more I think about taking a week off, the more I begin to like the idea. I haven't seen my little sister, Roxy, in forever. Same for my cousin Layla, Aunt Rita, and Grandma Ivy Jo. It sure would be nice to take a break from this mess to relax and chill with the fam.

"I can do that," I say finally, feeling more at ease. "It'll be so good to see you and the family again."

Heaven help Cassie and Sarah.

"It sure will," Mom agrees. "Roxy has been asking about you non-stop."

A grin plays across my lips as I think about my younger sister. At twenty-one, Roxy's young, dumb, and full of fun. Basically, an even more smartassed and sassier version of myself.

But my Mom's next words take me out of my reverie and hit me like a lightning bolt. "And I expect you to bring your fiancé."

"My fiancé?" I ask with a croak when I can finally find my voice.

"Yes! You know, Harold. Tall. Handsome. Rich. Good in bed. The one you've been bragging to me about for the past year." She lets out a little laugh. "Roxy's been dying to meet him . . . and so have I."

Shit, shit, shit!

I pause, the phone pressed against my ear, my mind racing in panic.

That lie. I should've known it would come back to bite me in the ass. I'm not one for long-term relationships, and I got sick of Mom trying to set me up with some man back at home she wanted me to meet. Knowing her, probably a son of one of John's friends. I got tired of it, so I told her I was engaged to get her off my back.

Stupid me.

I suck in a deep breath, about to tell her the truth, but I stop. There's no way I can admit that I was lying for the past year and show up at her wedding without a man. Absolutely *no* way. By now, everyone in the family has heard about my fiancé, *Harold*, and mom is going to be overly dramatic if I fess up now. Besides, she's getting married. She doesn't need to hear that I lied.

"Mindy?"

"I—" I began to say, not knowing how I'm going to get out of this one. At that exact moment, Brianna Adams, my best friend and ex-partner in crime—and now part-owner of the Beangal's Den—walks through the door, her adorable little boy, Rafe, balanced expertly on her right hip.

Suddenly, I'm struck by an idea, my face lighting up like a light bulb. "Of course, Harold," I say cheerfully, regaining my composure. "He'll be coming. He's been wanting to meet you for forever!"

I can practically feel my Mom beaming through the phone. "Perfect! I'll be expecting you both. See you soon, love."

The line goes dead, and I'm quick to pocket my cell as I wave Brianna over to the counter. She's halfway there when the disgruntled woman from earlier jumps up from her seat. Apparently, she's finished with her drink and not satisfied in the least.

"You were wrong," she says loudly at me, brushing by Brianna to get to me. "It wasn't worth the wait. I've tasted far better, like the Unicorn Frappuccino they serve at the place on the other side of town." She shakes her head angrily and almost yells, "You guys suck. I'm never coming here again!" Cutting her eyes at me, she spins around and walks off, nearly running into Brianna on her way out.

Brianna's forehead crinkles into a frown as she reaches the counter. "Having a bad day, I take it?" She asks.

My chest fills with warmth as my eyes fall on my good friend. Dressed in a white and yellow flower dress that has a low V-cut with her long brown hair pulled into a lazy bun, she looks absolutely voluptuous. Shit, had I known pregnancy could do that, I would've gotten knocked up years ago.

"Besides the A/C not working and being overrun for over half the morning? Business as usual," I say dismissively. With my mind on my idea, the dissatisfied customer is already old news. "We were a little behind earlier."

"I feel sorry for you. Someone's been called about the A/C," Brianna says. She pauses and frowns again. "And what the hell's a Unicorn Frappuccino?"

I roll my eyes. "It's all the rage right now. What rock have you been hiding under?"

"Have you tried it?" Brianna asks curiously.

I shake my head. "Hell, no! I have a friend who did and she was shitting glitter and rainbows all week."

"Mindy!" Brianna protests.

I shake my head. "I'm serious! It's a real drink."

Brianna looks like she's about to argue and then thinks better of it, shaking her head. "I'll take your word for it."

"Good," I say, reaching across the counter to tug on Rafe's small hand. He giggles as I shake it. He's a spitting image of both his parents, with adorable baby blues and dirty-blonde hair. "How's my little man doing?"

Brianna smiles, her eyes lighting up as she looks at her baby boy.

"Good. He's talking even more now and can almost form a full sentence."

"That's awesome." I grin at Rafe and soften my tone into a voice as sweet as sugar. "Can you say a sentence for Aunt Mindy? Huh, Rafey?"

"Hungry!" Rafe says, reaching for his mom's left breast.

"Rafe stop it!" Brianna snaps, grabbing Rafe's little arm before he can pull her boob out in public, her cheeks turning red. "Sorry," she mutters. "He does that all the time."

I shake my head. I know I shouldn't, but I can't help myself. "Takes after his Daddy, and I don't blame him, Jersey Maid. You look like you can feed the village with those milk jugs."

"Mindy!"

"Girl, I'm serious. What are you, a triple-D now? If I ever run out of creamer, I know just the person to call."

"I'm gonna leave!" Brianna threatens.

I let out a laugh. "Oh my God, lighten up, will you? It was just a joke."

Brianna scowls. "Well, you're not funny."

"Yeah, I am." The grin on my face slowly fades as I remember my idea.

"So how's Gavin?" I ask, clearing my throat. Gavin, Brianna's husband, is almost just as good a friend as Brianna is to me. A former football star, he's settled down into small-town life with surprising ease. But I would think it would be hard not to with the beautiful ranch they moved into. "He enjoying fatherhood much?"

Brianna nods, a smile coming to her face. "Very much so. He can't wait until Rafe is old enough to go fishing with him. He talks about it every day."

"What about work?" I ask, leaning in with intense interest.

Brianna gazes at me for a moment. "Well, with the money he made during his football career and his investments, he's not hard up for a job. He's taking it easy right now. The kids love the football camp he runs, mentoring disadvantaged children, and helping local actors—"

Brianna's talking, but I'm starting to zone out, my mind drifting to my predicament.

It seems she notices, and Brianna stares at me suspiciously. As my best friend, she always knows when something is up. "Mindy Price, what is going on in that head of yours?"

"Umm . . . I need to ask you something," I admit.

Brianna arches an eyebrow as I feel sweat begin to form on my brow. "Oh, really? What's that?"

I stand there silently, not knowing how to form my next words, my heart pounding like a battering ram. *Jesus, she's not going to make this easy.*

"Mindy," she presses. "I'm waiting."

I'm unable to part my lips. I don't know how to tell her about the lie that I'm caught up in.

"Mindy!" Bri cracks.

"Mindy!" Rafe echoes, pointing at me.

Just say it!

Closing my eyes, I take a deep breath. And when I open them, I finally ask, "Know any hot guys named Harold?"

CHAPTER 2

OLIVER

"*P*air of aces," I announce with a grin, turning my cards over on the wooden table and gathering the pot from the middle of the table in one giant swoop. "Bend over, buddy. Your ass is mine."

"Fuck, man!" Jason Woods, a twenty-four-year-old friend and fellow businessman yells, slapping his hand down on the table with enough force to cause some of my chips to go flying off, his face an angry red. "That's the second fucking time you called my bluff," he complains.

I sit back in my seat and appraise him, hiding a smirk. Jason's not a good poker player. He's okay when he's winning, but whenever he starts losing or is under pressure, I can read him like a book. With his tells, I can easily see if he's bluffing or if he has a good hand.

"He's a lucky bastard," Kevin White, another buddy of mine in his early thirties who's sitting beside me, agrees. Shaking his head, he rolls back the sleeves of his white dress shirt, his blonde hair glinting against the single light hanging above our heads. Having lost nearly all night, he's not as pissed as Jason is. But then again, Kevin never gets that pissed about anything. I bet he could lose his life savings and his reaction would be mild.

"Sorry, boys," I say with a grin and then joke, "I taught Phil Ivey everything he knows."

Jason lets out a derisive snort. "Dude, you're so full of shit. Your whole game is about sitting there with that cocky smirk on your face and getting lucky on the river."

I huff out a short laugh. "Don't hate. A win's a win."

"And a dick's a dick," Jason snarls.

"Hey, hey, now," Gavin Adams says sternly from across the table, shaking his head at Jason. Dressed all in black, he looks like the dark knight with golden hair as he scowls. "Let's not. We all know Oliver's good. We're all grown men here. There's no reason to get pissed when we lose. This is like the third time you've popped off after a loss, and it's getting old."

Gavin's words seemed to calm Jason at once. "You're right." He barely looks my way as he adds, "Sorry, Oliver. Tired of losing, that's all."

As a former football star and kind of a celebrity, Gavin has more clout with the friends in our circle. No matter how wrong he might be, they almost always agree with whatever he says. It's a nice perk, but it's got to get old with everyone being fake around you. I'd rather someone give it to me straight.

I toss Gavin an imperceptible nod of thanks, though I think I could've handled the situation just fine myself.

"All good," I tell Jason. "No offense taken."

"Yeah, cause you have my money," Jason mutters under his breath, but I pretend I don't hear it.

"Glad y'all got that out the way. Now can we fucking play?" Kevin says.

The blood rushes through my veins at his words, Jason's anger quickly forgotten. Looking at my stash, I rub my palms together in anticipation. "Let's do it."

I love playing poker and taking risks. The higher the stakes, the bigger the rush.

Rock climbing, sky diving, martial arts, poker . . . if there's a real risk involved, I want a taste of it. It hasn't always been this way, though.

As an executive at Steele Pharmaceuticals, I never wanted for cash. My father was the CEO and owner, and I was his right-hand man. I could have and do anything I wanted. But with that position of power came a fuck ton of stress . . . along with a lot of disagreements. The stress and the arguing got so bad that I eventually sold all of my shares of the company and quit after my seven-year tenure, leaving my Dad to run the company by himself.

My father was furious with me over my move. He thought my leaving at the height of our success was a huge slap in the face. But I couldn't help myself. If I'd stayed there any longer, we would've ended up at each other's throat and hating each other. I didn't want it to be that way, so I left.

A year later, I have a net worth of over ten million, living the small-town life. I even own a small home a few blocks down from my mother when I could be living large. It's been quite an adjustment for someone so used to the city. But it's nice to be able to help my mom, a poor single woman who chose not to accept a red cent from my wealthy father when they got divorced.

"Well, as long as you gentlemen don't start pulling out guns and shooting each other," says old man Joe, the sixty-year-old barber and host for our games, "I'm fine with it."

I chuckle as my eyes find the man sitting at the head of the table, dressed in dark clothing with a straw hat on. Old Joe has a large belly and a big mop of salt and pepper hair. He has one of those finely groomed beards that hides his face and makes him look like he's jolly even when he's pissed. He's the living punchline of the old joke, if a town has two barbers, go to the one with the bad haircut since he's the good one and the other one sucks.

"Let me get a smoke first," Jason says, taking out a cigarette and a lighter in one smooth flourish. He's about to light it when Gavin shakes his head.

"Not in here," Gavin says firmly. "If you want to do that shit, go outside."

"Come on, man," Jason whines. "Are you serious? We're playing poker. Smoking goes hand in hand."

"We have to tell you this shit every time. You're the only one who smokes here. Take it outside."

Jason scowls, still fingering the cigarette like it's his lifeline. "My wife doesn't care if I smoke."

"Yeah?" Gavin says, "Well, mine does. And I'm not going back home smelling like second-hand ass funk."

Jason mutters something under his breath, but he stuffs the lighter and the pack of cigarettes back into his pocket.

"How's Brianna anyway?" Kevin asks.

A light brightens Gavin's eyes and a slight smile comes to his lips. "Pretty good. She's having a blast raising our little man Rafe, but lately, she's been complaining about the baby weight that won't come off."

Kevin chuckles. "Tara does the same thing. But I think it fits her."

Gavin nods, a boyish smirk curling his lips. "I rather like it myself," he agrees.

I shift in my seat, feeling slightly uncomfortable. Talk of wives and babies always makes me feel anxious for some reason. I don't particularly have a desire to settle down with a woman and have children.

Not when my last relationship left me sour with how overly needy and clingy she was. She loved the way I fucked, but she loved the size of my bank account even more. When I found out what she was truly after, I dropped her faster than a hot potato.

Since then, love 'em and leave 'em has become my motto. Except lately, I haven't been doing much loving at all. I'm always too busy with my corporate security startup and helping my mom when she needs it.

In fact, it's high time I get some action. It's been awhile since I made a girl . . .

"So when are you going to settle down, Oliver?" Jason asks me, tearing me out of my thoughts. "You're the only guy at the table who's still single."

I clear my throat. Why do we always end up talking about this shit? Can't we just play the damn game without going into our personal lives? "I don't know. Haven't met the one yet."

Kevin shakes his head. "You're missing out, man. Nothing beats having a family to call your own."

"I could argue against that," I say in braggadocious tones, not letting any of my feelings show. "Being free to do whoever you want, whenever you want has its perks." I wiggle my eyebrows for maximum effect.

"So about that game," Gavin says, suddenly eager to change the subject, noticing that it's something I'd rather not discuss. "Let's play."

Joe deals me my two cards, and I look—Ace of diamonds and the Ace of spades. I wait while Gavin checks his cards. "I'll raise five thousand," Gavin says.

"Five grand? Are you out of your damn mind?" Jason asks, shaking his head. "Man, every time I get a decent deal, you just slam the pot with that shit. Fuck this. I'm sitting this one out."

"Yeah, me too," Kevin adds, turning his hand over and tossing it in. "Two-four off suit? I'm not an idiot yet."

Gavin's done that before, tried to bully the little bits of the blind by splashing the pot, but I'm not taking it this time. Not with paired aces. "Ten grand."

Joe drops the flop, and I see magic. Ace of hearts and two sevens. I've got a full house—three aces and two sevens. Gavin licks his lips, and I know I have him. I got exactly what I needed. He checks. I knew he was trying to steal the pot.

"You wanna raise the stakes? I raise twenty thousand," I reply, shoving in the chips. The odds of him beating my full house are slim to none, and I'll admit, I'd like to get one over on the former football star.

I can't believe it when Gavin calls my bet. "Call," Gavin says, his hands shaking slightly. Joe gives Gavin a look but shrugs as Gavin moves in the chips, and then he flips over the turn card.

King of diamonds. Gavin blinks, his eyes tight. "Check," he says.

Inside, I grin. I've got him. Even if he had two kings in his hand, he loses. "One hundred thousand."

There's not a sound in the room as everyone looks at Gavin, wondering what the fuck he's doing. Finally, he takes a deep breath and slides his chips into the middle. "Call."

Joe drops the river, and I feel a sense of concern. But then I see it's the ten of clubs. No chance in hell he can beat me, but his next words confuse the hell out of me. "Five hundred grand," he says.

Gavin gives me a tight smile and slides the money in. Has he lost his fucking mind? "This one's mine," he gloats.

"Hardly," I say with a laugh, pushing in my chips. "Call," Gavin grins again and turns over his cards. "Four sevens."

As soon as I see the pair of sevens, the air is ripped from my lungs

I stare at the cards in disbelief, feeling numb all over. He raised five grand on a pair of fucking sevens and then flopped four-of-a-kind? How lucky can you be? I can't believe it—he flopped a four of a kind. Around the table, everyone seems to be echoing my shock. Old Joe, Kevin, and Jason are frozen like statues, staring at me with surprise in their eyes.

I clench my jaw, anger rising from the pits of my stomach. It doesn't matter though. I accepted the bet and I lost.

I get up from my seat, feeling absolutely defeated, ignoring all the eyes on me. "I'll transfer the funds to your account in the morning," I say, keeping my tone even, even though I'm fucking pissed with myself. I don't know what the hell I was thinking.

It fucking sucks losing that much money, but it's not going to break me, though it's sure going to hurt.

"I'm done for the night. That's gonna put me on tilt if I keep playing," I tell them, turning to leave.

"Wait," Gavin says, standing up.

I turn, arching an eyebrow. "Yeah?"

Gavin glances around at the other men. "Are we done for the night? Let me talk to Oliver alone."

Without saying a word, Kevin, Jason, and Joe get up, gather their things, and leave the room, each one casting sympathetic looks my way as they file out.

"What's this all about?" I ask. "It's a lot of money, but you know it's not going to break me."

Gavin stares at me for several moments before asking, "What if you could keep your money?"

I frown. "What do you mean? I got overconfident and lost fair and square."

Gavin goes silent, studying my face. Finally, he speaks up. "I have a proposition for you."

"What—"

"You do a favor for me and we'll call it even."

I want to tell Gavin to go fuck himself. I'm a man, and I pay my debts. But a part of me is intrigued now, and I'm dying to see what Gavin has up his sleeve. "What kind of favor?"

Gavin steeples his fingers together, staring at me, appraising me.

"Well?" I ask, the anticipation killing me. "What is it?'

His next words shoot across the table like a speeding bullet. "I need you to pretend to be a friend's fiancé for a week."

I let out an incredulous laugh. I was totally not expecting something like that. "What?"

Gavin proceeds to tell me all about his friend, who's the godmother of his child and best friend of his wife, and how she's gotten herself into a bind because of a lie.

"Absolutely not," I say firmly when he's done, shaking my head. I'm not gonna lie, his offer is tempting. But there's no way I can accept it. I have too much lined up. Business meetings, lunch dates . . . and there were those repairs to my mom's attic I'd promised her I'd fix myself instead of paying some stranger to do it. "I'm not disrupting my life and plans to be some chick's cuckold for a week."

Gavin leans forward in his seat. "Just think of it this way . . . you get to spend a week with a chick for over half a million dollars."

"My half a million dollars," I say dryly.

"*Was* your half million," Gavin corrects "And you can keep it if you just do this one little thing."

23

I stare at him long and hard. His words are tempting enough, but it suddenly dawns on me how invested he is in this.

"You set this whole thing up," I accuse. "You knew I was the only single guy in our circle. You've been waiting all night to try to get me in this position."

Gavin manages to look guilty but doesn't say anything.

I begin to get up from my seat. "I'm done—"

Gavin reaches into his pocket and tosses a small photograph across the table. As soon as I lay eyes on it, my mouth goes dry. The young woman in the photo is drop-dead gorgeous, with beautiful golden brown hair, gorgeous green eyes that sparkles with mischievousness, and an impish smile to match.

"Yeah, so what? I was getting shit for cards and had to make a move. I didn't expect to flop those sevens—that was a miracle. Anyway, it's one week," Gavin nearly purrs, watching my intense interest in the photo. "And you have your money."

His words hardly register. I can't seem to bring myself to take my gaze off the picture. The playfulness in her eyes seems to call to me.

When I finally look away from it, I have only one question on my mind.

"What did you say her name was?"

CHAPTER 3

MINDY

"*Y*ou owe me," Brianna says as she hangs a right turn. "Like . . . give me your firstborn owe me."

I laugh. I can't help it. We're driving to her ranch, and it's an amazing day. The sunroof is down on her convertible, and for the first time in months, I feel like I'm getting back to normal. With the wind rustling our hair, I feel like a woman in my mid-twenties who has a million options in life. Not an overworked coffee shop manager stuck in day-to-day drudgery.

I was a little surprised when Bri came by to pick me up, telling me we're meeting the new mystery guy It's *so* not her style. She's always been the conscientious one of us. And despite all my needling, Brianna's been mum about how he looks. It's intriguing.

"How on earth did you find someone so fast?" I ask as we leave town and head out toward the ranch. Honestly, I didn't and still don't expect much. After all, who the hell would be willing to do this? There's likely not a man who could live up to all the hype that I've made "Harold" out to be.

"I didn't," Bri says with a twinkle in her eye. "Gavin did."

I'm a little surprised. I mean, Gavin's a friend and all, but damn, that's the sort of stuff you don't even expect from your sister. Actually, thinking of Roxy, she would hook me up with a guy . . . and I'd regret it.

As long as he can remember what I tell him, it'll be fine, I try to tell myself.

"Do I even wanna know how Gavin got Mr. Mystery Man to agree?" I ask, slightly curious. I remind myself to never underestimate Gavin Adams.

Bri smiles. "I'm not even sure myself. All he said was the guy owed him a favor. I didn't ask any questions."

"What *do* you know about him?" I ask, unable to contain my curiosity.

"I really don't know anything, Mindy. I'm as in the dark as you are. I jumped on it because, well, you got anyone else lined up?"

I stick my tongue out at her. "Bitch, you don't even know if he's hot?!" I can't help myself. I feel like a little school girl and it's so unlike me.

Brianna shakes her head. "I have no idea. But he made it seem like your problem was solved. Maybe it's an old football buddy . . . you could be shacking up with a stud for a week."

"Great, just what I need. A dumb jock who thinks he's—sorry, I know Gavin's not like that."

Ugh. I feel like I'm going on a blind date and I'm getting all antsy. I hate this.

Brianna waves me off. "I trust Gavin to not do you wrong. Just relax. We're almost there."

I'm not so trusting. We're always joking with each other, but I hold my tongue. I mean, I did have a role in hooking him and Brianna up. I hope he remembers that.

We get to the ranch, and when I step out of the car, Gavin greets us outside, a smile on his face. Bri scoops up Rafe from next to him, tickling him and making her son giggle while Gavin and I exchange hugs. "I can't thank you enough for what you've done for me," I tell him. "Miracle worker."

Gavin shrugs, smiling a secret smile that tells me he's got something up his non-existent sleeves. He's at home, and he's got no problem showing off the body that made him into a football star. If anything, he's even more ripped, if possible. "It's no big deal."

"So how do you know him?" I say suspiciously, getting right to the point. "Bri's keeping me in the dark."

"We're good friends."

I gawk at Gavin, alarm bells going off. Friends, sure. But this . . . "Good friends? You just asked him to be some stranger's fake fiancé and he said yes?"

Gavin smirks, that maddening twist of the lips that I know makes Bri both weak in the knees and ready to choke him. Right now, I'm ready to choke him. "We have an arrangement. That's all that really matters."

I scowl. He's really getting a kick out of this. "Well, where is he?"

Gavin steps to the side with a sweep of his arm, giving me a mocking half-bow. "He's waiting for you in the living room."

"Okay." Suddenly, I'm nervous. I was anxious on the way over, but now I'm nervous, and that's something I never feel. I mean, not about meeting guys. Guys have been easy to me ever since I realized that the combination of my smile and my boobs usually shorts out their big brains and turns on their little brains. Problem is, I always attract the wrong ones.

I start walking toward the front door and then stop, turning around when I don't hear anyone else moving. Instead, I see them staring back at me, Gavin still with that cocky grin on his face.

"Well, you coming?" I ask, annoyed. I get it—Gavin's pulling a bit of a joke, but this is taking it too far.

They both shake their heads. "I thought it best that you two meet and get to know each other," Gavin says. "We're gonna go for a walk."

"What?" I ask, shocked. "Brianna Adams, you're not gonna do this to me!"

Brianna shrugs, chuckling from something Gavin whispers in her ear before turning a saucy grin on me. "Mindy Isabella Price, don't tell me you're scared of meeting a man?"

I snap my lips shut. She has a point. I'm never scared of anything, especially not men. I stick my nose up in the air, turning on my heel with a harrumph.

"Fine. I don't need you. Bye, Felicia."

Brianna laughs as I spin around and march down the hall. Despite my show of bravery, I can barely stop my heart from hammering away in my chest. By the time I reach the archway, I'm covered in a sheen of sweat. I pause at the doorway, gathering myself.

Get ahold of yourself, Mindy.

Taking a deep breath, I start to relax. I'm in control. I've got this.

I walk through the doorway into the living room. "Hello?"

My breath stills in my lungs and my heart stops as the man in one of the chairs sets down the book he's been reading and looks up.

There, sitting in a leather club chair, is God. Well, he's not God, but maybe the dark, sensual reflection of Him . . . maybe the Devil? His coal black hair is accented by rich brown eyes that gleam with intelligence and a dark dangerousness that both chills and thrills me at the same time. He's wearing a white shirt with bulging biceps straining against the fabric, and I can see the swell of his chest muscles under his tanned skin through the deep V at his chest. I swear it looks like he's got a grapefruit stuffed in his pants as he sits there, his legs slightly apart like he owns the place, an amused smirk on his sensual lips.

Say something, you idiot!

I know I should speak, but it's like a cat's got my tongue. He's put me in a trance and he hasn't even said anything yet.

"Were you expecting someone else?" he asks with a slight chuckle, and I note the confidence in his eyes. The cocky curl of his lip. He thinks he's all that and the bonus prize, doesn't he?

I don't fucking think so.

I stand up straight and walk over. His eyes follow me, and my skin pricks, my normal confidence evaporating as I get another look at him. Holy fuck, he's hot. I sit down across from him, crossing my legs, showing him what I think is my best asset.

I gesture between us, trying to appear more confident than I feel. "I want to start by saying that I appreciate your doing this for me—"

"Gavin," he says, interrupting me. His voice is deep, rich, and soothing. It reminds me of the taste of smooth, delicious white chocolate. "I'm doing it for Gavin."

A flush comes over my cheeks. "Well then . . . doing it for Gavin," I say, still a little tongue-tied. "Sorry, this is all catching me a little off balance. Uhm, what's your name?"

The man chuckles, and his dark eyes gleam as he looks me over. "Oliver. And trust me, I was just as shocked when Gavin told me about it."

I feel like squirming. He's got me heating up, and all I know is his first name! "So, why are you doing this for Gavin?"

His eyes never leave my face as he replies, "I owe him."

I want to ask him to elaborate, but I can tell in his posture that it's something he doesn't want to talk about.

"Talkative, are we? Well, can you at least tell me *something* about yourself?" I ask. "Have you been married? Got any kids?"

He chuckles. "Never married, and last girlfriend was over a year ago." He scratches his chin, and for some reason, it makes him even hotter that he's not totally perfect. I can't help it. I'm relieved he hasn't been married. "I recently quit my job, actually," he adds.

"Why?" I ask. Here it comes, the big let-down. He spends his days playing video games and wants to be a YouTube 'star'.

He pauses for a moment, choosing his words carefully. "I had a disagreement with my boss and decided it was time to go on my own way. So I moved here. Mom has a bad leg and needed help around the house. I wanted to help her and maybe start up something here in town."

I nod softly. Better than I hoped. "That's admirable."

"I hear you work up at that coffee shop in the Grand Waterway," Oliver replies. "Enjoy it?"

I roll my eyes. "Most of the time. I've been hoping to open my own one day. There's a ton that we have to do to fit with hotel policies that I don't like. I've been saving and saving, and I mean, working with Gavin and Bri is great and all, but . . ."

"Running a business is harder than you think. If you think you work a lot now, wait until you have your own," Oliver says.

I stop, surprised. "Yeah, but it will be mine so—"

"You'll work harder?" he interrupts. "Yeah, at first you will, but then it'll become the same old, same old and you'll want to slop the work off on some other poor bastard."

"That's not my style," I say.

He shrugs, uncaring. "That's what they all say."

"Well, they're wrong," I say more sharply than I intended, and I realize it. "Sorry. But I don't shirk shit off onto my workers."

Oliver waves it off. "Don't be. At least you're being real. I imagine you won't be as soon as we see your family."

His little jab stings. But I feel like I have to do this next bit. "My mother, she's uh . . . she's marrying someone who has money. She's become a little snobby."

Oliver groans, rubbing at his temples as he gives me raised

eyebrows. "One of those?"

"Yeah. One of those." I pause, digging in my purse to bring out a picture. "I brought a picture book with names attached. This might be a little easier if you can recognize a few of them."

I toss it over to him, and he opens it and begins flipping through pages. "Aunt Rita," he mutters.

"You'll love her. She's a firecracker with a sharp mouth."

Oliver keeps going, pausing a few pages later. "Roxy? Cute name. She looks like you."

"That's my sister. She calls herself a younger, better version of me. But that's a lie." I swing my hair around, lifting my nose to the ceiling. "You can't top perfection."

He chuckles and flips through a few more pages then sets the book aside. "I can handle it. I'll give it a look over later."

"Also," I say, digging in my purse and pulling out a piece of paper, "I've prepared a list of rules, some dos and don'ts. Just so we're on the same page here."

I feel stupid. When I made it this morning, I didn't know I'd be walking right into a man who's literally sex on a stick, but he just flashes me a little grin. "Hit me."

I try not to tremble as I recite them. "First, when we're not in the presence of my family, you're not allowed to touch me. And if there comes a time where we display affection for show, only I initiate it. Also, in front of my family, you'll never lay a hand anywhere on my body that can be deemed inappropriate. Last, you'll always be respectful and laugh at my jokes."

My heart is pounding as I lower the paper. "I'll give you a paper with more, but that's all I could think of for now."

He chuckles, amused. "That's cute. But I'm going to let you know now, Princess, that I've never followed rules well."

I grip my throat as anger flares up. "What's that supposed to mean?"

He smiles. "We're supposed to be engaged, aren't we?"

"Yes, but—" I start, but Oliver cuts me off, his eyes quieting me in an instant.

"Okay then. Then let's be real. If I want to kiss you in front of your family, I will. If I want to grab your ass to show them what's mine, I will." His eyes bore into me with an intensity that seems to say, *and if I want to fuck you, I will. So get your pretty little head used to that idea, Princess.*

Oh, my God. What have I gotten myself into?

"I'm willing to pull off this little act for Gavin," he continues, "but I'm not going to act like some cuckold to make you look better."

I draw myself up, ready to unleash fury on him. Let him know that he can go fuck himself and I'll just fess up to my lie, but I'm interrupted by a sound in the doorway. It's Brianna in the doorway with Gavin, Rafe balanced on her hip. "Everything going okay in here? Have you two decided where you're staying on your honeymoon yet?"

Looking at the grinning Brianna and the adorable baby in her arm, I feel my defenses falling. Fessing up makes my stomach crawl, and I don't have much choice now. I can't find someone else and he knows it.

But looking at the smirk on Oliver's face, something tells me this might actually be fun.

"Yeah," I finally say to Brianna. I turn my eyes back to Oliver, giving him a challenging grin of my own. "Hell, I might enjoy doing some ball busting over the next few days."

Oliver gives me a smirk. One that says *like hell, you will.*

CHAPTER 4

OLIVER

I trail my finger over the photograph of Mindy, sitting back in my office chair and shaking my head. I shouldn't be doing this. I've got a lot to get done before I leave. Getting a company off the ground takes a lot of work, even with a large bank account. But instead of getting work done, I'm staring at this photo.

She's so fucking beautiful. I thought I knew what to expect, but meeting her in person was intense. As soon as I laid eyes on her, any regrets went out the window. I played it cool, though, not letting her know the effect she had on me.

My fingers trace over the lips of her picture. I can't wait to taste them. The way she tried to get all high and mighty with me makes me eager to show her who's the boss. If she thinks I'm about to follow all of her silly little rules, she's got another thing coming. I'm gonna take what I want, and judging from the look she had in her eyes, she's gonna love every minute of it.

My dick hardens in my pants and suddenly, I have to adjust my collar and loosen my tie. *Fuck*, I think to myself. *I haven't gotten this worked up in a long time. Get a hold of yourself, Oliver.*

But the only thing I want to take hold of is her ass. Grip those bubbly, luscious cheeks in my hands and pull her in close, taking her body and ravaging it for everything that it's worth. My cock throbs harder in my pants, dying to be let out even if I am in my office. I hold in a groan. I refuse to let her have this power over me.

But no matter how hard I try, I can't get her out of my head. Even worse, I'm actually looking forward to the trip. I need this. I'm gonna have her eating out of my hand in no time. Oh, the things I'm going to do to her. I bite my lower lip at the thought.

My cock throbs again, but I ignore it. I tuck the picture of Mindy underneath my briefcase and push the thoughts of her out of my mind.

I open my email on my laptop, trying to focus on the things I need to take care of. It's afternoon and I'm stuck in my office in the middle of town, trying to get my affairs in order before my trip. We're leaving in two days, and whether I need it or not, part of me wonders if I'm walking into a fucking trap. Mindy's mom must be a piece of work for her to have to lie.

There's a knock on my door, pulling my attention away. Martha, my part-time secretary, sticks her head in. "Mr. Steele? Your ride is ready."

"Thanks, Martha," I say. "You sure you can hold down the fort?"

Martha looks around our small, two-room office and chuckles. "I'm pretty sure," she says. "But sir, hiring a car?"

"He's family, and besides, it's a tax write-off," I joke. Martha is great for me. She's a natural penny pincher, and it helps balance my splurging tendencies. I know she's saved me a lot of money as we get Steele Security Solutions off the ground. "When we get back, I'll introduce you to him. Your daughter might like him."

Martha, whose daughter is nineteen and just starting college, laughs. "If he's anything like you, Mr. Steele, I'll have my shotgun ready."

I laugh. "You've got me all wrong. Okay, I'll be back."

Outside, the black Lincoln SUV with a driver waits, and I climb in. The driver and I say nothing as we head over to the university. I spend the whole time working on my tablet, relishing the peace and quiet. When we pull up outside one of the dorms, my brother Anthony sticks his head out of a third-floor window, a wiseass grin on his face.

"Don't you just look important as fuck?" he yells loud enough for the whole campus to hear.

I growl, already fed up with his antics. I know he's younger, twenty-one years old and still in college, but he goes out of his way to be a smartass and piss me off. When our parents divorced, he badly wanted to go live with my father, but my father wanted me to go with him instead. So Anthony went with Mom, and it was timing I guess that brought me home just as he started looking for his own freedom. He's going to college in town but staying in the dorm, and he needed to not have Mom to worry about.

"Get your ass down here, would you?" I yell back, knowing I look like an asshole standing outside a college dorm building in a suit and tie and yelling up at one of the students, but I can't help it. They've got locks on the doors.

"Two minutes!" Anthony says, and for once, he's actually on time, though I sort of wish he'd put on something besides a sleeveless T-shirt and jeans. He approaches the SUV, laughing at the magnetic removable logo on the side.

"Steele Security Solutions? Sounds like something out of a damn comic book. You got a super suit in the back?"

"Just get in," I grumble, making Tony laugh as he gets under my skin. I swear, every little brother in the world is born with the sole mission of pissing off their elder sibling.

"What, you missing the secretary and the morning blowjob?" he needles me, as always. "You're usually more patient."

"I've got shit to do, that's all. I'm going to be out of town for a week," I reply as the driver pulls away. "I've arranged for Martha to be looking in on Mom."

"Martha? She's nearly as old as Mom," Anthony bitches. "Can't you at least get some naughty little home helper instead? I've got vacation next week, asshole."

I check the urge to give him the beating my parents never did. He's a cocky little shit. "I'd have just asked you, but I know you're going to be spending your whole vacation chasing tail."

"Damn, Oli, that's harsh even for you," Anthony says. "So what's the deal? I can help if you need it. I mean, it's Mom."

I think for a second, calming down. "Okay then. Listen, I need you to take care of some things while I'm gone."

"Where are you going to—" Anthony starts, but I cut him off. My brother is all questions when he wants to be.

"That doesn't matter," I say flatly. "I need you to man up and take care of some stuff this week. Martha can take care of the office, but I need you on backup. And I need you to help out with Mom."

"When are you leaving?" Anthony asks, growing more serious. He's got some potential at least.

"In a few days," I say, not offering more.

Anthony shakes his head. "I can't. Dad wants me to check on a property for him down in Georgia. I'm flying out Tuesday."

"Fuck him," I say, sharper than I intend. "And fuck his grooming."

Anthony recoils slightly and goes silent for a moment. "Are you going to tell me what happened between you two? It's been months now, and neither of you will say what went down."

I clench my teeth, looking out the window. I still get hot under the collar thinking about the disagreements we had. "Another time." I make sure I say it with enough conviction so he won't press the issue.

Anthony's silent for a few moments before he replies, his voice quiet and intense. "You're an asshole, Oliver. And Dad's gonna be pissed when he can't count on me."

"That's too bad. He doesn't need you. Mom does."

"He wants me to take your place, you know. At the company," Anthony says. "Says he needs a right hand he can trust."

Anger surges through my chest. He gave me the same line of shit back when I was twenty-one and he was recruiting me. But Anthony doesn't understand. "That will be the biggest mistake you ever make."

"Seems like you're the one making a big mistake," Anthony replies hotly. "Look at you, giving up your stake in our father's company and moving here. And for what? Tell me one thing that's here for you."

"Mom," I say. Truth be told, the list ends there, but it's enough.

Anthony goes silent, guilt showing on his face. I know why. He wanted desperately to go with Dad like I did, to live the good life. But that would've left our mother all alone.

"You're right," he says quietly. "There's Mom."

I nod. "And I need you to spend time with her while I'm gone. In fact, I want you to stay at her house rather than the dorm. Martha shouldn't be the one taking care of her."

Anthony looks pained at that comment. "Damn, man. Travis said he was going to hook me up with this hot chick this weekend—"

The stony look on my face shuts him up. "I'm going to need you to stop making excuses. Take some fucking responsibility for once."

Before Anthony can start, I cut him off. "I was supposed to help her with fixing the lights in the basement. She twisted her ankle doing laundry and needs a few things done around the house."

Anthony swallows. "I didn't know."

"You don't call. You never check on her." I could go off on him about how he lives in the same town and neglects his mother. I checked in with Mom more when I was in college, and I was several states away. He lives in the same town.

"I've just been busy with classes. School work. This shit's harder for me than it was for you."

I turn away, looking out the window and ending the conversation.

I don't need to hear his excuses. I've always known that actions speak louder than words, and Anthony's actions have amounted to diddly squat when it comes to his relationship with our mother. Finally, as we pull up in front of Mom's house, I turn back to him, my voice quiet.

"There's more to life than just having a corner office, fucking chicks, and partying. Time to be a man, Anthony."

❄

"OH, MY WORD, MY TWO BOYS," MY MOM, JAMIE STEELE, SAYS AS WE step into the living room of her house. She tries to get up from her seat, an old raggedy recliner, but I quickly motion her back down, noticing her bandaged ankle.

"Sit down, Mom," I tell her, closing the door. "No pressure on the ankle, remember?"

I don't give her a chance to respond. I quickly make my way across the room, bend down, and pull her into my arms. It's been a few days since I last saw her, but she looks disheveled, her hair in disarray. She has fine frown lines going down the front on her lips brought on by cigarette smoke. Another thing Gavin and I agree on— I hate cigarettes, but I can't stop her. It makes her look a lot older than she really is.

Her eyes light up when I step away, and she looks at Anthony. "And Anthony too? What have I done to deserve this?"

"Oh, stop it," Anthony says sheepishly, coming forward to give her a hug.

"I can't help it," she says as she pulls away. "You never come to see me. The last time I had you both under this roof is when Oliver came home from . . ."

Her voice trails off and a distant look comes over her eyes. I know what she's thinking about. How I left her to be my father's pet child. I thought she'd be okay with Anthony, but he resented the fact that I was gone and took it out on her like any kid would, with lots of stress and backtalk. It was only the fact that he was a kid when he did it that saved him from an ass beating.

She didn't tell me how bad it was until I came back home. I was furious when I found out what was really going on. At the same time, I felt guilty. I felt like maybe I shouldn't have left. And to know that she didn't take one red cent from my father makes it worse. She lives off the meager income she gets from her job as an office manager for a trucking company. I try to give her money to help, but she's too prideful to take any. I barely convinced her to take time off work with her ankle.

"You know I'm sorry," Anthony says, and I think Mom's words hit him harder than mine did. "I'm going to try to do better. Oliver told me that you hurt your ankle."

"Yeah, I was trying to get the fabric softener refill in the basement when I fell," Mom says. "My own fault. You know, Anthony, if you'd be more dependable . . ."

I think Anthony's had enough. I went in on him the way over here, so I interrupt Mom before she can really get going. "Mom, Anthony's going to be saying with you for the week. I asked him to help out at my office, and then he said he wanted to spend some quality time with you."

Anthony gives me a grateful look as Mom turns to him, her face brightening in disbelief. "Tony? Is that true?"

He nods his head. "Yes. I'll help out with any work you need around the house. Help out with groceries, take care of the basement, all that."

"You'll see, Mom," I say. "Tony's going to be a great help while I'm gone."

My mom turns to me. "Gone? Gone where?"

I grit my teeth. I can lie to Anthony, but I can't lie to Mom. "Just going away for a week to a wedding."

My mom's eyebrows raise. "A wedding? Whose wedding?"

"A friend's. I'm going as someone's date." It's not a total lie but one I can get away with. I can hear Anthony grind his teeth, and I know I've got some explaining to do with him later. Not now.

"It must be someone important if you have to leave town for a week," Mom fishes a bit too eagerly. "It sure would be nice to have some grandbabies."

I almost blanch. She snuck that one in there with a quickness I wasn't prepared for. Babies are the furthest thing from my mind right now.

"It's totally not like that," I say, my tone firm, letting her know the discussion is closed. "I'm doing it as a favor."

My mom looks around suddenly, very excited. "Well, since I have you both here, why don't I make your favorite, cherry pie? Hmm? If nothing else, we can spend some family time together before you leave with some good home-style cooking."

My mom grins, and I'm so glad I forced Anthony to come. She's the happiest I've seen her in a long time. "Sure, Mom, as long as you stay off your ankle."

"Well, you know back in my day, there was a song about cherry pie. Mine's sweet enough to make a grown man cry," Mom boasts with a laugh.

Anthony groans, slapping his forehead. "Really, Mom? That's not what that song's about. Please stop . . ."

I open my mouth to comment, but right then, Mindy pops in my mind. Her long legs, her sweet lips. And I have to think that maybe that band had a point.

There's a sweet cherry pie, and I plan on tasting it.

CHAPTER 5

MINDY

"How did it go?" Brianna asks me. "When I walked in on you guys, it looked like you'd seen a ghost."

We're in my bedroom and I'm getting the clothes ready that I'm going to wear for my trip. I packed a lot of nice dresses, and now I've got a problem. I might have packed some nice things, but I've got to do some shopping to get a few more outfits that would be more in line with what my mom would expect.

Peering at myself in the mirror, I spin around and place my hands on my hips, fixing Brianna with a scowl. "I don't appreciate your sending me in there unarmed. He was an asshole."

Brianna lets out a laugh. "Unarmed? What did you want to go in there with? A shotgun? I've never known a man you couldn't wrap around your finger in about two minutes flat," she says with a snap of her fingers.

I shrug. "I dunno. A big fat dildo, maybe? So I could've shoved it up his cocky ass."

"Mindy!" Brianna protests. "What did I tell you about these words around Rafe? You can't be saying those things! He's started repeating every new word that he hears!"

"Sorry, Rafey," I say to the little boy who's sitting atop a mountain of my discarded clothes, playing with one of my sports bras.

I get lucky, as he seems to have ignored my foul mouth and instead pulls one of my sports bras on top of his head. "Look, Mommy! I'm a Duacone!"

"A what?" I ask, giving Bri a glance.

"Cartoon," Brianna says with a chuckle before looking back at me. "Still . . . why so mad?"

"Are you kidding? I was sweating bullets before I even walked in there!" I say, my face flushing. "He wasn't what I expected, and I'm just frustrated that he was able to get the upper hand on me."

"And I . . ." I clench my fists, my breath tight in my throat. "He got to me, okay?"

Brianna's jaw drops. "I can't believe I'm hearing this. Aren't you supposed to be Miss Fearless? The woman who takes life by the balls?"

"Balls," echoes Rafey. "I like balls!"

I mock-scold Brianna, sticking out my tongue. "Wanna tell me where your son gets his bad language again?"

Brianna scowls at me. "I'm so going to kill you."

I spread my arms defensively as Brianna glares murder at me. "I just wish you would've told me."

"Told you what?" Brianna asks, trying hard to be mad but looking like she wants to burst into laughter.

I gesture sharply, leaning in to whisper so Rafe can't hear. "That he was hot as fuck!"

Bri looks at me out of the side of her eyes before she shakes her head. "How was I supposed to know? I'd never met him."

"I don't believe you," I say. "You did that on purpose."

Brianna looks genuinely hurt. "I swear to you, I didn't. I never saw him before I walked into the room with Gavin. It was his idea."

I look into my best friend's eyes to see she's telling the truth, and I sigh, shaking my head but not smiling yet. "Never mind that. I seriously don't know how I'm going to live a week with that guy without killing him."

Brianna glances at Rafe, who's now quite happily turning my Under Armour sports bras into hand puppets, and leads me into my connecting bathroom. "Was he that bad?"

"You're damn right!" I growl, letting go for the first time. "You wanna know what he told me?"

"What?"

My hand goes to my throat, remembering his deep voice and the way that it both pissed me off and turned me on. "Basically, that he would do anything to me that he wants since we're supposed to be engaged."

Brianna gapes. "He did not!"

I nod, my skin flushed. It pisses me off that I'm getting hot thinking about it.

Brianna thinks for a minute, then chuckles. "Well shit, you said he's hot, right? That should be right up your alley."

I glower at her. "What's that supposed to mean?"

Brianna shrugs, leaning against the bathroom wall and grinning. "I recall a certain person urging me to sleep with Gavin when I barely knew him."

"But this is different," I protest. "Gavin was sweet. He wanted to court you, treat you like a princess. This guy . . ." I shake my head as the curl of his cocky lips appears in my mind. Oh, what those lips could do to my . . .

I shove the treasonous thoughts away, my chest heaving. "He's different. Let's just leave it at that."

"You all right?" Brianna teases, raising an eyebrow. "Feeling a little hot in here? Need a cold shower or two?"

I wave her off. "I'll be fine."

"Mmmhmm," Brianna replies. "So, should I close the door behind me so you can break out your purple friend?"

I scowl. "Please. He might be hot, but he's not *that* hot."

I smile, and we both start laughing at how bad my lie was. "I might need to take it with me though," I admit. "We're going to have to fake all this affection. From what he says, he's not exactly worried about keeping his hands to himself, but with how he was talking to me, I'm not about to sleep with him."

Right then, I see Rafey pull out a red number from the pile of clothes, a dress I bought years ago but have never worn. Even for me, it's pretty sexy and flirty.

"Oh, Rafey, I can just kiss you," I say, rushing over and grabbing it from him, but he hangs on like a toddler will. He giggles as I tickle him and deliver kisses to his head, letting go of the dress and letting me snatch it up without any more trouble.

I rush back to the bathroom and pull it on. It doesn't go with the undies I'm wearing today and I'm not wearing heels, but it gives me an idea. I come back out, spreading my arms and twirling a few times for Brianna. "How do I look?"

Brianna's eyes go wide. "I think you know how you look."

"Good," I say with a naughty grin, the plan cooking up in my head on the fly, "because I'm going to wear this tomorrow to meet Oliver."

Brianna looks at me like she's about ready to call the psych ward. "Seriously? You just said you weren't going to sleep with him, but then you're gonna wear something like that? Don't make me say what that dress is screaming. Not with Rafe around."

I make a face, wiggling my butt in Bri's direction as I check myself in the mirror. I know the heels I need to wear with this. They'd make me . . . oh, yeah. "I'm not gonna sleep with him. But two can play his game."

"Right," Brianna says. She grins as she gets the point of my plan. "You're going to grab the bull by his horn."

"More or less," I say as I place my hands on my hips, admiring the dress that hugs my curves like Saran Wrap. *Oh, I most certainly fucking will.*

CHAPTER 6

"*R*emember," I tell Tony as we pull up to the curb of the airport. I hired a driver again, both for convenience and to make sure Tony and I can talk. "Don't pull any bullshit while I'm gone or you're going to find your ass and your head meeting."

"Relax. I got it," Tony says, annoyed. "You've only said it a hundred times before."

"Good. Take care of Mom. We're all she's got," I remind him, more gently this time. "She needs us."

"Damn, Oli, you're just leaving for a week. Not a lifetime," Tony says with a grimace.

We pull up in front of the airport, and I offer Tony my hand as we come to a stop. "Take care. I'll be in touch."

Tony shakes, and I'm encouraged. He's got a man's grip. I get out of the car and grab my bags out of the back. With a wave, I slap the hood and watch the car take off.

I stop and look around. I got a text from Gavin this morning telling me that Mindy would be here before I was. But she's nowhere in sight.

I wait five minutes, and I'm about to pull out my phone when Brianna rolls up with Mindy, the sunroof down on her convertible. She gets out of the car and I have to fight to keep my expression neutral. She's wearing dark shades and a tight body-hugging red dress. She might as well be wearing nothing at all.

Blood pumps furiously to my cock as it instantly hardens. Good thing I'm wearing a sport coat.

"Hey, Oliver," Brianna greets chirpily as she gets out of the car. Mindy pretends she doesn't notice me, walking around to the side and bending over to get her bags out of the back, giving me an unrivaled view of her ass. I'm pretty sure she's doing it on purpose.

I swallow hard as fire runs through me. I see her toss a little glance behind her and then quickly look away as she slowly pulls her bag. I knew it— she's doing this shit on purpose.

Okay, Princess, you wanna play? Challenge accepted.

"Hello, Brianna," I say politely, trying to keep the strain out of my voice. "You're looking as beautiful as ever. Gavin's a lucky man."

She walks over, gesturing at me with a smile. "Looking good yourself, Mr. Fiancé. What is that, Gucci?"

I chuckle. "Thanks. I figured I'd play the part. Mindy's supposed to have this stud of a date, so I dressed down a little."

Brianna chuckles, then leans in to whisper to me. "Thank you for doing this."

I shake my head. I still don't get why this charade is needed, but whatever. "It's no problem. I think it'll be fun," I say, trying to restrain a grin from spreading across my face.

Brianna gives me a measured look, and I wonder how much her husband has told her about me.

"I think that's it," Mindy says, pulling our attention to her. She has a small hoard of luggage. She's packed for a month, not a damn week. "So where's the redcap?"

Brianna winks at me and stands on her tiptoes to pat me on my shoulder. "Take care of her for me, okay? She can be a handful."

I give her a polite nod. Regardless of the dirty things that dress makes me want to do to Mindy and her body right now, I can tell Brianna cares about her a lot. "I'll do my best."

There's a twinkle of mischievousness in Brianna's eyes when she turns away, and something tells me that she's laughing at an inner joke. Something tells me Mindy's got something up her sleeve.

"Bye, trick," Brianna says to Mindy, giving her a hug. "I'll miss you, even if it's only for a week."

"Bye, hussy," Mindy says, delivering a quick peck on her cheek. "Please control your language around my little Rafealicious while I'm gone. It's really getting out of control. I'd like to know some-one's raising him right."

Brianna turns to me, a mock scowl on her face. "You know what? I take that back. Have your way with her."

Mindy gawks, then laughs defensively. She wasn't expecting that one. "Oh, come on, you know I love you!"

"Nope, not listening," Brianna says, sticking her fingers in her ears as she walks around and jumps into the driver seat. "I hope you get hogtied and covered in honey!"

Oh, the ideas that brings to my mind. Mindy blushes too but waves it off with a laugh. "Whatever!"

"That's right!" Brianna says cheerfully. She starts up her car and gives us both a playful wave. "Bye, Felicia!"

She drives off, leaving Mindy looking almost shocked. "I'm so gonna kill you when I get back!" Mindy yells at the fleeing car, flipping the bird.

I chuckle at their antics. I don't know if they've always been this way. Gavin says that his wife used to be pretty shy, but she could have fooled me.

When Brianna is gone, I walk over to Mindy. I look her up and down, letting my eyes tell her just how much I like it. "Dressed for the weather?"

She looks down at the dress before giving me a saucy grin and putting on a terrible Scarlett O'Hara fake accent, teasing me again. "This little ole thing? I just threw it on."

Painted it on is more like it, I think, checking her out again. "It looks good on you," I admit, but not offering too much. I'm not going to let her think she has power over me and think I'm going to obey her little rules.

A blush comes over her face and she looks away. "Thanks." She turns back around a moment later. "Can you get my bags?"

"Just a second," I tell her, holding in my grin. I pull out a black velvet box from my pocket, raising an eyebrow. "You're missing something."

"What is that—" she begins to ask. Her breath catches in her throat as I open it to reveal a platinum engagement ring with two stones, emerald and diamond to match our birth months. Gavin was helpful. "Oh, my . . ."

I lean in close, pressing my body into hers, letting her feel my cock pressing into her side and whispering in her ear. She's trembling already, and I feel confidence returning. She's so going to be mine.

"For you," I say, meaning both my cock and the ring. I pull away a second later, grinning at the effect my moves have on her. "I'm sure it's just the right size."

She's red in the face and her chest is heaving as I take the ring out of the box and place it on her finger. A perfect fit, of course.

"Why—" she begins to say breathlessly when I step away, staring at the ring as if it's magic, and she's not sure if it's good magic or bad yet. "How did you . . .?"

"The details don't matter, Princess," I tell her. "We're supposed to be engaged. How would it look if you show up without an engagement ring?"

She looks like she wants to say something, but she knows I'm right. "You're right," she mutters so low I can barely hear her. "I guess I didn't think about that. Where'd you get it?"

I wink at her and throw her words back in her face. "That old thing? Oh, I just found it lying around somewhere."

I hold in my grin as she scowls at me and I call the redcap for her bags. We check in the airport and walk through the terminal. On the way to the plane, she says very little. I try to keep my eyes off her tight curves, wanting to keep the little edge that I've got.

But by the time we board the plane and get in our seats, some of her spark has returned. We're flying first class, of course, and she knows as she slides past me to the window seat exactly how much her ass is in my face. The flight attendant brings us some pre-takeoff drinks, and she turns to me, raising her glass.

"This ring is beautiful," she says, her shoulder brushing mine as she leans slightly in to toast me. Up close, I can smell her perfume and it smells like heaven. Running her finger along the band, she chuckles as she checks out the stones. "Nice bullshit story about where you got it though. So, you're a May baby?"

"I am," I admit. "Figured it'd help you remember."

"Nice idea," she says with a chuckle. "So where'd you get it?"

Damn, she really wants to know badly. Well, it won't hurt to tell her. "I got it from Feinberg's in the middle of town. He's got a good selection of stuff."

"It must've been a small fortune," Mindy says, biting her lip unconsciously.

"It wasn't cheap," I confirm. Actually, Feinberg will let me bring it back, minus a thousand bucks, but Mindy doesn't need to know that. Besides, the ring looks good on her hand.

I clear my throat as the plane begins to taxi. "So what's this place like?"

"Summerfield?" Mindy says, looking out the window for a moment. "It's a rich bay town, sorta like the Keys or Martha's Vineyard. Oh, by the way . . . for the next week, your name is going to be Harold."

"Harold?" I ask, raising an eyebrow. "You must be fucking kidding me."

"You got a problem with that?" Mindy asks in challenge. "Seriously, it's what they're expecting."

"I'll go by Oliver," I say firmly. "There's no way in hell I'm answering to Harold."

"But . . ." Mindy says, stopping when I shake my head.

"We'll say Harold's a bad joke of a name you gave me. For something being especially . . . hairy."

Her mouth opens and shuts like a fish and I hold in a grin.

"Nothing wrong with being called Harold," she grumbles after a moment, having to get the last word in. "I had a goldfish named Harold. By the way, did you rehearse the names?"

"I looked at it a little." To be honest, I couldn't focus much on anything but Mindy.

She sucks in a breath, frustrated. "Okay, let me give you some tips. Mother can be bossy. She'll try to run all over you. Grandma pretends to be dumb, but don't let it fool you—she's as sharp as a tack."

"Anything else?" I ask. Sounds like Mindy's not going to be the only fun I have this next week.

"Listen to me and follow my orders and you'll be fine."

I have to grin. She should know by now. "What did I tell you about that, Princess?"

Mindy hums and turns back, her hand brushing her cup and

dumping half a Sprite with ice in my lap. "Oh, Harold, I'm sorry!" she says with an overly dramatic gasp.

Before I can react, she gets a napkin and dabs at my crotch. Her strokes barely brush the top of my dick, and it twitches, wanting nothing more than to get rid of the two layers of fabric between me and her soft fingers.

I grab her hand a second later when the shock wears off, putting it firmly in her lap. "I got it," I say. "You should be more careful."

My cock is straining against my pants so much it hurts. She was intentionally brushing her hand up against my cock. My cheeks are flaming, and I have to use the photo book to hide my crotch as the plane makes the final turn and starts down the runway, accelerating into the air.

"I really am sorry," Mindy says with faux sincerity as we reach our cruising altitude. "I so didn't mean to do that."

Yeah, right. The little triumphant smile I see on her face says it all.

This is fucking war.

CHAPTER 7

MINDY

*M*y heart pounds in my chest as the limo rolls to a stop in front of Wentworth Estate, parking on the circular driveway. It's like something out of a storybook, or maybe even a painting. Lush green grass is perfectly trimmed on the huge manicured lawns. Three statues adorn the lawn, all of them classically-themed pieces, one of them of a man on a horse. If I remember what Mom told me, it's supposed to be a Wentworth who won the Congressional Medal of Honor back in the Civil War or something like that.

"It's beautiful," I breathe, momentarily stunned.

"It's nice," Oliver agrees.

For some reason, his lack of gushing pisses me off. He sounds so casual about it all.

I'm still smarting over what he did. Pushing his body into me when he gave me the ring, intentionally pressing his big, hard . . . wait, what am I thinking? I shove the thought away, my face turning red.

Jesus, will it ever stop?

We're not even a day in and I can already cut the sexual tension with a knife. My body is on hormonal overdrive, and I've still got six days, eighteen hours, and too many damn minutes before we're done with this charade.

"You okay?" Oliver asks, seeing my trouble. "Did the plane ride upset your stomach or something?"

I wave off his concern, not letting on to my desire. I can't let him know just how much he's affecting me. "You can save the hero act for a bit. I'm just a little nervous, that's all."

The corner of his lips curls up into a grin and I grit my teeth. I got the last laugh on the plane, but somehow, I know he has the upper hand now.

"Hey, don't worry about me," I say. "Remember the back story?"

"Yeah, yeah," Oliver says, rolling his eyes. He doesn't understand yet. Mom and Grandma both have minds like tape recorders and the cross-examining skills of a lawyer. They'll tear him apart if he starts screwing around. "You only said it a million times on the way over here. We've been together a year. I walked into your coffee shop and told you that you were the most beautiful thing I've ever seen. Short and sweet."

A flush comes to my chest. The words sound nice even though they're fake. "Yeah, something like that. Don't forget about you dropping to your knees when I said yes."

Oliver's smirk turns into a genuine smile, and I feel my flush deepen. "Don't worry," he says, giving me a reassuring, smoldering look. "They're going to buy every word. We'll see about going to my knees though."

Somehow, his words don't give me comfort. It's like everything he says has layers of meaning, and no matter what, my mind wants to think of sex. Like him covering my body in kisses and being on his knees, his lips . . .

The door opens and the driver, an old man named Sam, stands ready for us. "The Wentworth Estate. Please watch your step on the gravel, Miss."

I step out, relishing the cool breeze that blows in lightly from the east, caressing my soft flesh as I take in the scenery. It's a beautiful day with sunny, clear skies, the large French Provincial mansion looming against the azure sky. If I weren't so nervous, I'd be amazed.

"Don't worry about your bags," Sam says when Oli makes a move to grab them out of the back of the limo. "The house staff will get them and make sure they're delivered to the proper bedroom."

Oliver gives me a look. "The house staff?"

I just shrug. I knew John had money, but I've never cared enough to find out exactly how much. I was expecting a nice big house, not a damn castle with house staff. "I'm just rollin' with it."

"If you'll come with me," the driver says.

Sam leads us to the cobblestone walkway that leads to the huge double-door entry of the mansion. As we head up, Oliver places his hand on the small of my back. Warm currents begin to ripple out from his touch, and I squirm on the inside, flustered.

"What are you doing?" I whisper out of the side of my mouth, alarmed by what his touch is doing to me. How am I supposed to share a bedroom with this man for a whole week?

"Being your fiancé," he whispers back, grinning at me. "Come on, Princess. Let's meet the fam."

He says it so sweetly that I almost wish it were true for a second. A part of me likes being on his strong arm, though I'd never admit it to him.

By the time we reach the double doors, my forehead is dotted in sweat. My heart is pounding in my chest like I just sprinted a half-mile or something. Truth be told, I'm overcome with sudden anxiety.

Too late to worry now, I realize as Sam puts his hand on the twin handles of the front door. *I'm in too deep.*

The large door springs open before the driver can turn the handles, and out steps my mother with a small barking dog, a fluffy white Pomeranian at her side. Sam springs out of the way, pretty spry for a guy his age, which is a good thing or else he'd get run over.

"Mindy, my darling!" My mother sings, stepping forward with her arms outstretched. The woman is practically dripping in diamonds, with a matching necklace, bracelet, and earring set over top of her white brocade dress that flows down her body all the way to her ankles. "It's been so long!"

"Mom," I say as we embrace. I smell her perfume, and it smells expensive as hell. "I've missed you."

I pull back and feel tears forming in my eyes as I survey her. Her face looks different from when I last saw her. The wrinkles that had begun to show around her eyes are mysteriously gone, along with her forehead wrinkles. It's a little weird, and I wonder if

Mom's just feeling youthful from love or if she had a little help from Botox.

"You're lookin' good. Not as good as me, but you'd do just fine in a singles bar on Ladies' Night."

My mother laughs. "Yeah, well, that's in the past for me. You look good too, honey. I never could have worn a dress like that at your age."

"Who's this little lady?" I say, gesturing at the dog who's running circles around our feet, barking and carrying on in an attempt to deflect attention away from my dress. I feel nervous enough feeling Oliver's hand still on my lower back. I can't decide if I want his hand higher . . . or lower.

"Oh, that's Bertha," Mom says with a dismissive wave of her hand, "a puppy John got me several months into our courtship. She's a handful, but I can't imagine this place without her."

Weird name for a tiny little dog if you ask me, but hey. Mom turns her gaze on Oliver, her eyes widening as if noticing him for the first time. "Mindy, you never said your young man was this hand-some. Why, you're practically perfect!"

"He is," I mutter, not quite sure what I'm agreeing with. I step away from Oliver, using hand gestures to complete the introductions. "Harold this is my mother, Mary Jo. Mom, this is Harold."

Oliver grins, taking my mother's hand and gently kissing the back of it, his eyes twinkling. "It's a pleasure, Ma'am. They say that a man can see his future wife when he looks at her mother . . . and I'm a lucky man."

My mom looks at me approvingly, sounding slightly out of breath. "Ooh, Mindy, I like him."

"Don't be fooled," I say under my breath before replying, "Thanks, Mom."

Mom shakes her head, running her hand down the length of Oliver's arm in admiration as if he's a toy on display. "You must work out a lot, Harold. You'll like the gym, I hope."

"Oliver, please," he says gently. When my mom looks at him in question, he chuckles. "I prefer to go by my middle name."

She looks at me, her eyes accusing. "How come you never told me that?"

"I . . ." I'm at a loss for words when Oliver saves me.

"She's always forgetting things," Oliver cuts in. "She even forgot the day we first met and when I decided to honor my grandfather by going by my middle name."

I turn a dark scowl on Oliver, trying to tell him to stop it with my eyes.

He grins at me and winks, but before I can reply, I hear a voice from the doorway. "Well I heard that you had your mother's beauty, but that just doesn't do it justice. It's good to finally meet you, Mindy."

A white haired, distinguished-looking man steps through the doorway, dressed in a fine gray suit and tie, everything about him perfectly groomed.

"Honey! Mindy, this is John, my wonderful fiancé," my mom gushes as John takes my hand and kisses it, his mustache prickling lightly on my skin. It tickles, and I have to smile a little as he steps back, clasping my hand in both of his and smiling.

"Nice to meet you, John," I say politely.

"It's a pleasure." He turns to Oliver, sizing him up the way men do and looking impressed. "And is this Harold?"

"Oliver," Oliver corrects as he offers his hand, and the two men shake in another one of those male measuring sticks, both looking like they passed the other's test. "I recently decided to go by my middle name."

"Well then," John says, gesturing inside. "Come on in. Let me give you the ten-cent tour."

My breath is taken away again as we step fully into the foyer. Gleaming marble floors, impossibly high ceilings, and a winding staircase make the entryway look like a grand entrance to heaven.

"Wow," I breathe. "So which king did you rob to get all of this stuff?"

My mom clasps her hands together with pleasure. "It is like a palace, isn't it? The first time I stepped inside, I felt like I'd had my Cinderella moment."

"Nice place you've got here," Oliver says, again sounding not as impressed as I thought he'd be.

"Everything is—" I start before Oliver pulls me to a stop, cutting off my words.

"It's nearly as beautiful as my little Princess," Oliver says, taking me by surprise when he pulls me close, and before I can do anything, he kisses me on the lips. His kiss is intense, powerful, and before I know, it I'm kissing him back, even as his hands pull me against his hard body. I feel a growing heat rising again between my thighs. I'm left breathless, chest heaving when he pulls away. I flash murder at him as he whispers in my ear, "Payback for your little stunt on the plane."

I can hardly listen. My body is hot, and I know my nipples are tight and aching inside my dress. I'm probably poking through the thin bra I wore to show off the dress. My cheeks burn, and I'm so embarrassed to be turned on in front of my mom.

"You okay?" she asks me, amused. "Young love is so passionate."

"I'm fine," I stammer, pushing away and not wanting to. "He caught me off guard. And someone forgot we had garlic chicken on the plane. Tic-tac next time, honey?"

Oliver flashes his mocking smirk at me before giving Mom a raised eyebrow. "I always leave her breathless. Sorry, I couldn't resist. Your daughter's too beautiful."

John chuckles at that. "I'm liking you already." He pulls out a cigar and inhales as he runs it under his nose before sticking it in the corner of his mouth. "Trust me, I'm so glad I can get these legally now. They're a bad habit, but I allow myself one or two a week. Cuban, imported directly from Havana. Come, Oliver, let me get to know my eventual son-in-law."

Oliver smiles. "Got any Cuban rum to go with that cigar?"

"How's Jamaican? And do you like cars?" John asks, his eyes twinkling merrily.

Oliver laughs. "Of course I do. When I was a kid, I had all the best sports cars in my toy collection."

John seems giddy like a schoolboy, and he claps Oliver on the shoulder, charmed already. "Come with me and I'll show you my garage. I'm sure there's something there you'd like. Let these ladies catch up."

The two of them head off, Oliver giving me a wink. After they leave, Mom leads me through the mansion.

"Where is everyone?" I ask as we leave the foyer. "Where's Roxy? And where's this *staff* I'm hearing about?"

"It's not all that," Mom says with a shrug. "John sent the staff on duty to town together. I wanted to do something special for dinner. As for Roxy, she's with your aunt out getting their dresses for the rehearsal dinner."

"I can't wait to see them," I tell Mom honestly. "It's been too long."

Mom shows me around the house, and as we do, I feel a question that's been on my mind for a long time bubbling to the surface. Finally, I have to ask. "Mom?"

"Yes, honey?" Mom asks, stopping in front of the eighteenth-century German grandfather clock that she's been going on about for a while. "What is it?"

"Mom . . . do you love him?"

She gives me a questioning look. "What do you mean, Mindy? Do I love John?"

"Yes," I say, letting my fears out. "Most of the time you talk about him, it's about his money. His things. His stuff. You come to the door looking like you've stepped out of an old Elizabeth Taylor movie or something . . . but what about John?"

Mom nods, looking at the bracelet on her arm, then chuckles. "If John lost it all tomorrow, if we had to hock these diamonds, if we were left with nothing but the clothes on our backs and the feelings we share . . . I'd still marry him. I love him, Mindy. It's just hard for me to put my feelings about John into words, so I talk about his things instead. You don't know how strange it is, telling my adult daughter about how I'm left feeling like a schoolgirl again, a . . . what's the word Oliver used for you?"

"Princess," I say automatically, and Mom laughs.

"Yeah, that's how I feel. I'm fifty-four, and I feel like a princess," Mom says, reassuring my fears. "So, what about Oliver? He seems to be very into you."

"I . . . well," I start, lost in thoughts over Oliver's kiss. My lips still tingle and my body feels warm even at the memory, and I stammer for words. "He's great."

"Seems more than great to me. He seems like a catch," Mom says, but before she can say anything, there's a booming sound as the doors to the estate are thrown open and a voice I've long missed calls out.

"MOM! We're home!"

Roxy. Oh my God, I've got to go back into performance mode. Roxy's going to want to see Oliver, and he's going to want to kiss me again, and my body . . . I'm babbling in my head and I can't stop it.

"Mindy?" Mom says, shaking me back to the moment. "Hey, you okay? You looked pale there for a second. Was it the airline food?"

"No . . . no, I'm fine, Mom," I lie, wishing it were just the airline food. Fine? I'm not fine, and now I have to deal with Roxy and Grandma.

Shit

CHAPTER 8

OLIVER

"Oh, my darling niece," Aunt Rita coos as she comes forward and wraps her arms around Mindy. We're in the waiting room just outside the dining room. John and I spent a good hour in the garage going over his pretty sweet collection, and now it's time for dinner.

Mary Jo made us all wait outside for the rest of the family to get acquainted with me while dinner was being prepared. I'm glad I dressed the part. This family seems to like dressing up. Chalk one up to my father's constant social skills lessons. I can go back to being a blue blood very quickly.

There's a few more people here now. Behind Aunt Rita, Mindy's grandmother is with two girls, one who's nearly the spitting image of Mindy except that her hair's shorter. She must be Roxy. The other looks like she'd prefer to be anywhere else but here.

"Hey, Auntie," Mindy says excitedly, taking her in an embrace and delivering a kiss to her cheek. She takes turn embracing each woman then steps back, giving her aunt a questioning tilt to her head. "Where's Uncle Charles?"

"He's outside having a smoke," Rita replies, sighing and rolling her eyes. "No matter what I try, I just can't get that man to stop. You take a pack away, he's got seven more hidden."

John, I see, has a guilty look as his hand unconsciously pats the suit pocket where he'd put his cigar case, and I'm glad I didn't take him up on his offer. I seriously doubt he's going to pull another out for as long as Rita's around. Meanwhile, Rita turns her eyes on me, and I can feel the question burning in everyone's eyes. "Who is this fine young man?"

"This is Oliver, my fiancé," Mindy announces proudly, gesturing to each woman in turn. "Oli, this is my Aunt Rita, my cousin, Layla, my sister, Roxy, and my Grandma, Ivy Jo."

"Nice to meet you ladies," I say, flashing them all a charming smile. "And thank you, Princess, for remembering my name this time."

Ivy Jo holds out her arms at me as Mindy gives me an evil look. "Don't stand across the room, young man. Come give an old lady a hug."

I chuckle and do as she commands. "Who am I to resist the charms of a beautiful woman like you?"

"Oh, stop it," she murmurs as she pulls me into a hug and runs her hands up and down my back, finishing with a pinch of my butt. "Nice and strong, just like old Johnny used to be."

"Grandma," Mindy says warningly and casts me a sympathetic glance. "Let's not molest my fiancé before dinner, please?"

I chuckle. "It's okay. Sometimes, it's nice to eat your dessert before dinner," I tease. Mindy blushes slightly, and I give Grandma my full attention. "Johnny's your husband?"

"Was," she corrects, but I can tell by her voice that it's an old loss. "He's worm food now, but boy, do I enjoy remembering the days when he used to hike these old legs back and—"

Mindy coughs loudly, shaking her head, while Layla grabs her grandmother by the shoulders and pulls her to the side, shutting her up. "Uh, she gets that way."

"No problem," I reply with a laugh. "I love doing some hiking myself," I say, looking over to make sure Mindy heard me.

Layla gives me a grateful nod while Mindy turns a deeper shade of red, and Roxy steps forward, peering at me with wide eyes. "Oh, my God, he's gorgeous!" she exclaims to Mindy. "Girl, you got a keeper. No wonder you wouldn't stop bragging about how good he was in bed."

Mindy scowls murder at her sister. "Roxy, please don't—"

Roxy shakes her head, not listening. "Shoot, I might have to go back home with you if they're serving up dishes like this." She gives me a look. "You got a brother? You know, for the longest time, I swore you were just the battery-operated fantasies of a girl who wasn't getting her needs met. Glad to see I'm wrong."

"Ignore her," Mindy half pleads, half commands. This is hilarious. "She's just being silly."

"What?" Roxy asks, giving her sister a smirk. "So anyway, about there maybe being a younger version of you . . ."

I chuckle. I like her already. "Yeah, I have one, but you'd want to kill him after five minutes. I have a feeling Tony would like you though."

"Why's that?" Roxy asks, her eyes going slightly wide.

"Well, he kind of likes anything with a vagina and a pulse."

Mindy glares at me with eyes that seem to say I want to kill you, but Roxy just laughs. She's enjoying the banter.

"I hear you're a singer," I say. "What do you sing?"

Roxy lights up like a light bulb. "Yes, I have my own band. We sing on Friday nights and weekends at a bar in town called Trixie's. Lots of rock, but we mix in pop too—we kind of have to depending on the night."

"Really?" I say honestly. "That's impressive."

"Little Roxy has a beautiful voice," Rita says. "Why don't you sing a few lines for the man?"

"Please, let's not," says Layla with a roll of her eyes. "I can only handle so much ass kissing at once."

I ignore Layla and give Roxy a smile. "Go for it if you want."

Roxy looks like she just hit the jackpot. "I can," she says with a dimpled smile. "What do you like? Beyoncé? Taylor Swift? Katy Perry?"

I laugh. "I'm more of a Johnny Cash man myself, so I'll let you choose."

"Honey, I don't do country. But I can start singing some Fifth Harmony and Mindy can start twerking for us. Remember your last birthday when you got drunk and they started *Worth It?* Oh, my God . . ."

71

Mindy places her hands on her hips and opens her mouth to berate her sister when the doors to the dining room swing open and Mary Jo appears in the doorway, clapping her hands and beaming at us all. "Dinner's ready!"

We go into the dining room, where I see that Mary Jo has actually gone to the trouble of putting place cards out for everyone. While I help Mindy with her chair, a short, tubby man who smells like every nasty, old ass smoky bar in the world comes in, walking by me and spewing clouds of noxious odor behind him. "Sorry I'm late."

Rita tries to hold back her disgust as Charles sits next to her, but I can understand. The man smells like he didn't have one cig, but the whole damn pack. "Charles, if you don't mind?"

"Piss off," he growls, and I'm about to say something about being respectful, but I feel Mindy dig her fingernails into my thigh as she gives me a small shake of her head. I get it. I don't know these people and it's not my place, but it's hard to watch the disrespect.

"So how long have you worked for Honda?" Grandma asks as we wait for the servers. "I didn't know they have an office in town."

"Oh, since I graduated school, and I have to commute," I say quickly, keeping a smile on my face. Mindy gave me some details, but a lot of it I'm just making up on the fly. "It's worth it though, small-town living and all that."

"And how did you first meet?" John asks.

Mindy smiles and tries to take the lead. "Well, you guys have to listen to this. I was in the coffee shop, my hair all messed up. He walks in and says I've been—"

"Actually, I came into the coffee shop and was sitting down.

Mindy started flirting with me, asking if I worked out. I was surprised by her boldness, but I liked it. I had to give her my number when she asked me for it."

"That sounds like my Mindy," Ivy Jo winks. "Forget the clothes—check out the biceps."

"I don't blame her. I'd have been offering free fraps and singing *Call Me Maybe* if I'd had the chance," Roxy adds with a grin. "And I hate that song."

"Now, now, Roxy," Mary Jo says. "I think you've embarrassed your sister enough."

"Just kidding, Mom," Roxy says, obviously not apologetic. "But seriously, Oliver, you do look like you work out. I'll play the guy here—so whatcha bench?"

"I really don't know," I reply. "I'm more into martial arts than lifting."

"Really? You didn't tell us you were dating Bruce Lee," Roxy teases Mindy.

Beside me, I feel Mindy go stiff, and I don't have to look to know she's cutting me with her eyes. She reaches over and puts her hand on my thigh, giving me a fake smile, when there's a commotion at the other end of the table.

"Jesus!" Ivy Jo squeals as we hear a yelp, and suddenly, Bertha goes running around the dining room in fear. "Mary Jo, you get that HEFFA on a leash or I'mma skin it and make me a coat! Or maybe a rug!"

"Bertha, you behave!" Mary Jo snaps, and Bertha runs out. She looks at me apologetically. "Sorry."

"Oh, it's no problem," I say easily. "You don't like dogs, I take it?" I ask Ivy Jo.

She raises her nose to the ceiling. "I'm more of a cat lady myself."

I chuckle. "My dog would never let me own a cat."

"Oh, yeah, your golden retriever," Mindy says. "What was his name?"

"Her name was Hershey, and she was a brown spaniel," I say casually, chuckling as I look at Mary Jo. "What was it I said about her being forgetful?"

I don't have to look in her direction to know Mindy is cutting her eyes at me again. But I ignore it, enjoying conversation with her family. Besides Charles, I think I like everyone in the room. They're certainly not the cultured one-percenters you'd think of with a place like this, but they are real. And I'll take real over a pedigree any day.

Everything is going fine and smooth when Mindy suddenly sets her napkin aside and gets up from the table. "Can I speak to you outside?" she asks, walking to the doorway and turning around to give me a look that says *Now*.

"Sorry," I say, flashing a wink at everyone. "Relationship goals."

There's a polite chuckle from the group as I leave the table, following Mindy out the back door. We step onto the marble patio, and I take a second to admire the layout of the back garden. It's beautiful, with a clear sky and the stars starting to come out in the purplish sky. It's going to be amazing later.

Before I can comment on it, Mindy whirls on me, her voice barely contained. "What the hell are you doing?"

74

"What do you mean?" I ask innocently, trying not to laugh. Watching her upset like this is just glorious. "I'm being your fiancé."

Mindy shakes her head, and I must admit she's hot as hell when she's pissed. Hotter than she normally is. "Don't play dumb. You know exactly what you're doing."

I shrug, purposely still trying to piss her off. "I thought what you said was boring. Come up with better stuff next time."

"Boring? Come up with better stuff?" She grabs me by the shirt, getting right in my face. Her eyes are sparkling with anger, and again I think, damn, she's hot when she's pissed off. I so need to make her mine.

"Listen here, you muscled up, arrogant bastard!" Mindy hisses, shaking me and snapping me back to her words, "You're supposed to be here doing what I say, not trying to humiliate me. That had better be the last time you slip up or I'm gonna introduce your balls to Grandma's nutcracker collection, got it?"

She moves to turn away, but I grab her arm, pulling her in close. Lowering my lips until they're a fraction of an inch from her ear, I grind my hips against hers, letting her feel my cock as it quickly stiffens. "What did you say you wanted to do to my balls?"

She's flustered, her face going red. Her lips are parted, and in the light, I can see her eyes go darker. She's torn. She wants me, but she also wants to slap me. I'd give it to her right here on this balcony, make the choice for her, but I know there are others inside. I'm not going to push my luck that much.

I move my lips until I'm just a fraction of an inch from hers. She mewls like a kitten almost, and I know she wants to close the gap, to kiss me again. Right when our lips are about to touch, I hear steps at the entry and Mary Jo comes out, her voice cutting through the tension between us.

"Everything all right out here?"

At the sound of her Mom, Mindy tears away from me, her breathing ragged.

"Yeah, Mom," she says, not even able to look at me. "We'll be there in a minute."

Mary Jo gives us a questioning look, then shrugs. "Okay. But the duck's on the table, and I'd like to get things started. You know how Grandma is with her pills. We can't delay dinner too long."

She goes inside, and Mindy turns back to me. "Don't touch me unless I tell you to. I still haven't forgotten that stunt you pulled back at the airport and that kiss you gave me."

I chuckle, wiggling my eyebrows. "I'm sure you haven't, Princess. I'll admit, you kiss pretty damn good, too."

My comment only riles her up more. She swirls and stomps back into the mansion, giving me another breathtaking view of her ass in that tight dress and those heels. In my mind, I can imagine pulling her dress up, bending her over, and seeing just how soft the skin of her ass really is.

I shake my head, adjusting my cock to make sure I don't stick out too much when I go back inside. As I step back into the house, I can't keep the grin from coming across my face. Crossing the foyer back toward the dining room, I mutter softly, "You'd better get used to it, Princess."

CHAPTER 9

MINDY

"*T*hat meal was wonderful, Mary Jo," Oliver says beside me, stretching his arm out along the back of the leather loveseat. "Thank you and John for your hospitality."

I shift around, trying to minimize the chances of contact between me and Oliver, but the loveseat is too damn small and his arms are just too damn long. We're sitting in the library after dinner, relaxing and sipping some after dinner drinks. Mom wanted everyone to have a little bit of family chill time after dinner, but I'm so ready to do anything but chill.

Sitting next to Oliver, I'm fuming on the inside while trying to look as calm as possible, smiling on the outside. But really, I'm still smarting over what he pulled at the table. Even after we came back, he would trip me up when he could, never directly saying I was wrong but subtly steering things. Every time Roxy or Grandma had a question, I could see Oliver putting his own little twist on things, just enough to make me look foolish if they remembered what I'd told them before.

I could literally grip his balls right now and squeeze. Just grab them right through his trousers and yank. But I hate that the very thought of touching his balls and his cock fills me with desire.

John gets up, stretching. "Well, I think I'm going to turn in. No offense to you all, but I have one more day of work to do before I officially go on vacation. Have a good evening."

Mom smiles at Oliver, charmed to the bone by him. At least *that's* gone well. "Well, Oliver, I'm so glad you could make it here to spend some time with us. I can see why Mindy is so taken by you."

"My word, Mary Jo," Grandma remarks with a cackle, "you keep on with much more of that and your nose is going to turn brown."

Mom blushes, and I understand what Grandma means. Mom can't seem to stop praising him.

Roxy lets out a snort and a giggle. "I still want to see if this Tony is as bad as Oliver makes him out to be."

If he's half the cocky bastard his brother is, I think to myself, *you're better off hanging out with the gay guys at Trixie's.*

Ivy Jo waves a hand. "I'm just so proud that Mindy has found her a nice handsome man to treat her right. And he has money too." Grandma beams at me for a moment before asking. "Should I be planning for great-grandbabies anytime soon?"

My heart skips a beat. Babies? Is she kidding? "Uh, Grandma—"

Oliver chuckles, grabbing me around the shoulder and squeezing me close. "Maybe not soon, but we sure have been practicing, haven't we, Princess?"

He winks at me, and I can't help it. I bite my lip at the idea of 'practicing' with him. But still . . . I could just kill him.

It's hard not to scowl, but instead I just grin. "Uh, honey," I say, gesturing at Roxy and Layla, "not in front of the children."

Roxy sticks out her tongue, but I'm quick to change the subject. "So Mom, what about the wedding—"

"Oh no, Mindy Price, I'm serious," Grandma persists. "When's it happening? I'm not getting any younger, you know, and not everyone gets to be a great-grandmother." She looks at her other two granddaughters. "Unless one of you two wants to give me one first."

Roxy grabs her sides. "Oh no, Granny Goose," Roxy says in between holding in laughter, "don't go putting designs on this uterus. I don't need that kind of pressure on me, not when I just barely climbed out of the womb. Why, I'm perfectly innocent!"

"I seriously doubt that," I mutter under my breath, and Oliver chuckles. I'm annoyed with him, but I can't help but be charmed by his handsome smile.

Roxy shakes her head. "Besides, I still have a lot to do before I have a baby. Queen Bey might be able to have a couple of kids, but she's already the queen. I've got a way to go yet."

"A baby's the last thing Roxy needs. She needs to get a real job first, at least," my mom says.

"I resent that. What's wrong with singing?" Roxy complains.

Mom frowns. "I think it's sweet and all that you like to sing, but baby, the odds of ever actually making it big are slim."

"Tell that to the people down at Trixie's," Roxy rebuts, sounding hurt. "They love my voice."

"I think it's admirable that you have the guts to try and find your own way," Oliver says, and I hear something in his voice that I haven't heard before. He sounds legitimate, like it's not for show. He looks directly at Roxy as he talks, the rest of us forgotten. "I think you should keep going for it. Don't get roped into a job, a life you don't want, just to fulfill someone else's idea of what you should do. Trust me on that one."

Oliver seems to have silenced everyone, but Grandma finally speaks up. "Let's just leave the poor girl alone. She's young and has more than enough time to figure everything out."

"Thank you," Roxy says with relief. "Now can we please get back to the subject at hand? Babies—when are *y'all* gonna have babies?" Roxy says, turning to me. Oh, I could kill her. I think I can. The law might be on my side. I'm temporarily insane. "Cause y'all look like you'd make a litter of beautiful ones."

"We're waiting until after we're married," I say. I give Oliver a meaningful glance. "We want to do things right and all."

I figure that as soon as we're gone from here, I'll call Mom and tell her that Oliver and I had some issues and broke off our engagement. I'm sure it will upset them, but I really didn't expect things to get this deep.

"Well hopefully, that's sooner rather than later," Grandma says. "You might think I'm still a spry chicken, but I'm just about plucked and ready for the fryer." She looks around and smirks. "Not that I can't think rings around all of y'all though. But on that note, I think it's time for bed."

Grandma starts to get to her feet, but before she can heave herself up, Oliver's there guiding her up. "Thank you, young man. Handsome and a gentleman. Good night, you all."

"Goodnight, Grandma," I say, watching Oliver give me a smoldering look as he sits back down. When he settles in, I lean over and whisper to him softly. "That was nice of you."

"She's funny," Oliver whispers back. "I like her."

"I think it's time we all retired," Mom says, also rising to her feet. "We have a packed schedule this week. Breakfast is served at eight in the morning. I expect everyone to make it, even if you're just eating some Pop Tarts." She arches a brow at my sister. "I'm looking at you, Miss Roxy Price. And show your sister and Oliver to their room, will you?"

"Of course," Roxy replies, jumping to her feet. "We made sure to give you guys a nice, private room far from everyone else so you can't disturb everyone with the wild sounds of whips and handcuffs," she says with a big wink and nudge from her elbow to my midsection.

"Oh, we left those at home," Oliver quips, making me blush as we let Roxy lead us up the stairs.

"You guys really make a cute couple," Roxy says. "You could be a couple in a movie or something."

"Thanks," Oliver says. "We get that all the time."

"I was serious about your brother. No pressure, but I'm a little hard up," Roxy says with a laugh, and I'm surprised. My outgoing little sister, hard up for a date? Then again . . . Oliver's brother, if he even exists? No chance in hell.

"Trust me, you don't want to do that," Oliver says, and I feel an awesome wave of relief wash over me. He's not a total asshole.

Roxy lets out a sigh as we reach the guest bedroom. "Damn. Oh, well. Here it is."

Roxy, swings open the doors, stepping inside with us. "Welcome to the . . . I think John called it the Morgan Bedroom. No clue why."

The room is huge, with a giant picture window that dominates one wall and a balcony outside, white walls, and a huge gray four-poster, canopied bed in the middle. The rug is gorgeous, and every carved twist of wood, from the details in the door frame to the gilded edges of the molding on the ceiling, screams luxurious. I look around, and I notice that our luggage is waiting for us beside the Cherrywood dresser.

"Goodnight, you two," Roxy says, mischievously wiggling her eyebrows at us. "Don't make too many bumps in the night. Or at least, muffle the screams when you do."

Before I can protest, Roxy turns and walks out, closing the door behind her. I step toward the door and turn, realizing that I'm alone with Oliver for the first time since meeting him in the living room at Gavin's.

The moment hits me, and I realize that I'm faced with the situation I've been dreading. This room is so extravagant, so why isn't there a sofa in here that I can make him sleep on? The room has everything but a damn sofa.

"This is . . . nice," I remark, trying to stall. I walk around the bed to the other side of the room, studying the night through giant French doors. "We'll have a great view in the morning."

"We will," Oliver agrees, and I turn around to see him beginning to unbutton his shirt.

"What are you doing?" I ask, my voice unsteady. "You can't be serious!"

He gives me a look before pausing. He's got his shirt half opened, revealing a set of super-hard abs and tanned skin beneath.

"I'm unbuttoning my shirt. What's it look like?" Oliver asks. "You know, I can't exactly go to bed in a sports coat and khakis."

My mind is flooded with thoughts of all the dirty, sexy things that could happen if I let them. I'd normally be down for a night of fun with a man like him, but I just can't get over his cockiness. My pride's getting in the way of a good fuck. But lying in a bed with him with only a few inches and some cloth between us? Asshole or not, his body is irresistible.

I grab myself by the arms, squeezing, trying to ward away the desire flowing through my body as the image of his lips burning into mine flashes in my mind. My pussy clenches as I remember the kiss from earlier that seemed to promise paradise. Oh, fuck.

I'm not caving on the first night. No fucking way.

I set my face as hard as I can and stab a finger at the floor. "I think you should sleep on the floor for tonight. I'm not sharing a bed with you."

Oliver looks at me like I'm crazy before letting out a chuckle. "Like hell. I'm a man, not a dog. If you want to sleep on the floor, be my guest."

He pulls his shirt all the way off, tossing it to the side. In an instant, I have a full view of him. Every muscle on his torso is defined and flows like a piece of artwork from one to the next, and all of them are saying *fuck me, Mindy.*

My knees give a wobble as they become weak. Sweet baby Jesus. He is on fire.

I place my hands on my hips, trying to be strong. "Yeah, that's exactly why I want you to sleep there. You are a dog, and I don't fucking trust you."

On one hand, I'm pissed that I can't let my pride go. I want to get in that bed and lick him from head to toe, but beyond his being an ass today, I'm scared. I'm scared what would happen if I sleep with him. And it's totally not me. I'm on guard because he's different. He feels . . . I can't decide if the right word is dangerous . . . or special.

And he's not really my fiancé, I remind myself. *It's pretend*.

"When are you going to learn, Princess?" he says, walking over and placing his hands on my waist. "I don't follow your orders." He leans into me just a little, invading my space, and whispers in my ear, "And I think you like it." I can hear the smirk in his voice.

His body is so hot that my temperature is rising. I can see the ridges between his muscles, ridges I want to trace with my fingernails and scratch lightly, just the way I know he'd like it. I look up at his full, sensuous lips, and I practically feel them on my skin.

Fight it, bitch!

I pull away, my chest heaving and my face burning. "Keep your hands off me." I try to sound firm, but what comes out sounds more like a moaning whisper. "Remember my rules."

My words sound so weak. I'm having a hard time even thinking straight, and Oliver grins as if he's saying *you'll be changing that tune soon*. "If that's how you want it."

"Yes, that's how I want it," I rasp, not even trusting myself to look at him. I stare at the door instead. "You need to follow the rules."

No, you don't! Take me now! my body seems to scream. *Touch me, tease me, make me scream your name!*

"I'm going to go change," I mumble, trying to calm down. I go get my bag and walk into the adjacent bathroom. I stare at myself in the mirror, taking a big calming breath. I throw cold water on my face, hoping it'll shock my system back to normal, but after patting it dry, the same lust-crazed, barely in control reflection still looks back at me from the mirror.

"Okay, Mindy. Get yourself together. You're stronger than this. Stop letting him know he affects you and he'll stop," I whisper, but the girl staring back at me says I'm a fucking liar. And I'm pretty sure she's right.

I go through my bag, finding my brand new nightgown. I bite my lip. I shouldn't wear it. It's only going to make things worse. But fuck him. He's got me all worked up, so now it's his turn.

I take my gown out, a little red number I got from Victoria's Secret, and put it on. The satin slips over my skin and I feel sexy, my nipples hardening as the lace rests against the tops of my breasts, and I quickly brush my teeth, looking at myself in the mirror. I've made a lot of strong men go to their knees with a lot less than this, and Oliver Steele is no different. I can make him beg and then shut him down. Or at least I'll be in control when I fuck him senseless.

I walk back out, strutting with each step and not saying a word.

Oliver's sitting on the bed in just his boxers, and he pales when he sees me. He swallows a lump, and I have to smirk a little when I see another lump twitch and grow between his legs. "Uh, you're wearing that?"

I hide my grin as I walk over to the bed and sit down. "It's my favorite nightgown. If you've got a problem with that, I guess you need to pull on some sweatpants or something," I say with a raised eyebrow and a pointed glance down at his crotch.

His eyes burn into mine. My nipples get even harder, and I know he can see the diamond hard points. I don't care. His lips seem to twitch, and I know he's imagining sucking on them.

I pull back the blanket and lie on the sheets, stretching just a little bit, displaying what he isn't going to get tonight. Oliver stares slack-jawed for a second before lying down, and then I see it. Lying down, there's no way to hide it anymore. That huge fucking bulge.

His cock is straining to get out, and I'm both glad and regretful he's wearing boxers without a front fly. I'd love a peek, but it's hard enough already to not to want to pull it out. My mouth waters—I can't help it—and Oliver notices my swallow.

"If that's what you want," he says with a deep growl to his voice. There's no teasing, no fucking around now. One word from me, and he'd fucking ravage me.

"It is," I say, my breath rasping again. I turn away, pulling the sheet up and over me before squeezing my eyes shut. Desire burns through me. Oliver clicks off the light, and the minutes pass like years.

I can't sleep. Several times, I almost roll over and grab it, reach for him. But I fight back the feeling. I can't give in. I'm not gonna let him win. But why does it feel like I'm the one losing tonight?

CHAPTER 10

OLIVER

I wake up in the early morning sunlight to the sound of running water and a hard cock. Rolling onto my back, I let out a soft groan, opening my eyes. The ceiling is so high that it gives me vertigo for a moment, and I close my eyes again, reaching over to feel the warm sheets next to me.

The spot beside me is empty, Mindy's soft, sexy body nowhere I can feel. I turn my head and open my eyes, seeing nothing but rumpled sheets that still hold her scent and warmth. She must be taking a shower.

I slept like hell, maybe the worst night of sleep I've ever had. Every time I would close my eyes, they'd fly open again at the slightest sound she made, hoping that every movement was her turning to me, giving in to the moment. I groan again, gripping the bedding and wishing she were right here and ready. I'd punish her with the wood she gave me all night long.

I look over at the bathroom, my mind drifting into fantasy mode, but after a night of maybe an hour or two of sleep at most, I don't give a shit.

I lie in bed, trying not to think about her in that nightgown when she walks out. Thankfully, she's dressed in blue jeans and a white scoop-neck top, but damn, she still looks hot as fuck. My eyes are silently and quickly undressing her as she saunters across the room and sits in the chair near the window. She bends down to pull on some socks and gives me a look down her top at the valley between her tits. My cock twitches again, and I'm glad the blanket's over my waist.

"Sleep well?" Mindy asks, and there's a hint of a smile on her lips. I know she thinks she's won, but she's dead wrong. I can see in her eyes that she's just as sleep-deprived as I am.

I yawn, placing my arms behind my neck. "Pretty damn good," I lie. "Haven't had a night's rest that good since the Delaney sisters." I kick my legs a little, and the blanket slides down to my knees. I don't do anything to hide my hard-on now, even squirming my hips slightly as if I'm moving to get comfortable. Mindy's mouth drops open a little, and I know what she's thinking about. "You?"

"Oh . . . fine," she says, her eyes falling to my cock before jerking away. I see red come to her cheeks and I smile.

"It's a quarter till eight," she says, her voice small as she suddenly focuses on making sure the tongue on her shoes is just perfect. "You should get ready. Mom was serious about everyone being there for breakfast."

"Leave any hot water for me?" I ask jokingly. A mansion like this could probably heat enough water for a hotel and not have a problem.

"Should be enough," she says, still refusing to look at me. She fusses with her shoes a little more, then stands up. "I'm going to head down."

"No," I say, rising from the bed, and she looks at me with surprise. "Wait."

"What—" she starts, then crosses her arms underneath her breasts, frustrated. "Why?"

"Don't you want us to be more cohesive? We need to go down to breakfast together."

"Uh, yeah, I guess," she says, biting her lip again, and she looks so cute. I smile and swing my legs over, giving her my back as I go over to my bag. "So . . . I guess I'll just hang out. Hurry, please?"

I chuckle. Please, now? Progress. "I'll be ten minutes."

I gather a change of clothes, some nice black dress pants and a white dress shirt, and walk into the bathroom. I take a quick cold shower, half to take care of my dick and half to wake me up. After a quick shave, I brush my teeth and step out, feeling more in control of myself.

Mindy looks up from sitting on the bed, picking at her nails. I see something flash in her eyes and she says, "You look . . . refreshed."

I grin. "Thanks. Listen, about last night—"

"You don't have to say anything," she says, giving me a slightly regretful half smile. "What we've both been doing is wrong. But we made it through one night. We only have six more to go. Let's just drop anything that came before and get through this without killing each other."

You mean fucking each other, I say in my head.

89

"Agreed," I reply instead, though I know it's all a lie. There's too much tension between us. There's only one way for this to end up, and that's her playing cowgirl on my cock.

Still, I smile and offer her my arm. "Ready?"

She looks at my arm for a moment before she takes it, rising to her feet. We leave, and part of me feels good with Mindy on my arm. Maybe we're pretending, but I could get used to pretend.

We go downstairs, but before we enter the dining room, Mindy plasters a heavenly smile on her face.

"Good morning," Mary Jo chirps as we walk in. "Thanks for making it on time."

I look around and quickly notice that not everyone is here. Aunt Rita and Ivy Jo are here, along with John, but Charles, Layla, and Roxy are missing.

"Good morning, ladies . . . and John," I say with charm. "Lovely morning, isn't it?"

"Did you guys sleep well?" Mary Jo asks.

"Absolutely wonderful, didn't we, babe?" I ask Mindy. "I slept like a baby," I add.

Mindy nods. "Mmmhmm. That bed was really comfortable and the room was gorgeous. I loved the view from the balcony. I felt like I was sleeping at the Ritz Carlton."

"I hope some baby-making action was going on," Ivy Jo mutters. "Less viewing. More screwing."

I chuckle as everyone seems to ignore her. I guess she's earned the right to say whatever the hell she wants at her age.

John sets down his spoon, standing up from his plate of grits and eggs to give Mindy a hug. "I'm glad you both enjoyed your room. You know we just had it redone? My father had turned it into my playroom when I was a child. I just couldn't see doing that anymore, so I had it restored and upgraded."

"It's lovely," Mindy says, looking around. "Hey, where's Roxy?"

Her mom scowls, and I have to laugh. Mothers everywhere are the same. "Late to breakfast, as usual. I swear, that child . . ."

"And Uncle Charles?" Mindy asks, hoping to stop a rant before it begins.

Rita shakes her head. "Honey, you'll be lucky if he's up by two. He usually skips breakfast. It's those damn cigs. He has no appetite."

"Good morning, lovelies," a cheery, singsong voice says. Roxy walks in looking bright faced, a disgruntled Layla behind her. "How are my favorite people?"

Roxy goes around kissing everyone before sitting, totally ignoring the daggers her mother is staring at her. Meanwhile, Layla sort of slumps into a chair, still looking like she'd prefer to be anywhere but here.

"Would've been better if you were here on time," Mary Jo finally says, stabbing at her eggs like she's ready to murder the chickens they came from.

Roxy looks over at us, giving us a saucy grin. "So how did you two sleep?"

"Everyone seems to be asking that," I say, reaching over and hanging an arm around Mindy. "We slept great."

"Like a baby," Mindy agrees, letting my hand stay for a bit.

Roxy looks disappointed. "I didn't hear screams and whips at all. Major letdown, you two. Get with the program."

"We're not here for entertainment," Mindy grumbles, rolling her eyes and taking my hand off her shoulder.

Silence falls over everyone for a few minutes as breakfast is eaten, and I must admit that whoever Mary Jo has cooking for everyone has skills. Roast duck is easy. Good grits are hard.

As Roxy scrapes the last of her insisted on granola out of her bowl and crunches down, Mary Jo rises to her feet and claps her hands together. "Enough dilly-dallying. There's so much to do and not enough time to get it done. We've got to get flower girl gowns, and there are decorations and dealing with the caterer . . ."

Roxy sticks her hand up, sort of, interrupting her mother. "Mom, I think it would be better for everyone if we worked in groups. Keep you sane."

Mary Jo brightens. "That's actually a great idea, Roxy."

Roxy sticks her tongue out at Mindy. "You're not always the pet!"

"Girl, please," Mindy says, waving her away. "I'll go with you, Roxy. Keep you out of trouble."

"And I'll go with them," Ivy Jo adds. "Keep these old bones youthful."

Mary Jo looks like she's about to protest but relents with a nod. "Well then, can you three deal with the dresses? Rita and Layla, come with me to get the decorations."

"And Oliver can come with me for a ride through town," John says. "I want to show him a few things and get his opinion on some others."

Mary Jo claps her hands together, pleased. "Okay. That sounds great. Be back here by one for lunch."

As everyone is getting up from their chairs, I pull Mindy in close. "Bye, Princess," I tell her, giving her a kiss on the lips. This time, she isn't as shocked, and I'm surprised when she kisses me back quickly.

"Goodbye, handsome," she tells me, giving me a cute little smile that stops me in my tracks for a moment. I think I'm having just a little too much fun with this roleplay. "See you in a bit."

I get up, and John and I make it outside and jump into his classic Mustang convertible, cherry red, of course, and we head into town. The engine purrs as we cruise, and I have to admit, it's a great car.

"That Mindy is quite a handful," John says as he drives, the top down and just the engine providing background noise. "Just a more grown-up version of her younger sister. But what I love about them most is that mischievous sparkle in their eyes. They're always ready to hit you with a joke that will have a grown man giggling."

I chuckle. "I can't argue with that. You'd be surprised how often she knocks me on my heels."

"Do you love her?" John asks me directly as we pull up to a stop sign. "No offense, but I'm about to be her stepfather. I'd like to know she's going to marry a man who will love her, not just be a good match."

I hesitate. Love is such a strong word. I know I'm supposed to be pretending to be in love, but to actually answer a direct question, I feel uneasy. But I can't help but answer with what he wants.

"Yes," I say. "Heaven and stars above, I love her very much."

John studies me for a moment, then nods. "Good. Then don't ever let her go. Girls like her only come around once in a lifetime. So to hell with the rules. You make sure you hold her, please her, and give her everything she desires."

"Desires," I muse as John pulls away. *Desires indeed.*

Hopefully, she gives in to that desire sooner rather than later. Another night of her dressed in that nightgown and I'm going to have a serious case of blue balls.

"Oliver?" John asks. "Did you hear me?"

"Hmmm?" I reply, glancing over at John. "Yeah. I was just thinking how stupid rules can be, and that you're right. Mindy deserves her wildest dreams."

"Good," John says, turning his attention back to driving. I look out the car window again, not really watching as the greenery rolls by. I'm thinking about Mindy. And rules. The only thing separating me from her is a flimsy barrier of rules she's put up between us.

And if I want to get the rules to change . . . I need to change the game.

CHAPTER 11

MINDY

*A*s Roxy and I ride with Grandma, I know I'm in big trouble. I can't stop thinking about the way he kissed me.

The way that his hands felt on my waist, and the way his thumb brushed over my cheek when our lips parted. It's fake, but it felt so real. I can still count on one hand the number of times he's kissed me. The scary part is that each one is getting better than the last. The really scary part is that I'm looking forward to the next one more and more.

It's more than the way he uses his lips or the way his body feels pressed against me. It's the look in his eyes. There is real desire there, and something else too. Something that scares me.

But last night was a real test of faith. I think I deserve entry to the gates of heaven because I'm a goddamn saint for resisting him. Call the Pope or something, because I felt like Eve, and Oliver's big fucking dick was the forbidden fruit. I didn't partake, so now I need to be rewarded.

"Yoo-hoo! Earth to Mindy!" Roxy says, waving her hand in my face.

I'm snapped back to attention. Roxy's driving us down the road in her white convertible with the sun roof down. The wind ruffles through our hair, and the weather is amazing. You couldn't ask for a better day, really. With clear blue skies and the sun warming our skin, everything is just right. Off in the distance, I can see the deep blue ocean. This place is nothing but beautiful. If I had to name a place to live, I think I would love to live here.

"Yeah?" I ask, setting aside my thoughts about Oliver and the creeping fantasy I have of him and me and this place. "What?"

Roxy grins, raising her voice to talk over the wind. "You look like you're in another world. Was the sex that good?"

I scowl at Roxy. "You do realize your grandma's in the back seat, right?"

"Are you serious?" Roxy asks, glancing in the rearview mirror. "She says and hears things far worse than that, ain't that right, Grandma?"

In the back, my annoyance grows as Grandma cackles. "Honey, I might be old, but I ain't dead. I've had more than my fair share of rides in the rodeo back in the day and put more than my fair share of cowboys away wet at night."

"See?" Roxy says as I wish I could just crawl into a hole and die. And Brianna thinks *I'm* forward? "Hell, I'd have her twerking on ladies' night at Trixie's if I could."

"Don't you dare," I say, feeling like the most mature person in the vehicle. "You're not about to have my Maw-Maw down there looking like some geriatric Nikki Minaj."

Roxy laughs, and silence reigns for a moment. "So, how have you been?" I ask Roxy seriously. "I haven't gotten a moment alone with you since we got here. You doing okay?"

"I've been good," Roxy says, giving me a smirk and a shrug. "But Mom's been giving me hell for taking a year off college to pursue singing. What else is new? She doesn't approve of anything I do unless it's something she wants."

Her words resonate with me. Aren't I pulling this whole charade to please my mother? I'm making an ass of myself in front of my family just so I can appear to have found a man. "It's just her way," I say.

We make it to the dress shop. It's a small little place in a strip mall between a karate studio and an eyeglass shop. I'm not sure at first, but when Roxy leads me inside, I see that everything's high-end. "This looks expensive as hell. I'd feel like I was slumming it in a Vera Wang," I say. "Jesus, this thing costs more than what I make in two months."

"Good thing I have John's credit card then," Roxy says with a chuckle, patting her hip pocket.

"What do you think of that?" I ask.

"What do I think of what?" Roxy asks as Grandma settles into one of the well-padded chairs and hums to herself.

"Of Mom marrying him?" I ask.

I know the conversation I had with Mom, but I want Roxy's opinion too. She bites her lower lip for a second as she thinks before answering. "He seems like a really sweet man. At first, I didn't think that they made a good match. He's laid-back, and as you know, Mom can be pretty . . . high-strung. But for the most

97

part, they've meshed pretty well. And despite all the bullshit, Mom's really the same inside."

"That's good. As long as she's happy," I say as I finger a tight little party dress. It'd look great on me, and I can just imagine myself dancing with Oliver . . . wait, what the hell?

"That's always what's most important," Grandma says as I quickly let the dress go. Now is not the time to think about Oliver. "Because if you ain't happy, everything and everyone around you will be miserable."

Roxie lets out a snort. "I know that's right. Preach, Granny Goose! You're on a roll today!"

"And if the shoe doesn't fit, don't wear the stinky thing," Grandma says, egged on by Roxy. "Cast it out!"

Roxy laughs as the salesperson comes over, looking like someone cut a fart in church. "May I help you?"

"Yes, we're here to pick up some dresses," Roxy says. "The name is Wentworth?"

At the mention of John's name, the bitch face disappears and a giant smile comes out. "Of course! I'll have them out in a second."

It's not quite a second, but they're back in a jiffy. They're certainly high-end. I seriously doubt any flower girls in history have worn dresses quite this level before.

"These are cute," Roxy says. "These would be great for your wedding too, Mindy!"

I want to have enthusiasm, but It's hard to even think about. There won't be any marriage. At least, not with Oliver. "Yeah, that would be cool."

"What's the matter?" she asks, noticing my tone. "You don't seem too excited. Aren't you looking forward to your wedding? You two just seem so perfect for each other."

Looking at my sister's encouraging smile, I feel like a fucking fraud. I should have known this fake-marriage thing wouldn't be so casual. I catch Grandma looking at me. She tears her eyes away when I see, but in that instant, I'm reminded that Grandma has been around for a long time. She's raised two daughters and a son, buried a husband and her son, and the whole time has been smart as a whip. She sees things other people don't. I need to be careful.

"Of course I am, but we haven't even set a date yet." God, I sound guilty, I know it.

Roxy shrugs, turning her attention back to the dresses. "Fine. I didn't mean to upset you."

I just want to hurry up and get this week over with. I feel like time is crawling, every minute is a year of mental agony already, and every mention of sex, Oliver, weddings, or babies is like a stab right in my gut.

We spend the next hour checking the dresses, but in the end, everything looks good. The tab makes me blanche while Roxy doesn't bat an eyelash at letting them swipe John's card. Instead, she just laughs as we carry the dresses out to the car. "Man, I really wish we could have gotten some of those party dresses. I saw you eyeing one. You'd look great in it. Not as good as me, but good."

"I'd make you look like a little girl playing dress-up," I tease back. "Oh, wait . . . you ARE a little girl playing dress-up."

"Bitch," Roxy says with a laugh, and I feel good again. On the way back, I forget about my worries as we all catch up on each other's day-to-day lives.

When we reach the Wentworth estate, my stomach is grumbling and I can't wait to get some food. We both help Grandma out and bring the bags in, setting them in the den where I guess Mom's starting to gather the stuff.

"We're home!" Roxy sings when we walk back into the foyer. "Looks like Mom, Rita and Layla, and the men aren't back yet. Let's go wait in the TV room. You've gotta check out John's system. They should be back soon, but seriously, Min, you need to see this thing. It's nearly the size of a movie screen!"

"I hope they're quick, 'cause I'm starving," I say, following Roxy into the entertainment room. Her description was a bit over-the-top. It's not the size of a movie theater, but still, a seven-feet-tall projection screen is pretty damn sweet. "Wow, imagine watching Ryan Gosling on this thing. He'd be life-sized."

"Imagine watching porn on this thing," Roxy says with a laugh. "The guys' dicks are life-sized."

"You . . ." I start before just shaking my head. "Just please tell me that you watch it by yourself."

"Well, duh."

Before I can reply, I hear a yell from the foyer. "We're home!"

Thank God for a mother who insists on making her lunch appointments. We go out where Mom and Aunt Rita are handing off their bags. "How'd you girls do?" Mom asks. "Been back long?"

"Everything went well," Roxy reassures Mom. "They're in the den. You guys?"

"Good. We got almost everything," Mom says before scowling. "They just won't be able to get in the *Toro* sushi that I wanted."

"Oh, that sucks," I reply, trying not to sound annoyed. Jesus Christ, Mom. When I was a kid, you'd have been happy with Chicken of the Sea, and now you won't be happy unless the fish were given massages before getting filleted. Jeez, no wonder you couldn't trust the wedding planner to do everything. There's no way any one human could remember everything you want for this thing.

Mom catches my tone, though, and chuckles. "Okay, Mindy, point taken. All right, lunch time. You guys wait—"

"Oh," Roxy says next to me, her hand pressed against her chest. "Talk about Prince Charming."

I turn to see Oliver walking in carrying a bouquet of roses. My heart does a backflip as he walks over to me, a beaming smile on his face. "I brought something for you, Princess," he says, handing me the roses. "They're not as beautiful as you . . . but then again, nothing is."

I stare at the bouquet as if it's a vase full of snakes. Still, his words have an impact, and I'm shocked. What's he up to? "Th-th–thank you."

"Oh, my God. That's so sweet," Mom says, fanning her face to prevent smearing her mascara, tears in her eyes. Every woman in the room has watery eyes with the exception of Layla, who looks like she's going through great lengths not to roll hers. Even I'm feeling a bit choked up, and looking into his face, I'm having to remind myself over and over that this is all an act. He's just pretending. He *has* to be.

"You're welcome," Oliver says, his deep voice dripping like honey. He leans down to give me a firm kiss on the lips. His scent envelops me. It's a bit spicy from his cologne, but underscored with his unique manly flavor. I love it, and pretend or not, my body responds.

When he pulls away, I almost feel like I need a ventilator. My head is swimming, I'm confused, not able to think, and I can feel my cheeks burning. To hide my embarrassment, I bury my nose in the roses. Maybe it's the moment, but they smell better than any roses I've ever seen.

"That was so sweet of you," Mom repeats. "You really are a gentleman."

Oliver grins and flashes her a smile. "I try."

"Can we clone you?" Roxy asks, and while I know she's just being silly, I swear she sounds like she's all gaga too.

Oliver laughs, shaking his head. "Sorry, Roxy, I don't think that's possible yet."

"No, seriously. Can we clone? I got a cup that you can donate your DNA—"

"That's enough, Roxy!" I say firmly.

"Selfish, stingy . . ." Roxy's words trail off as she makes a face, then turns and walks toward the dining room.

"Hold on, Roxy," Oliver says. "John and I were talking, and we've had the tables set out on the second-floor balcony. We're going to do lunch out there. The day is too beautiful to let it go to waste."

Mom looks at John, beaming. "That's a great idea! You two make a great team, John. It's going to be great having Oliver as your son-in-law."

"Thanks, honey," John says, "but it was all his idea."

Oliver turns his eyes on me and smiles. It's not a smirk, and it's not mocking or joking. It's a smile that makes me weak in the knees. "It's nothing, really. I do it all for her. My Princess deserves the absolute best."

I tear my eyes away from his gaze, my cheeks flaming. My heart feels fuzzy. Weird. I'm so confused and conflicted. I know this is all supposed to be fake, but Oliver is turning up the heat, and my heart, among other places, thinks it's real.

If he keeps this up, I'm going to be clawing his back and screaming his name before the week's out.

CHAPTER 12

OLIVER

"Here you go, Princess," I say, pulling out the seat for her. Out on the balcony, I don't think I could ask for a more perfect lunch time. The sun's high in the sky and the skies are a perfect blue. Past the back lawn, you can see the wall that borders the estate before the land drops, and the ocean begins. It's not too warm, not too cold, and the breeze has just a hint of salt on it. I don't think I could have scripted a more beautiful or romantic location for lunch.

Mindy's cheeks flush as she sinks in her seat. The staff have set up small tables for two or three people around the balcony as if it's an outdoor restaurant. Each couple has their own table while Roxy, Layla, and Ivy Jo share a third, leaving one for me and Mindy.

"Thank you," she says, her voice small.

I wink at her. "My pleasure. You look lovely, by the way."

I take my seat as a cool breeze flows in from the ocean, and I inhale deeply. "Jeez, this place is like a paradise."

"It is," Mindy agrees, enjoying the cool air with a satisfied look. "This was all your idea?" she asks quietly enough so the others don't hear. She doesn't need to worry—she'd have to be talking pretty loudly. There's comfortable space between the tables.

I nod. "It was nothing. Everything was already planned. I just suggested we do it out here."

"Why?" she asks.

"Because you deserve it," I say with a smile. "And I wanted to have a nice lunch with you."

She stares at me, unconvinced. "I can't tell if you're playing or if you really mean it anymore, Oliver."

"Maybe a little bit of both," I tease. "Maybe I don't really know myself." And that's the truth. I might be getting a little carried away, but maybe I actually mean it.

"Yeah, which means it's bullshit," she says. "You strike me as a man who always knows exactly what he's doing and what he wants."

"Isn't that what you want?" I ask.

She starts to respond, but the kitchen guy comes out with the menu for everyone. He goes around to each table, leaving the menus and then taking the orders for drinks. John's going all out. We're practically at a restaurant.

There's only a few selections of wine. Mary Jo is saving the best stuff for the actual wedding. I take a quick look, then hand it back to him. "Can I have the Darioush Chardonnay 2010 for us, please?"

The man nods, pleased. "Certainly, sir."

Mindy immediately glowers at me when he's gone. "Who said you could order for me?"

"I did," I say firmly. "I'm supposed to be your fiancé, remember?"

"How y'all doing over there?" Roxy calls from her table. "Enjoying the view?"

"Just fine," Mindy yells back, flashing a quick smile. "How about you worry about what's on your own plate?"

"Smart ass," Roxy yells.

I laugh. "You two are a riot. I bet you two were cats and . . . well, cats when you were kids."

"Oh, you haven't seen anything yet." Mindy scowls. "It's tame right now because people are around. It's an all out rumble when it's just me and her. Or it used to be."

"What would we do without our younger siblings?" I ask, my mind briefly going to Anthony and wondering if he's doing what I asked him to do.

He'd better, I tell myself, *or when I get back, we're going to have more than just a little talk this time. I really should find time to give them a quick call, but it's been impossible so far.*

"Repent," Mindy jokes, "for thou art cursed with the younger sibling. And with great wailing and gnashing of teeth, the elder siblings were thus cursed."

I can't help but to laugh. "Something like that."

"Nah, I'm just joking," Mindy says more seriously. "I don't know what I'd do without that girl."

"Then why didn't you come here with them? If a coffee shop is your thing, I'm sure John could've set you up."

Mindy frowns. "Because when Dad died . . . I just felt paralyzed. Like, I didn't know what to do with myself. Then running the coffee shop gave me something to focus on. Mom moving away was like a relief at the time. When she was around, it reminded me of him too much."

"I'm sorry to hear that. But I definitely understand where you're coming from," I tell her honestly. "My parents . . . they're not together either."

She peers at me closely, looking at me with real concern. "What happened?"

Before I can reply, the waiter returns with my drink. I look over the menu quickly and decide. "I'd like the lamb kebabs with couscous and grilled vegetables. Mindy?"

"That sounds . . . actually, I'll have the same," Mindy says, giving me a little smile. "What? You were right on the wine, so I figure I'll trust you on the food too. So . . . you were saying?"

"My father doesn't speak to me," I say when the waiter is gone. "We had a disagreement back at the company."

Mindy fingers her wine glass. "You know, there's a lot I don't know about you, Oliver. Hell, I didn't even have time to Google you. What was the disagreement over?"

I hesitate. This conversation isn't going in the direction I want it to go. I'm supposed to be turning up the heat, not turning up the mush. "I'd rather not talk about it. At least right now."

Mindy frowns. "That bad?"

"It was." There's silence for a few moments as I fidget, trying to think of anything to steer conversation away from me, but thankfully, Mindy doesn't push things any further. Finally, I glance around the balcony at her family. "So how do you think it's going?"

Mindy looks around, thinking deeply before replying. "I think everyone is pretty much fooled, if that's what you're talking about. Well, except for Grandma, but she's always wary. But you need to stop with the tricks."

I hide my grin behind the glass. "I'm done with those. Nothing but complete obedience from me from here on."

"Why do I think you're mocking me?" she asks suspiciously. "And why is it that almost everything you say seems to have a double meaning?"

"It's a talent of mine, one of many, I might add," I say with a grin. "When I was in school, they always told us never to talk yourself into a corner. Always give yourself another possible explanation in case things go wrong. So . . . well, I'm having fun—aren't you?"

"I most certainly am not," Mindy says, blushing and tucking a lock of her rich brown hair behind her ear. "I mean . . ."

"You're playing the game as much as I am," I finish for her. "And that's fine. It's no fun playing a game without a good partner to play it with."

"Why did you do this?" she says suddenly, trying to duck out of the way the conversation is going. "What is it that Gavin has on you?"

The ability to hide pocket sevens and the devil's own luck on the flop, I think, but I don't tell her that. "Well, he and I have known each other since soon after I got back to town. And he did something big for me, so I owed him one. I'll be honest, I thought he was insane when he first proposed it, but then . . ."

The waiter interrupts us, bringing our plates. He sets them down before leaving, and I give Mindy a nod. "*Bon Appétit.*"

"*Salud,*" Mindy says, reaching for her wine. As she does, her hand hits the bottle of sauce that the waiter had brought for our kebabs, and it tips over. "Shit!"

Before I can react, sauce has splashed all over my plate, and I'm pretty sure I have some of it on my shirt. Mindy blushes, reaching for her napkin, but I wave her off. "It's okay, really."

"Really?" she asks nervously, and I look at my right hand, which got covered in sauce all over my index finger.

"Really. Here, try some for me," I say, holding out my finger to her. "Tell me if it's too spicy, or else I might end up with hiccups all afternoon."

"No way," Mindy says, stopping when I put my finger against her lips.

"Do it," I say, lowering my voice. "Open your mouth."

Her eyes darken as she opens her lips, and I slide my finger into her mouth, my heart quickening and my cock jumping to rock hardness in a split second as she licks my finger. Her lips are velvety soft, and her tongue . . . it's beyond words. It's devilish, erotic, and as she sucks my finger in deeper, I can tell she likes it as much as I do.

"Hey, get a room over there!" Roxy yells from her table.

Mindy freezes, pulling her head back and her face blushing furiously. Not saying a word, she gets up and runs into the house. I'm on her heels in half a second, ignoring the fact that my cock is tenting my pants or the impending argument between Roxy and her mother as I follow Mindy inside.

She's quick, her shame and my hard-on giving her an advantage until I catch her just outside our bedroom. I grab her arm and pull her to a stop, where she spins against the wall, her eyes wide and desperate. "You said you were done with that!"

"I didn't say you could leave," I say, moving close to her. I step even closer, putting my arm out and trapping her against the wall. "Who gives a shit what Roxy says? Everyone ignores her antics most of the time, it seems. You were enjoying it as much as I was."

I reach out and stroke my finger down her cheek, and she's practically trembling beneath my touch. "Stop," she half moans, half whispers. "Just stop!"

"Why?" I ask, leaning in closer. We're less than two inches apart, and I can feel the heat and the tremble of her breath on my skin, and I want her so badly I could take her right here in the hallway. "You're running from what we both want. What we both need."

A soft sigh escapes her lips. "We're not supposed to be doing this."

"There's nothing wrong with it," I whisper, leaning in closer. "There's nothing wrong with having a little bit of fun."

I move in closer, and our lips touch again. Our kiss is soft at first before growing hot, and I trail my lips down her neck, licking and feasting on her skin. She's delicious, and she melts into my touch, her hands pulling me closer as I close my hand around her left breast, feeling her hard nipple under my fingers and pulling on it.

"Oh, sweet God," Mindy moans, her thighs parting as I slip a knee between them, and she starts grinding against me. "What the hell are we doing?"

"What you need, Princess," I moan, moving my hand from her breast and down her belly to unbutton her jeans. I slide my hand inside and run my hand over the slick satin of her panties. She's soaked, nearly dripping wet as I slide them to the side and slip two fingers inside her while the heel of my hand rubs against her clit.

I know I shouldn't be doing this here in a hallway. Someone could walk by and see us. But I'm filled with so much desire I don't want to fucking move. And the danger of someone seeing adds to the excitement.

"Oh, fuck," Mindy moans, her fingernails digging into my shoulders as I nibble on her ear.

"You know you want this as much as I do," I whisper in her ear, rubbing the secret spot inside her quickly as I rub my thumb over her clit. "Say it. Say you want it."

"No," Mindy moans, trying to fight it and losing. "I can't . . ."

"You can. Say it. Say you want to feel my cock pumping into you and making you scream. You know how good it'll feel stretching you open and making you—"

"Coming," Mindy moans as her pussy tightens around my fingers. She clamps her lips on my neck, stifling her cries against my neck as she bites down, and I hiss, the pain addling to my strokes as I keep her coming, melting against my hard body and clinging to me, needing me . . . wanting me.

When she sags against the wall, spent, I pull my fingers out and run them under my nose, relishing the scent before I lick them clean. "So fucking delicious."

"Fucker," Mindy half gasps, half curses me, even as a satisfied grin crosses her beautiful face. "That was totally against the rules."

"I told you, I don't like rules," I say, stepping back. Mindy doesn't move. Her legs are still shaking from the intensity of her orgasm. I turn and start walking down the hallway before I stop and look back. "And Princess?"

She can't even speak, but her eyes find me.

"Next time," I say, giving her my best intense look, "it's not going to be my fingers. You're going to be coming on my cock."

CHAPTER 13

MINDY

I lean back against the wall, buttoning up before someone sees and trying to catch my breath. My legs are trembling from the aftershocks of the orgasm Oliver gave me, and my heart is still hammering in my chest. And the intensity of his promise as he walked away . . . I can't help but wish he would've dragged me into our room and fucked me senseless.

I suck in a trembling breath, rubbing at my throat where I can still feel the burning kisses he left on my skin. My panties are soaked. I need to change them. His eyes held sweet promise the whole time, his fingers ripping a climax from me that was otherworldly.

This is getting out of hand. I wasn't supposed to feel this way, I want him to take me. To possess me. And I don't care about any of my fucking rules anymore. I want him to break them all.

"Are you okay, darling?" a soft voice says behind me.

I nearly jump out of my skin when I look to my right to see Grandma looking at me with concern.

What the hell? How the hell did she sneak up on me? She can barely move.

I swallow and flash a cheery smile. "I'm fine."

"You sure?" She persists. "You ran away from your table like a bat out of hell. The dessert wasn't even served yet."

"I just needed to clean up what spilled on me. I didn't want it to stain."

She's quiet for a moment, letting me squirm in my obvious lie. We can both see my shirt is unchanged. Finally, she looks at me. "Is everything all right between you and Oliver?"

"Of course," I say. "Why wouldn't it be?"

Grandma waves her hand lightly. "Oh, I don't know. It just seems that you're not happy when asked about him. To me, that's a sign that there is trouble."

"There's nothing wrong between me and Oliver. If anything, I'm just a little high-strung about Mother getting married. After what happened to Dad, I never thought I'd see the day." While the last part's true, I'm just trying to deflect her curiosity. The truth is . . . there might be trouble, but not what she's thinking. There might actually be something building between us.

Grandma shakes her head. She loved Dad like a son. "I never thought so either, but you know people have to move on with their lives. It wouldn't have been fair if she sat there and lived in the memory of your father and never started living her life again. Look at me. I never remarried, and a part of me regrets it."

This is news to me, and I feel compelled to take her hand in mine.

"Oh, Grandma, I had no clue that you were lonely. You always seem so strong and independent."

"That was just the shell that I put around myself. Every morning I wake up alone is terrible. It gets to you after a while," she says.

I shake my head, tears forming in my eyes. "Grandpa would've wanted you to be happy."

"You know, Mindy, for the longest time, I thought the opposite. But then I realized that I was projecting my fears onto my deceased husband. I felt guilty because of my own feelings. By the time I realized my truth, it was too late. Now I would be happy and just settle for a great-grandbaby."

Damn, *that* again. Why, oh, why am I to be saddled with these expectations? It's not fair to Grandma, but it's also not fair to me, and it makes me feel even more like a liar.

I do a nervous chuckle, trying to buy for time. "Well, maybe we'll surprise you."

It makes me sick to my stomach saying it, but I don't know what to say. "Babies do tend to sort of just . . . well, happen."

"Well, as much as I would love that," Grandma says, "I wouldn't dare ask you to do it to make me happy. If it happens, it happens. The most important thing is to live your truth. Because when you do that, the universe will make all the things you want happen."

Live your truth. When I'm living a damn lie. I can't believe I allowed myself to get into this! What was I thinking? I'm too used to joking about things and brushing things aside. I didn't stop to consider the feelings of others who would be caught up in my web of deceit because I didn't think it was that serious.

It's hard, but I manage to plaster a grateful look on my face. "Thank you so much for your words of wisdom, Grandma. Don't know what I'd do without you." I pull her into an embrace, holding her frail body tight. "What can I do to ever show you how much you mean to me?"

"How about visiting me more often? You don't want to wait around. The next time you see me, they might be carrying me out in a cardboard box."

"Oh, stop it. I'll do better. I promise."

"That's what I want to hear," Grandma says. Standing on her tiptoes, she gives me a kiss. "Now come back out here and get your dessert. The others will be wondering where you went."

"Okay, I will," I tell her, turning toward my room. "After I go to the bathroom to tinkle."

She nods at me and totters off. I sigh in relief as soon as she's gone. This is turning out to be harder than I imagined. I thought it would be easy to come back, crack jokes, and hide behind all the bluster. Oliver isn't making it easy by being so irresistible.

Just a few days, I tell myself. *This will all be over. I'll tell them Oliver and I are done. And this will just be one bad memory.*

I go to the bathroom and clean up, changing my panties. He's so going to pay for that.

Back outside, there's a commotion going on. Grandma is waving her arms, yelling at Mom, while Bertha is going off like she's on crack, and it takes a moment for me to figure out what's happening.

"I told you about keeping this dog on a leash!" Grandma is snapping, pointing at Bertha, who is circling her and barking at her like she's intruder. I look, and my breath catches in my throat as I see that Grandma's slacks have been ripped, although I don't see any blood. "That heffa doesn't like me!"

"I got it," Oliver says, rising to his feet and letting out a piercing whistle. Bertha stops in her tracks, sitting on her haunches. Slowly, Oliver approaches her. When he gets close, he bends down and picks her up with ease.

"There, there, girl," he says, stroking her gently. "Time to put you in time out."

"Wow," Roxy says, shocked by how easy Oliver handled the problem. "You're a dog whisperer too?"

"Glad someone could tame that little heathen," Grandma mutters, retaking her seat. "If I'd known Mary Jo was going to let that ball of fur run wild, I would have brought my cat, Giselda, to put her in her place."

I ignore Grandma for the most part, my heart fluttering as I watch Oliver hold and stroke Bertha. I don't even know why. I'm okay with pets, but the way he's holding the dog in his arms, almost like it's a baby, is doing weird things to my ovaries.

I walk over and sit back down at the table. Oliver follows me over, still holding Bertha.

"That was something else," I say to him as he sits down in his seat. The dog looks like it's silly putty in his hands, nuzzled against his chest. It's hard to act like nothing happened after he just finger-banged me in the hallway, but I have to pretend like nothing did, both because it's my family and because I need to maintain my sanity.

"I have a way with dogs," Oliver says with a smile, looking up at me. His eyes seem to say to me, *and with women.*

A flush comes to my cheeks and I look away. I can still feel his fingers inside me, and I want more. So much more.

Oliver gives me a questioning look. "Are you okay?"

"Yeah," I lie through my teeth, giving him a sickly, weak grin. "I just . . . I could use a little bit of that Panna cotta."

"Here," Oliver says, taking a bite of his before sliding it over to me. "Take mine. I think Roxy has devoured the rest."

"Thank you," I say automatically. Oh, God, I'm thanking him now?

The Italian custard is delicious, and as I eat, I watch Oliver. I'm afraid. I came into this week thinking this would all be easy. That Mom would be so much the center of attention that I wouldn't have to keep building lies on top of lies. And if I got lucky, maybe even get a little play cock.

Now, my defenses are crumbling, and I'm constantly thinking about babies and the idea of Oliver's thick, juicy . . .

I'm hanging on by my fingernails at the edge of a bottomless pit, and I don't know how much longer I can keep it up.

CHAPTER 14

"*A* blob!" Roxy guesses excitedly as Layla spreads her arms out, wiggling them around before making big circles with her hands. I have no idea how Roxy's getting blob out of it, but then again, I have no damn clue what Layla's trying to say either.

We're sitting in the living room playing Charades after dinner. It was nice, too. There was no gaming between us, just a good time. Mindy seemed to enjoy herself. She smiled, and as we talked, I felt myself being drawn to her more and more.

Not that I'm going soft. I can't stop thinking about the feel of her tight, slick pussy on my fingers or the way her teeth bit into my skin when she came. Now, playing Charades and having her next to me, I'm . . . torn. Good guy, bad guy, or just be the guy for Mindy? I can't decide anymore, except that I fucking want her.

"Fat ass!" Roxy yells, pulling me back to the game. "Mindy has a fat ass!"

Layla drops her act, throwing her hands in the air. "I meant to say

Mindy has a big brain. That she's smart!"

"You're horrible!" Mindy says with a huge laugh. "You couldn't wait to do that. I've seen you trying to get it in for three rounds now."

Roxy laughs. "You know I was just playing. If anything, you could gain some back there."

"I don't mind Mindy's curves myself," I say, rubbing her thigh. "They're in all the right places."

Mindy blushes, but before the next round can start, my phone rings. I pull it out to see that it's from Gavin. Showing Mindy the caller ID, I excuse myself and go outside to the patio, where it's another picture perfect night. "Gavin, what's up?"

"Hey, Oliver, I was just calling to see how things are going," Gavin says with a chuckle. "Brianna and I haven't heard from you two. We got worried."

"It's going pretty good, actually," I say, leaning against a wrought iron fence and chuckling. "We're playing Charades, believe it or not."

"Really? Doesn't sound like your style," Gavin says. "Any sparks between you and Mindy? At each other's throats?"

I chuckle. Oh, there's been sparks all right. "Nah, we're good. I'm not going to lie, there were a few hiccups at the start, but everything's going well now."

"I'm glad to hear that." There's relief in Gavin's voice, and I know he cares about Mindy beyond her being his wife's best friend. "I'll be honest, I wasn't sure if you could pull it off. Have you checked in on your brother yet?"

"I need to call him after this, actually. I've been meaning to. Do you know if my house is still in one piece?"

"From what I can tell. At least nobody's called the cops yet."

I shake my head. Hopefully, Gavin's joking. "Well, I'd better take care of that then. Mindy's mom is all about family time, so I won't have a lot of time. Take care, man."

"You too. And be good to her, okay?"

"You know it," I say, hanging up the call. I tap my phone against my chin for a moment, then dial Anthony's cell. It's a good sign when he picks up on the second ring. "Hey, Tony?"

"Oli, I'm dyin' here," Anthony says. "She's kicking my ass."

I chuckle. "If she could kick your ass, I wouldn't be worried. You doing okay?"

"Let's see," Anthony says under his breath. "I'm doing laundry, cleaned the whole house top to bottom, and so far, the closest thing I've had to getting laid was some late night downloaded porn. How do you think I'm doing?"

"Sounds just fine to me," I crack, and Anthony laughs. "Seriously, though, Mom's doing okay?"

"Yeah, we're doing fine," Anthony says. Suddenly, music comes on in the background, and Anthony scrambles. "Sorry, I had my game on pause. The network just put me back in."

"What else have you been up to in your free time?" I ask, not really caring about his game.

"Nothing, just chilling and doing my best to take care of Mom, that's all. She's saying I should go out Friday night, so maybe I'll bounce then. Hey, speaking of that, you bang that chick yet?"

I ignore his question, and Anthony gets the message. He changes subjects. "Hey, Martha wants me to go with her to look at some property that you said you want to look at."

"I think she can do that fine by herself," I reply. "Don't worry about it."

"Well, she's insisting. Don't you trust me? I looked at a lot of property for Dad."

I sigh, nodding as I reply. "Okay. Go on, but no shenanigans."

Anthony laughs. "Dude, I can be serious when I need to be. You gotta have faith in me."

He's right, and Anthony needs something to do besides porn, video games, and helping Mom around the house. "That's what scares me. All right, man, you take a look and tell me about it when I get back. Take care of Mom."

I hang up from him and go back inside, where I find that the game's wrapped up and everyone's gone to bed except Mindy, Layla, and Roxy. Layla's got a drink, while Roxy is leaning back, her legs kicked over the arm of her chair, laughing at something. "What'd I miss?"

"Roxy sent everyone to bed with her silliness. She answered John's attempt at 'John Wayne' with 'my sister likes anal'." Mindy rolls her eyes. "You're worse than me, you know that? You have no filter," she says, looking at Roxy.

Roxy throws her hands up. "Yeah, well, we all suck at that game. Someone had to bring the fun."

Mindy shakes her head, yawning. "Well, I'm a little tired too. I think I'm going to bed with my future husband."

The way she says those words makes my heart pound in my chest. Her future husband. Does that mean she's going to perform her wifely duties? My cock twitches in my pants and excitement courses through my veins. Her future husband. Damn.

I get up off the sofa and help Mindy to her feet. Her hand stays in mine, and I swear her fingers squeeze mine even after we get up. I barely pay attention until my calf bumps the coffee table, and I turn to see Roxy grinning. "Good night, ladies," I tell them.

Roxy's grin widens. "Goodnight, lovebirds."

We walk upstairs to our room, and I'm feeling blood rush through me every step of the way. This isn't teasing like before, and it certainly isn't the aggressiveness that I gave her earlier. Mindy's fingers are entwined in mine the whole way, and her demeanor seems different.

She's ready.

"What's up?" I ask softly to make sure nobody overhears us. "Charades bore you to death?"

"No," Mindy says, giving me a deep, longing look. "But after earlier, we both know things are different. And I'd rather do it this way than someone walking in on us."

I lean in close, and Mindy pauses for only a second before putting her hand on my neck and pulling me in for a kiss. Our first kiss was nearly forced, and the second was in front of her family. Earlier, I kissed her neck and she was passionate, but it was just sex.

This is smoldering. Her tongue slides over mine, and I taste her mouth. I feel her press her body against mine as her hand pulls me in deeper, and we're both promising the other things with our lips that words can't even begin to explain. She moans softly into my mouth and I groan back, my cock throbbing in my pants as she cups me, and we pull back. She turns and starts up the stairs, her voice shaky. "How's that?"

"Not bad," I grin, letting her know it was amazing. I take her hand again. "So what did you think of today?"

"It was an interesting day," she says as we reach the door to our bedroom. "I loved how you handled Bertha. That was sweet."

We go inside, and I close the door, pushing Mindy against it, not pinning her but just keeping her there by the force of my eyes alone. "What else did you love?"

Her lower lip trembles as she looks at me. We both know what we want, and while it feels dangerous, I don't care. I need her, and the rush I get from having her this close is bigger than anything else I've felt in my entire life.

I place my hands on her waist, tugging her away from the door and close to me, pressing her body against me and looking into her beautiful eyes. "You haven't answered me yet."

Mindy doesn't answer. Instead, she puts her arms around my neck and I know I have her. She's mine. The girl who has excited me since the first time I saw her picture is totally mine.

I lean in for the kill, intent on working her body from this side of the moon to Sunday, when there's a knock at the door.

You've got to be fucking kidding me.

CHAPTER 15

MINDY

J pull away from Oliver with a gasp, my skin prickling with desire. I want him so fucking badly I can practically taste it.

I shiver. Ever since dinner started, I felt like I was just going along, doing what came naturally, waiting for this moment. From the moment I stood up and took his hand, it was like my mind was on cruise control.

But can I control what comes after?

"Don't answer that," I say breathlessly, leaning back in to kiss him again.

Oliver begins to shake his head when I hear Roxy's muffled voice. "Mindy, open up. I know you're not asleep yet. You guys literally just left the living room."

I roll my eyes, cursing my sister. I turn around and take the two steps to open the door. Roxy is standing there with a smile on her face while holding Bertha in her arms. "What?"

"Ooh, I hope I didn't interrupt anything," she says, a mischievous sparkle in her eyes.

I want to choke her. "Oh, yeah, I was just about to pull out my strap-on. Oli's got a fetish, you know."

She slaps me playfully on the arm. "You liar!" She looks over my shoulder at Oliver. "She's lying, right?"

"You'll never know," Oliver says.

I nod at Bertha. "What's this?"

Roxy grins again. "After Mr. Dog Whisperer here showed his skills today, I thought this would be the best place for her for tonight. So . . . here."

She thrusts Bertha forward, and I step back, totally disbelieving. "What are you doing?"

Roxy nods. "Grandma was going to kill her, and Mom wouldn't let her stay in her room tonight because she had an accident or something. She kept running and pawing on Maw Maw's door. That used to be mom's room. I tried to take her with me, but she kept whining and I want to be able to sleep."

"And you think she's gonna be fine here with a couple of strangers?"

Before Roxy can reply, Oliver walks over and takes Bertha from her hands. "It's fine, we've got this. Goodnight, Roxy."

I turn to glower at him, but when I see the small dog in his arms, my heart melts. "Yeah . . . goodnight, Roxy."

Roxy beams at Oliver. "Thank you. You have a heart of gold, unlike Miss Evanora over here."

"Goodnight, Roxy," I repeat forcefully. "Love you."

I gently shut the door in her face. I hear her mutter some insult on the other side of the door, but I can't make out what it is. Instead, I turn to Oliver. "You must really like dogs."

He nods, petting her. "I always had golden retrievers. Loyal to a fault and greatly behaved. Bertha's no retriever, but she'll do in a pinch."

Bertha snuggles into his arms, and I swear she's claiming him as her own. I just can't get over how cute she looks in his arms.

I reach out and stroke Bertha's soft fur. She's not as bad or as annoying as she was earlier, or maybe it's just who's holding her. "I love seeing you hold her."

A slight smile turns up Oliver's lips as he stares down at the dog. "Do you, now?"

"Yes. I can see the soft, vulnerable side of you. And it makes me . . ."

He looks up at me, and there is fire in his eyes. Fire that heats my body again in an instant. Soft and vulnerable? No, those aren't the right words. Protective, nurturing . . . those words might be better, because I don't think anyone in their right mind could call Oliver Steele soft.

"Makes you what?" he asks, his voice low and magnetic.

Sweat beads my brow as my heart pounds in my chest. "Want you even more," I finish.

I can't believe I admitted that! To hell with it. It's true.

Oliver gently sets Bertha on the floor and takes my hand, leading me over to the bed.

"Then why not enjoy the benefits of having a fiancé?" he says, running his fingers along the curve of my left earlobe. "You know, I have a special talent."

"What's that?" I moan as his fingers find the little spots along my skin that send sparks shooting through my body.

"Let me show you," Oliver says, urging me back. I resist for a moment, but my body can't fight anymore, and I sit down with Oliver kneeling on the carpet. "See? You always wanted me kneeling at your feet."

I giggle as he pulls me down into a kiss and I'm swept away. His tongue is liquid fire in my mouth as he nibbles and sucks on my lips, his hands stroking my thighs and urging my knees apart. He pulls me close, leaving open-mouthed kisses down my neck, my heart pounding in my chest as he comes closer and closer to the edge of my sundress. "Oliver . . ."

"Not yet," he teases, pulling back and laying a kiss on my knee. "Trust me."

The bed's just the right height for Oliver as he kisses the inside of my left thigh, his eyes sparkling mischievously as he kisses higher and higher toward the aching, quivering heat of my pussy. Just when I think he's about to dive in, he pulls back, switching to my other leg, leaving another trail of kisses and licks that has my hips jerking before he's even touched my pussy.

"Lie back," Oliver says softly, putting his hand on my chest. I don't want to. I feel the overwhelming desire to watch him, but I find a couple of the pillows and grab them, tucking them under my head as I obey him, lifting my hips as he rolls my panties down my thighs.

The first touch of his tongue on my pussy lips is electric, and my hips jerk all on their own as he strokes his tongue up my lips before kissing and sucking his way back down. Oh, my God, if this is what he means by a special talent . . .

Oliver's tongue has the devil inside as he licks and kisses my pussy, stroking me first with feather-light strokes before dipping deep inside me and growling hungrily as he sucks. I can't control myself, my hands clawing at the bedspread and my thighs squeezing on his head. He grabs my knees and pries them apart, pushing them up and rolling me until he's got me nearly bent in half, staring into his eyes and the glistening shine of his mouth.

"That was just a preview," he purrs, smirking. "Now the fun starts."

Grabbing my dress, Oliver pulls it up over my head and tosses it aside as he starts licking and sucking harder. My body is practically on fire, and I throw my head back, staring sightlessly above me as my body is swept out of control.

Oliver's lips find my clit, and I know I can't help myself, Grabbing the pillow behind me, I quickly pull it over my mouth to muffle my cries as Oliver nibbles and sucks on my clit. I've never felt anything this good before. His tongue is as fast as a humming-bird's wing on the tip of my clit.

This isn't a build up to coming. I've been strapped to a rocket that just lifted off. Oliver's hungry muffled growls are the final straw as he bites my clit just hard enough, and I'm sent into spasms as I come hard. The pillow muffles my screams as I buck and my feet kick helplessly against his broad, powerful back. Black roses bloom in front of my eyes as I run out of air, and I'm on the verge of passing out when my orgasm finally passes. Oliver pulls the pillow from in front of my face, coming up and kissing me.

"Told you I had a surprise," he teases lightly in between gentle kisses.

We squirm higher up onto the bed, Oliver peeling out of his shirt and pants, giving me time to breathe as he climbs into the bed with me, kissing my lips again before kissing down my neck to my breasts. His talented mouth is put to good use as he licks and teases my nipples, not too hard, not too soft while I stroke his hair and feel his skin under my fingertips. He strokes me with his hands, his fingertips running over my hip and down my thigh to my knee before he kisses back up, nibbling on my neck.

"Mmm," I sigh warmly as I pull his head back to kiss him on the lips. Our lips meet again and caress each other until I urge him onto his back. He lies back, sliding an arm behind his head as he looks at me with an amused grin.

"I see you're recovered."

"Now it's my turn to show you my special skills," I tease, reaching for his underpants before stopping. "Wait . . . condom?"

"In the nightstand," he says, chuckling. "I kinda prepared."

I reach over, laughing quietly as I find a pack of condoms and lube, setting them next to him on the pillow before scratching my nails down his chest and lightly kissing his lips as I reach for his boxers again. "Now, let's see . . ."

My words die on my lips as I reach into his boxers and pull out his cock. His cock is perfect. Long, thick, and with a head that is flared just right. My mouth goes dry as I think of how good he's going to feel inside me. "Give it a kiss. It won't bite," Oliver teases. "Unless you're afraid?"

Oh, you won't get that out of me, I think with a light growl as I kiss down his body, biting his nipples just a bit harder than needed as I slide down his body to his cock, looking him in the eye. I kiss the head before licking, dragging my tongue over the silky soft flesh as I work my way down to his perfect, egg-shaped balls, sucking them into my mouth before blowing on them lightly and kissing my way back up, sucking just the tip of his cock into my mouth before holding my hand out.

"Tease," Oliver complains lightly, but he hands me the condom. Using just my mouth, I roll it down his cock, swallowing most of him as I get the condom down as far as it will go before pulling out and grinning.

"I'm planning on your taking it out on me," I retort as I lie on my back again, lifting a leg. "That is, if you can."

"Oh, Princess, you have no idea," Oliver growls. Straddling my left leg, he holds my right leg up as he positions himself, the tip of his cock just starting to stretch me open. "You ready?"

There's something in his words that reassures me, and I nod, smiling more gently than I thought I would. Oliver reaches up and takes my hand, pushing forward. His thick cock spreads me open, and it's so good that I moan from deep in my chest. "Fuck . . ."

Oliver slides all the way in, my pussy clenching and squeezing as I adjust to him. He's amazing, swirling his hips as he stretches me open and setting my body on fire. He reaches up with his left hand, squeezing and massaging my breasts as he starts to pump in and out of me slowly, taking his time relishing my body. "Mmm, you are good."

"So are you," I gasp as he pinches my right nipple. "Hard, Oliver. Please?"

"You only have to ask," he says with a light laugh, his hips speeding up. His cock reaches deep into me with every powerful thrust, and I can hear the headboard start to bang against the wall. I'm too lost in this overload of pleasure to care, though. I just hope Roxy and the rest the family can't hear it as Oliver starts fucking me harder and harder.

His hips smack into mine as he holds my thigh against his chest, pounding me hard, sweat springing out on my forehead. It feels so intense, my body is lit on fire. I'm groaning again uncontrollably, turning my head to bury my face in the pillow to try and stifle the moans when Oliver pinches my nipples again.

"Uh-uh, Princess." He grunts as his cock slams in and out of my pussy. "Look at me."

I turn my head to look into his eyes as he speeds up, the sweat glistening on his skin like diamonds as he hammers me, wiggling his hips back and forth with every thrust and lighting every nerve inside me on fire. I'm being swept away again, but I want to feel one more thing. "Oliver . . ."

"Now!" he moans, and the single word triggers my second orgasm, my body shaking as my pussy squeezes him tightly. I feel his cock swell and the throbbing pulse of his coming, Oliver's eyes rolling up as he grinds into me, the condom catching it all. A whisper in my mind says I don't want the condom, but it's soon overwhelmed by the intense feeling of my orgasm, and I collapse into the bed senselessly.

I feel Oliver pull out, and then the sound of him getting out of bed to take the condom off. I lie there with my eyes closed until he comes back with a warm, slightly damp washcloth, cleaning up my body. "You awake still?"

"I'm surprised you didn't fuck me to unconsciousness," I whisper in reply as I lie on my back, watching as Oliver carefully wipes down my body before running the cloth between my legs. "Where's the condom?"

"Chucked it in the trash," he says, jerking his head. "Didn't want to risk clogging the drain."

I nod, still gathering my wits as he goes back to the bathroom before coming back and sliding into bed, wrestling the sheets until I'm spooned with him, sighing happily. "You're pretty damn amazing."

"You too," Oliver says, kissing the back of my neck before yawning. "Listen, about this . . ."

"Friends. With benefits," I say, taking his hand and placing it on my chest. "No more fighting, okay? Let's just have fun and enjoy the week?"

"I can do that," Oliver says, but I hear something in his voice, or maybe it's just that annoying whisper in my own head again that says after what just happened, maybe being just friends isn't the best idea.

Either way, I yawn again and chuckle when Oliver echoes me, kissing the back of my neck once more. "Goodnight, Oliver."

"Goodnight, Princess Mindy."

＊

I WAKE UP TO WHAT SEEMS LIKE A DREAM. MY BODY IS SPENT, BUT IN a way that feels amazing. Turning over, I see Oliver, his left arm tucked behind his head and his glorious body stretched out, his eyes fluttering behind his eyelids. "Wake up."

Oliver smiles lightly but doesn't open his eyes.

"Rise and shine, sweetie," I whisper playfully, running my fingers over his chiseled abs to slide underneath the sheet. I find the thick tube of his cock and stroke it with my fingers, wrapping my hand around it and stroking him.

He grows hard quickly, and I hear him chuckle. "Rise and shine for sure."

I look up to see his beautiful eyes taking me in, and I snuggle closer, kissing him. A single soft kiss quickly turns into a deeper one, and Oliver pulls me close, finding my ass and squeezing it in his powerful hands.

"One more before we shower?" Oliver urges, and I pull back, letting go of his cock. "Why?"

"We have breakfast," I say regretfully. "We don't have time for this. You know how Mom is."

"Bullshit," Oliver teases. "You know you want it."

I moan as he pulls me back in for another kiss, and I have to force myself to pull away again. "Don't tempt me. I want to feel that cock of yours inside me again. But we don't have time."

"You sure?"

"No," I say, laughing slightly. "Trust me, if we had another half hour . . . but it'll give me something to look forward to later."

He gives me a warm smile, then nods. "Later."

I stretch, knowing my body's on display for him but enjoying the way he takes me in. I'm about to go to the bathroom to take my shower when I notice Bertha lying over in the corner.

"Bertha, dear, are you okay?" I ask, worried.

Instead of popping up and being her normal hyperactive self, she just lies there, looking dejected. "Hey, I think something's wrong with Bertha."

Oliver gets up and comes over. He runs his hands over her sides and even opens her mouth, looking at her teeth and down her throat. "Nothing seems to be wrong," he says after inspecting her.

"Mom's gonna be worried sick."

"Hold on," Oliver says, but I'm too worried to listen. I don't want anything to happen where Mom's wedding could be ruined. I have no idea what could be wrong. I pet the dog, who wiggles in my lap a little but doesn't do much else.

"Uh . . ."

The catch in Oliver's voice causes me to spin around, and I see him squatting in the corner, inspecting something.

"What?" I ask. "Tell me you stubbed your toe."

"I think I found our problem," he says, displaying the empty trash can that has several bite marks around the rim. I think back and try to remember what could have been thrown in there, and then it hits me.

"Oh, my God," I moan, picking up Bertha and looking her in her little doggy face. "You ate the fucking condom?"

CHAPTER 16

OLIVER

"*Y*ou've gotta be fucking kidding me," Mindy demands of Bertha with a disbelieving laugh.

I laugh. "That has to be it. Unless someone came in here and stole it."

Mindy laughs so hard. "So fucking gross!" She shakes her head. "Poor Bertha. But . . . is she supposed to be feeling this way, though? Like, can't dogs eat anything?"

I shrug. "She should be okay. It's not gonna kill her. My dog ate a beer-soaked pair of socks one time and was sick a little, but he was fine after he hacked up the fuzz ball. It was funnier watching him stagger around drunk."

Mindy laughs lightly. "Your sperm must be doggy kryptonite then."

I laugh. "Aren't you glad I didn't make you swallow?"

Mindy chuckles, blushing hard. "Seriously, though, what do we do about this? We have to be down there for breakfast in like twenty minutes," she says.

"Let's just go down there, have breakfast like normal, and then we'll take her for a walk. She'll be fine. She just needs to poop it out."

Mindy giggles. "I hate that it happened, but I can't help but laugh."

I have to laugh too. "It makes for a great story to tell our grandkids." I pause after the words leave my mouth. Grandkids. It was almost as if I was talking like *we'd* have grandkids. Am I really that deep into character after a couple of days?

The mirth flees Mindy's face as well, making an uncomfortable silence, as if the same thought came to her. "I'm gonna go get ready."

"All right," I agree, squatting down next to Bertha and rubbing her belly.

Mindy hurries into the bathroom. We both take our showers and are down in the dining area within the next twenty minutes, just making it. I'm dressed casually in jeans and a breezy shirt because I'm in the mood to relax today, and Bertha's already caused enough stress.

Mindy has on a sundress, a cute little light blue thing that hugs her body. She looks beautiful in it, flirty and sexy with just the right amount of skin showing. I have a fleeting memory of the way those arms clung to me last night, and I have to take a few deep breaths before I can continue.

"Remember," I tell her before we step in the dining room. "Act normal. Anyone asks, we let Bertha out to do her business in the middle of the night."

"I'm not sure that'll be believable," she says before I open the door. With the magic of a natural actress, her face lifts and she puts on a big smile and her voice lifts cheerfully. "Good morning, Mother!"

Everyone is in the dining room for once, with Uncle Charles slouched over a big bowl of what looks like Lucky Charms and looking like death warmed over, while the rest of the family at least looks like they're enjoying the good food the kitchen has to offer. Mindy goes in, giving her grandmother a kiss on the cheek, then her mom.

"Y'all look good this morning," Mary Jo says, her eyes sparkling as she takes us in. "You certainly got up on the right side of the bed this morning."

She most certainly did. On my side.

"Thank you!" Mindy chirps, and I feel a tremor inside. "You look good too, Mom. Everyone's looking happy this morning. Except Uncle Charles, but at least you got some early morning swag going on with that getup."

Rita gives her niece a look. "Swag? You are blind, girl. More like sag."

I nudge Mindy a little. I told her to act normal, not try to distract by overcompensating.

Thankfully, Mindy takes my nudge and shuts up, still smiling. "You sure are happy this morning," Roxy remarks. "You guys must have really rocked the boat last night. Nice job, Captain Oliver. I'm so jealous. I'm about to go down to the beach and find me a nice cabana boy."

I love how this family just rolls with all of Roxy's antics, paying her no mind. I guess after both Mindy and Roxy, they're used to it. John's certainly adapted quickly.

"Hey, Oliver, let's make sure Mary Jo's got us cleared for free time," John says from the front of the table. "I'd love to give you more rides in my pride and joy. My Honey's to-do list is longer than what I get some days at the office."

"I'm not that bad," Mary Jo says. "I'm just . . ."

Suddenly, Mary Jo stops mid-sentence and glances around. "Where's Bertha?"

"Hopefully, stuck on a beach raft and floating away in the ocean," Ivy Jo mutters.

"I gave her to Mindy and Oliver last night so she could sleep with them," Roxy says, looking over at us.

Mindy glances at me, but I'm already on it.

"We let her out in the middle of the night. She was clawing at the door and whining," I say smoothly.

"Well then, where is she?" Mary Jo asks, worried. "She never misses breakfast."

"Calm down, Mary Jo," John says. "She's probably just playing in the garden like she did when she got out over St. Paddy's Day, remember?"

She ignores him. "Bertha!" she calls, "Where are you, honey?"

"Act normal," I whisper in Mindy's ear. I can see the nervousness on her face. "Mary Jo, Mindy and I will find her after breakfast. Don't worry, I'm sure she's around here somewhere."

It settles her enough, and we finish our breakfast in peace. After we're done, Mindy and I go to our room, trying not to practically run. Bertha's still there, her tail flapping around. That's a good sign at least.

Mindy picks her up and tries to cover her with a blanket, but Bertha hates it and squirms so much that I'm worried she'll raise a fuss if we insist. Finally, I grab a towel and throw it over my shoulder, taking Bertha and holding her in my arms so that the towel lies over her and mostly obscures her.

"Let's go," I say. "You take the lead."

I feel fucking ridiculous trying to sneak out of the house with a little dog. But still, this shit is funny, and I can't help it, I start humming the *Mission: Impossible* theme under my breath as we make our way down the stairs. We're clear all the way to the back lawn when Roxy's suddenly on our ass.

"Hey guys! You guys . . ."

I try to hide Bertha, but the dog lets out a little bark, alerting Roxy, and she stops, smiling for a moment before giving us a suspicious look. "Bertha! Mom has been looking all over for her."

"We found her. Taking her for a walk," Mindy says, hoping to end the conversation.

"Can I come?" Roxy asks excitedly, seeming to ignore the fact that I'm *carrying* Bertha.

"Uh . . . no," Mindy says, giving me a desperate glance.

Roxy scowls. "Why not?"

"Because we'd like a little couple time to ourselves," I say with a fake embarrassed chuckle. "A nice walk with our little friend here."

Roxy can't come up with a reason to argue. "Well, give me her if you're so intent on being with each other. I'll take her to Mom and you two can go get your outdoor freak on."

Mindy glances at me, at a loss for words. I think quickly and shake my head. "Actually, Rox, I told your mom I'd find her. I could use the rub on my rep."

Roxy gives me a grin and a nod. "Okay, okay. Buttering up to Mom some, huh? I don't think you need it, but whatever. Have at it."

Roxy goes inside, and Mindy shakes her head when she's gone. "Why couldn't she have just listened to me from the get go?"

"Little sisters never listen to big sisters. And what can I say? I have that charm the ladies love."

I expect some sort of rebuttal but she lowers her lashes. Her reply is almost too soft to be heard. "Yes, you do."

We walk down to the beach, and as soon as we're out of sight of the house, I squat down, setting Bertha down. She walks around, sniffing everything, but definitely not interested in pooping yet.

"Fuck me," Mindy groans, then laughs at her words. "No matter what Roxy said, that's not an invitation. Not yet."

"Later," I remind her, and we start walking. "So, Mindy Price, tell me about yourself. I mean, beyond what I know."

"If you tell me about you," she says, looking so sexy in her sundress that I forget for a moment the reason we're down here. "What do you want to know?"

"Fair," I reply, grinning. "So . . . first kiss. How old were you?"

"Eighteen," Mindy says, and I stop, gawking.

"What, did they send you to an all-girls' school or something?" I ask, trying to imagine how a girl as beautiful as Mindy Price got all the way to eighteen without even kissing a guy. "Was every guy in your school blind?"

Mindy laughs, shaking her head. "Nope. You can thank the orthodontist. I had some pretty badass hardware in my mouth for a few years. Hard to kiss a girl when she looks like an extra in a Mad Max movie. You?"

"Twelve," I admit, shrugging. "Junior high dance. It was a dare. Trust me, I wish I had a better story. It was terrible."

Bertha starts doing the dance, and I stop. "Wait . . . I think we've hit the jackpot. Come

on, Bertha, baby, show me the money."

Mindy turns her head, shading her hand over her eyes. "Oh, my God, this is so fucking gross. I'm a coffee vendor, not a plumber," Mindy says. Bertha finally squats and does her business. "Damn, did it come out?"

I squat down, grabbing a stick and poking in the mess. "There it is."

"I should've brought a barf bag," Mindy says, gagging. Bertha is herself again at least, running around and doing the little shake. "Well, I guess we got lucky. She looks fine like you said. Come on, let's go back."

"Hold on," I say, reaching out and taking her wrist. "Q and A isn't done yet, is it?"

Mindy looks down at my hand, then smirks. "Guess not. So, tell me, how many girlfriends did you have in school anyway, Mr. I Got My First Kiss At Twelve?"

I feel heat creep up my neck, then chuckle. I asked for it. "Zero."

"You liar!" Mindy says with a laugh. "There's no way you didn't have a girlfriend. Or ten!"

I shake my head, sobering up. "God's truth, not even in college. My father . . . well, he pushed me hard. Since my folks were divorced, he turned all of his focus on me. Nothing was ever good enough. All Conference in football? Should've been All State. Three point eight GPA? Should've been four. I was so stressed by him that keeping a *real* girlfriend was pretty much impossible."

"I noticed you emphasized *real*." Mindy comments, and I shrug. I won't lie. "Thank you for not lying."

"What about you?" I ask, trying to change the focus. "I mean, even with the mouth hardware, your personality had to have gotten you plenty of attention."

Mindy laughs and hugs her body. "I've always been wild, but in that department, it wasn't always so. In High School, I was the out girl. I was 'that' girl."

"What do you mean?" I ask, feeling drawn to her, I step closer, putting my arms around her waist from behind, and she snuggles against me.

"*That* girl, you know? The girl who's fun to hang out with but nothing more. I was the walking, talking personification of the Friend Zone. That changed later, but yep, that was me then."

I smile, kissing her neck. She moans and reaches back to grab my jeans, pushing her hips into my rapidly hardening cock and making us both gasp.

"Wait," Mindy says, pulling away and turning to look at me, her lip trembling and her dark eyes wide with arousal and desire. "What about Bertha?"

"She can watch." I chuckle, reaching for Mindy and pulling her closer. "She won't run off."

"And if someone sees us?"

I growl lightly, pulling her against me and kissing her neck. She moans, arching her neck, and I lift her up, whispering in her ear. "Then let them watch and be jealous."

I reach down, massaging and squeezing the taut swells of her ass, hungry for her body. Bertha yips and yaps but gets distracted by a gull, leaving me with nothing to focus on but Mindy's body. I stroke and caress her, tugging on the straps of her dress as she pushes away. "What?"

My fears of her backing away are relieved as she drops to her knees, reaching for my belt. "I know you wanted this last night," she says with a chuckle. "And this morning too."

My eyes widen as she frees my cock out of my pants and kisses the head, licking around it for a moment as she pumps my shaft before sliding it between her sensual lips. I moan as she swallows more and more of my cock before pulling back. A naughty glint shows in her eyes as she starts pumping my cock in and out of her mouth, bobbing her head while she reaches under and fondles my balls.

She's amazing, her tongue light as a butterfly's wing but with every touch sending massive tingles up my cock all the way to my head. I want to grab her hair and throat fuck her, but something holds me back. I'm rewarded when Mindy works more and more of my cock into her mouth until she has me all the way in, the head of my cock lodged in her throat while she makes little gagging sounds of pleasure.

Mindy pulls back, looking up at me with hungry eyes. "I want you to come in my mouth."

"Why?" I ask, and she laughs lightly.

"Because after this, I want you to fuck me . . . and I don't think you've got a condom on you. So you can finish on my ass."

Her words send another tingle up my spine as she starts sucking my cock again, faster and faster while her right hand pumps my shaft. I'm groaning, my knees shaking as I try to stay on my feet. Time stretches out, and I cry out, scaring the gulls and almost overwhelming the sound of the waves crashing twenty yards away as my orgasm crashes over me and I fill Mindy's hungry mouth with my come. She sucks greedily, my eyes rolling back as she milks me, massaging my balls until the last drop is gone. Pulling back, she gives me a naughty grin before smacking her lips. "Yummy."

I spread out the towel we used to cover Bertha, but it's not big, and Mindy looks at it for a moment before shaking her head and pulling her panties down her long legs before kneeling on it and looking over her shoulder at me. I read her eyes and drop behind her, kissing her ass as I reach between her legs and massage her dripping wet pussy, sliding a finger inside her as my body recovers.

I kiss closer and closer to the deep valley between her ass cheeks as my finger pumps in and out of her while Mindy moans,

145

lowering her elbows to the sand. I hear Bertha come back, yipping before stopping and wandering off again.

My tongue reaches out to tickle her ass crack, and Mindy gasps but pushes back into my hungry mouth as I wonder . . . have I found the perfect woman? Some women are so shy about this, but Mindy loves it as my tongue circles closer and closer to the puckered knot of her asshole, and when my tongue touches her, she groans from deep inside. "Oh, another time . . ."

I mumble my reply into her ass as I finger fuck her pussy, licking and sucking on her until my cock is hard and throbbing again. I quickly line up behind Mindy, pulling my finger out and reaching up, grabbing her hair for a hold as I thrust deep into her in one long stroke.

Last night, I marveled at how perfect Mindy's pussy felt wrapped and clenching around my cock, but that was with a condom on. Now, my mind is blown away as I feel her fully, and my body cries out in joy as sensations I've never even imagined fill my body. "Fuck, you feel so good."

My hips take over on their own, pumping my cock in and out of her pussy as she moans in front of me, looking back over her shoulder and grinning at me with lust-crazed eyes. "Give it to me, Oli. Fuck me raw. Make my pussy scream."

Her constant stream of filthy words drives me on like whips on a thoroughbred, and I hammer her deep and hard, grunting with every thrust of my cock as I watch her eyes, seeing just where to stop and riding that line, my hips smacking against her ass. I pull her up, biting the curve of her neck as she moans, lost in a haze. "You're mine, Princess."

"Yours . . ." she moans, and I slow down, pulling back a bit as I push her down again, thrusting my cock in time to the waves, drawing out the ecstasy for both of us. Mindy squirms, pushing back into me after a few minutes, and I speed up again.

It's hard not to come inside her. Mindy's body is heaven as she squeezes me, her pussy gripping around my cock as I push her higher and higher. I listen, grinding my hips against her as I speed up, until she cries out, her pussy clamping around me. She's so tight and thrilling as she comes that I barely pull out in time, another hard jet of seed splattering on her ass before I can turn and leave the rest of it on the sand. I tremble. My cock aches from coming so hard twice so quickly. I can't believe how much Mindy pushes me.

I think about what we just did. I wasn't trying to seduce her. I'd totally intended to bring Bertha down here, get the condom out of her, and go back.

I didn't mean for this to happen. It wasn't just fucking on the beach.

But that's what this week was supposed to be. Take the girl out, show her a good time, and clean her pipes if we wanted to.

But not this. Not like this. I never even thought it was possible.

"Oliver?" Mindy asks, and I look up at her, seeing her tentative, concerned smile. "You okay?"

"Yeah," I lie before getting to my feet. Okay? I'm far from okay. I'm starting to wish this were real. "Come on, let's keep walking."

CHAPTER 17

MINDY

*I*t's a little late for lunch, just after two in the afternoon by the time we return from the beach. Walking up the pathway, I feel natural reaching over and holding hands with Oliver. Bertha's running at our heels and circling us, and I have to stop as we climb the stairs from the dunes up to the main property.

The estate looks so beautiful. The sun is still high in the sky behind the house, making it blaze in front of the sapphire blue sky, and I feel my breath taken away. It's just gorgeous. I wonder what it would be like to have all of this, raising a family here. It would be paradise. If only . . .

I suck in a deep breath, trying not to think about it. I know I'm getting carried away with the fantasy. This isn't real. But damn, did his being inside me feel real. The way his hands felt on my body. My neck still burns from his kisses.

It was everything I've dreamed it could be. More than I imagined. I've been with men. I'm no virgin, but none of them were anything more than a fuck or a passing thought. None of them were more than a physical exercise, a release of primal need.

I've always kept a shell around me to protect me from the very thing I'm feeling right now. But I have to wonder if I'd be feeling this way if we weren't pretending to be engaged.

As if sensing my thoughts, Oliver smiles at me, squeezing my hand. My heart skips a beat, warmth flowing in my chest. "Don't worry," he says reassuringly. "Nobody's gonna blame us for being out for so long. I just hope Roxy told your mom we had Bertha."

I nod, knowing I need to get ahold of my emotions. It's scary to be feeling anything when this charade is over in a few days.

We don't even reach the steps before Roxy's out the front door to confront us.

"Where the hell have you been?" Roxy demands. "Mom has been going nuts. I told her you went on a walk, but when it stretched for hours, I started wondering if we were gonna have to send out the Baywatch crew." She pauses, then looks back and forth between the two of us before grinning, reading our expressions. "What did you do, ride a surfboard?"

"No, I got eaten by a shark," I joke. "What's it to you?"

Roxy waves it off, chuckling, "I just wondered. You said you were going on a walk."

Oliver chuckles. "We just walked down to the dunes and watched the waves a little. It was gorgeous."

Roxy rolls her eyes. She knows we had enough time to walk halfway to the next town if we'd wanted. "Well, I'm glad you two lovebirds had fun. But Mom wants to see you."

"Why?" I ask.

"She wants help with stuff. I don't know. Decorations, I think, and they have to go up this afternoon and evening. You know how she is—everything needs to be her way, and she refuses to hire it out. I know she wants Oliver to help move that big ass sound system."

"Easy enough," Oliver says. "I'll handle it so John and Charles don't have to."

Roxy shakes her head. "Good. Because let me tell you, they probably won't be much help. I love them both, but those two geezers can't do much heavy lifting."

I have to laugh. She's rude but she's right. "Roxy!"

"What?" she asks innocently. "I'm just sayin'."

Inside, Mom is happy to see us and gives Bertha a gigantic cuddle. "There you two are! We're preparing to go to the reception hall. We've got staff moving stuff there but still need some help." Bertha squirms in Mom's arms, turning to lick her face, and I have to snicker as Bertha gets a noseful of foundation. Mom doesn't seem to mind. "I was so worried about you, snookums!"

"Lord have mercy, I was hoping that rat catcher was gonna stay gone," Grandma mutters, sitting in a chair and fanning herself. "Most peaceful couple of hours my whole visit."

"Quiet, Momma," Mom says, setting Bertha down, where she immediately begins hopping around like her normal self. "All right, let's get going. Oliver, John and Charles are waiting for you in the garage."

Everyone starts filing out of the room. When it's just the two of us, Oliver turns to me. "I really enjoyed this morning," he says softly.

"Besides the dog poop investigation, I did too," I say before I give him a smirk. "You really ought to be careful where you plant your seed."

He laughs. "I know the best place to plant it next time."

A flush burns my cheeks, remembering the unbridled passion on the beach and the way we seem to crash like the waves themselves. He grabs me and pulls me in, giving me a kiss that leaves me wanting more. "See you at the reception hall," Oliver says.

Outside, I get in the SUV with Sam, the driver, behind the wheel. All the women are in it, and Roxy's already called shotgun. "Let's roll, Sam!"

"So what's this place like again, Mom? I know you told me about it over the phone, but I forget the details," I say, turning to her. She's behind me with Grandma.

"You'll love it. It's not that far, only about five miles away. It's on the beach in a little cove," Mom says. "You're really going to love it."

When we arrive at the hall twenty minutes later, it doesn't disappoint. The outside is amazing, a beautiful giant adobe, almost Caribbean-style structure sitting just on the edge of the sand. The inside of the hall is gorgeous with huge windows along the eastern wall that give a breathtaking view of the ocean. This place looks like something out of a fairytale wedding . . . but that's what Mom's getting.

"I'm speechless," I breathe as I look around the inside. "Forget the reception. I'd love to have my wedding in some place like this."

"All right, ladies, let's get to work!" Mom says. "Lots to do, and not a lot of time to do it in!"

Roxy and I are given the task of hanging up some electric lights shrouded in lace, and we get to work with the ladder. As we get the strands tacked, Roxy chuckles. "You know, you and Oli should use this place. You guys are just so beautiful together."

"You think?" I ask, my heart aching. Before, I could easily lie, say he was just a bastard who has a hot body, but now, the truth hurts. He's a sham of a fiancé, but he's got everything I've ever dreamed of a man having. Face it—he's a catch.

My cell buzzes in my purse, saving the day. I pull it out. It's Brianna. "Hey, Rox, can you handle this for a few yourself? It's my bestie."

Roxy glares at me, a thumbtack in her mouth. "Hurry!"

"How you doing, girl?" Brianna asks as soon as I pick up the line, and I feel a grin start before my worries start up again. Brianna knows what this all is. Maybe she can help.

"Good. I guess."

"What's wrong? You sound down," Brianna says, and I hesitate. I don't know if I should tell her the truth. "Come on, Min, I know you well enough even over the phone. Aren't you having fun?"

"Oh, I'm having fun," I admit. "All I can handle."

"How's Oliver been?" Brianna asks. "Behaving?"

"No," I say with a little chuckle. "But good. Very good."

"I know that tone, Mindy. Something you need to tell me?"

"Well . . ." I say, wondering how much I should tell Brianna. "At what point did you start thinking you had feelings for Gavin?"

"Oh, it's *that* sort of problems," Brianna says. "Well, to let you know, I think it was about three seconds after I saw him the first time."

"Come on, I'm serious!" I protest. "When?"

Brianna's voice grows somber, and I can imagine that intense look on her face that she has when she's worried about me. "Mindy, it doesn't really matter. It happened. So what's the problem?"

"You know this isn't . . ." I start before lowering my voice. "You know this isn't supposed to be real!"

"And I was supposed to be a one-night stand or a sport fuck," Brianna reminds me. "Look how Gavin and I turned out. If you're feeling something for him . . ."

"Hey! Get off the phone and help me, you lazy skank!" Roxy yells. "I'm not doing all of this my damn self!"

"Roxy?" Brianna asks, and I chuckle.

"How'd you know?"

"She reminds me of some foul-mouthed, cute as hell coffee shop manager I know," Brianna says. "Seriously, though, if you like him . . . don't wait and give yourself the drama I did. Tell him."

"I'll keep that in mind," I reply. "Thanks. Love you, Bri, but I gotta go before Roxy starts throwing tacks at me. Bye."

I head back over toward Roxy, but before I can get halfway across the hall, the doors open. I see Oliver carrying a huge set of speakers, one in each hand, the DJ behind him.

"Over there," she says, and Oliver gives me a sexy little grin and blows me a kiss as he heads off across the hall.

I get back over to help Roxy, who climbs down from the ladder, handing me what looks like paper lanterns. "Here, you hang. I'll hand you the next ones," she says, grumbling. "You know how hard I've been working?"

"Sorry," I say, climbing the ladder. I start putting up the lanterns but get distracted in my thoughts. I think about what a good man Oliver is. With the dog and all that, I could totally see settling down and . . .

I try to push the thoughts away. I have to remember this is fake. In a few days, it will all be over. I just need to enjoy it for what it is—a fun vacation fling.

But it's not that easy. The passion. The connection. All of that feels real.

Maybe Brianna is right.

Roxy waves her hand in front of my face.

"Mindy?" Roxy says. "The lanterns?"

"Huh?" I ask, looking away and blinking. "What's that, Rox?"

"I know you love your fiancé's ass and stuff, but we need to get this done."

I chuckle as we go back to work, doing my best to deal with the questions running rampant in my head.

But there's one thing I know for sure. I don't know what's real anymore.

CHAPTER 18

OLIVER

The bedroom lights are low, and I marvel as I run my fingers down Mindy's arm, enjoying watching the goosebumps rise on her skin. "How do you keep doing that?" she asks, smiling. "Two days of us having sex, and you keep surprising me. I know it's coming and you still make it happen."

"A secret." I chuckle, looking into her eyes. "And you've got great skin."

The past few days have been paradise. With most of the big stuff done, we've had some more time to just spend together. Most of it has been spent talking.

The more and more time we spend together, the more I grow confused. At first, this was all fun and games. But it's turned into something more. Being here with her, getting to know her and her family, I've enjoyed every minute of it.

Sure, some of them are wild. Her sister has sex on the brain way too much, her mother's a bit too worried about money, and her grandmother gives exactly zero fucks what anyone thinks about what she has to say.

But they're real, and they love each other. All of them. And Mindy herself . . . she's more than a Princess. She's an angel.

She reaches up, cupping my face to look into my eyes. Her breathing is still ragged from our early morning quickie, and watching her naked body on top of the sheets, I can't believe that I've had the chance to be with her as often as I have. "That was great," she says, shuddering. "You take my breath away."

"Good," I say, delivering a kiss to her lips. "Because I plan on doing that a lot more."

She smiles for a moment, then it slowly fades. "A lot more? We only have a few days left. Reality's coming, and it's coming too damn fast."

I feel a little jolt. It's now Friday. It's the day before her mother's wedding. Honestly, it feels like our last day together. Our return flight is Monday morning, but I'm sure Sunday will be spent preparing to go home and spending a lot of time with the family. It'll be the hug and kiss goodbye time and a chance to wish Mary Jo and John off on their honeymoon. They're flying out Monday too.

We don't even have all day today. Today is already packed with rehearsals and trying on stuff. This will be our last leisurely morning. And it's hard to admit, but I don't want it to end.

"Yeah," I murmur, my chest feeling like I've got a lead weight pressing down on it. It's taking away my breath and making it hard to even say what I want to say. I want to tell her that the dream doesn't have to end. I want to promise her more than just a fantasy week on the ocean.

But I can't form the words. How can I tell her that I don't think this is fake anymore? Our engagement might be fake, but what I'm feeling damn sure isn't.

"What are you going to do when you get back?" she asks softly.

"Probably check on Mom first, then make sure my business isn't in total shambles before it ever gets off the ground," I say, slightly troubled. Last week, making Steele Security a name in the corporate world dominated my thoughts and my efforts. Now, it just doesn't seem as important as spending time with Mindy. "Then I'll make sure my little shithead brother hasn't burned down my house. I asked him to watch my place."

She smiles. "I'm sure everything will be okay. If he's anything like Roxy, he's a pain in the ass but comes through when your back's to the wall." She sighs and turns on her side, running her hand down my slightly stubbled cheek and making my morning shadow crinkle. "But I'm not gonna lie. I'm not looking forward to going back to that damn coffee shop. I've been having so much fun, and the days have flown by."

"I've been having a blast," I agree. "I've really enjoyed my time here."

A flush comes to her cheeks and goes down her neck to her chest, and she bites her lip, smiling slightly. "Thank you. It means a lot, and you make me feel good. And to think, the first time I met you I wanted to choke you."

I chuckle. "Yeah, well, that was hot. I loved how you walked in there with your little list, thinking you could tame me. It was . . . cute."

Mindy smiles and traces my jaw with her fingers like she's trying to memorize me with her touch as much as with her eyes. "Who's to say I'm not just doing this to wrap you around my finger? An insidious plan to make you my love slave?"

"Who's to say I'm not doing the same? When I first saw you, I told myself you thought you were a queen and I was going to have to be your king. How am I doing?"

Mindy laughs. She runs her hands down my body, making my skin prick. "I can't complain, that's for sure. I don't think I've ever been this satisfied."

I don't need compliments, but her words still warm me on the inside. Her opinion matters to me. It makes me feel important.

Her eyes flicker for a moment before they dim, and I see her gaze grow distant. She's thinking about something. I've grown close enough to her over the past few days to know that look.

"What is it?" I ask her. "Whatever it is, you can tell me."

Her lips part, and she struggles for the words that I can sense even before she tries to form them. They're foolish, but I want her to say them. I want her to tell me that she truly wants me, that perhaps there's a chance for something back home. I don't know how I'd react, but to hear her say those words . . . I need it. I need her.

She looks away, turning over and wrapping her arms around her body. "It's nothing."

"It's something," I say, spooning behind her and feeling her amazingly soft skin press against me. I bring my lips to the back of her neck and nuzzle, knowing just where she likes to be touched already, just how much she likes that little spot right where her hair makes a little V-shape at the nape of her neck. I kiss and nibble, wrapping my arms around her and stroking her arms. "You know you like it. Tell me what's on your mind."

She lets out a soft little moan, arching her back to slide her right breast into my hand and pressing her ass back against my cock. "Jesus, you know what you're doing. But really . . . it's nothing."

"Oh, really?" I say playfully, trailing my free hand down her thigh, enjoying the feel of her soft flesh. "I think you're lying to me."

"What gives you that idea?" she asks breathlessly, gasping as I pinch her nipple and tug on it lightly. "Fuck . . . I didn't know I could get this hot so quickly again."

"I can feel your pulse racing," I murmur, kissing her neck again. "Under my lips."

"That's just because of what you're doing to me." She gasps. "And we both know where your hand's going."

I grin, recognizing the deflection. "Well, if you're not gonna tell me, I can stop. Or I can continue."

She squirms, still not answering me. I pull her tighter against me and press into her. I roll her onto her back and get on top, kissing her lips with more passion. She melts, and I pull back, grinning. "Got anything to say?"

Silence.

"Okay, if that's how you want to play it," I warn her. I bring my lips to her neck, trailing kisses down her body. She arches her back, her head pointed to the ceiling as I stroke her skin with my hands while I kiss down to the hard buttons of her nipples, sucking on them and biting them lightly before I make my way down her belly. Then I stop. "Still nothing?"

"Okay!" Mindy gasps. "Please, don't stop!"

She needs this, we both need this. But I don't want to rush things. We're not going to have many more intimate moments. Fuck everything else. If we have to bring it all to a close in a few days, and this is the last chance for me to show her what she is, what she's starting to mean to me . . . then that's what I'm going to do.

"Oliver, let's make this quick. They're waiting."

As I go down between her legs, my mouth watering at the heavenly scent already wafting from her wet pussy and ready to devour her, I growl, looking up into her eyes. "Let them wait."

CHAPTER 19

"Oh, Mom," I crow, tears coming to my eyes as she steps out of the dressing room in her wedding gown, her arms held out wide. She looks glorious. The beautiful white gown hugs her figure, all lace and classy design that makes her look elegant. The full train scrapes the floor, and she looks like she's walking on a cloud as she crosses the polished hardwood. Tears cloud my eyes as I search for the words to tell her how she looks, but I can't. "You're beautiful. Absolutely radiant."

It's hard to believe that it's already Friday afternoon. After missing breakfast and sleeping in with Oliver, it's been pedal to the floor the whole time. Doing rehearsals, getting last minute adjustments to our dresses, and checking that Sam and the other staff are on the spot with bringing in dozens of people from both sides of the family.

Now, we're all dressed in our gowns for the wedding, doing the last dress rehearsal and fit, making sure things look good. Aunt Rita, Layla, Roxy, and Grandma are all together with us, sitting around the room, and all of us are amazed at Mom as she comes out.

"Beautiful is right," Rita says, putting a hand on her chest. "I can't wait to walk you down the aisle tomorrow."

Grandma cackles lightly. "Yeah, my baby is beautiful, but my word, Mary Jo, your butt looks like it grew three sizes."

Leave it to Grandma to work in a wisecrack. Mom waves it off, knowing it's the design of the dress itself, and of course, Roxy puts her own two cents in.

"Yeah, Mom. You got so much booty in that dress you're gonna be making John holler tonight," Roxy adds, thinking she's funny. It's definitely not something I want to think about, and I doubt I'm alone. Roxy looks cute though in her white knee-length Valentino dress, flirty but still sexy at the same time. It hugs her upper body before flaring itself at her waist but doesn't go full party dress mode and keeps the poof under control. It's perfect for her.

"Oh he'll be hollering all right," I say with a grin, "hollering for her to shut up about where they're going for the honeymoon. You thought about where you're going yet?"

"Probably Hedonism, where they can get their freak on right there on the beach," Roxy says before Mom can answer. It's been one of the only secrets left . . . where they're actually going on their honeymoon.

"Oh, stop it," Mom says, laughing. "You two are such a riot. I love you both."

Roxy and I go over to Mom, the three of us doing a group hug, and I can't help but tear up a little at it. "We love you too, Mom."

We walk out of the dressing room for rehearsals after Mom lectures all of us about what she wants. I can tell Grandma wants to tell her to shut up a few times, but we all just listen, knowing it's her show. It's crowded in the chapel near the reception hall, with staff going around everywhere. There are family members I haven't seen in ages, and I know that tomorrow's going to be all playing catch-up with them. Some of them, like my cousin Jamie, I'm looking forward to. Others, not so much.

"Hey, check it out," Roxy says, jostling my elbow. "Stud alert."

My breath catches in my throat as I follow Roxy's guiding hand. I see Oliver standing with the group of men, talking like he's part of the family. He's just come out of the dressing rooms, and the rest of the room fades away as I look at him.

He's gorgeous dressed in his tux. It fits him in a way that makes him look debonair, relaxed, and powerfully seductive. More than ever, he looks like the devil in a tuxedo. My heart is doing back flips. He is so damn handsome. He sees me and blinks for a moment before giving me a smile and a nod.

"You'd better be careful," Roxy jokes, nudging me again. "I think John's niece is eyeing Oli."

I look around, and Roxy's right. She's practically ogling him.

Bitch better stay away from my man, I say to myself.

Is he my man?

"Wow, you look so handsome," I tell him as I come up. He grins and takes my hand, another thrill running through me at his touch.

"And you look beautiful yourself," he says, delivering a soft kiss to my cheek. My chest gets fuzzy as emotions start running through my body, a mix of panic and arousal and confusion that makes me both smile and want to scream at the same time. He places a hand on my hip, and now desire's added to the mix. When we first came here, it felt weird being on his arm. But now I wear that badge proudly, excited and happy to be here with him.

"I wish there weren't so many people . . ." he says quietly, his voice dripping with need. I know he's not trying to seduce me. He's just being honest. But he's making my blood boil, and I bite my lip. I want to melt into him, to find the nearest empty room and ignore the rest of the world. I want to turn the entire universe into a bedroom, a space where Oliver and I can indulge in each other's bodies and maybe our hearts too. But not here right now. It's too much, and we both know it.

"Later," I promise him, hoping there is a later. I hope there's more than a later, but that's a foolish hope. "By the way, Mom wants us to sit in the front row during the ceremony."

"She didn't want you to walk her down?" Oliver asks, slightly surprised. "Why?"

I shake my head. "I told her to let Rita do it. Grandma was gonna do it but she was scared about falling in front of everyone. I didn't want her to have to pick between me and Roxy. Besides, Rita and her . . . they've always been pretty close."

"I see," Oliver says, looking around as we reach the front of the chapel area. "This is pretty nice."

I nod. "I'm loving it. It's gonna be clear weather tomorrow too. So it's going to be a gorgeous day."

"Well, I know it's only been a few days, but I'm glad. Mary Jo deserves as perfect a wedding as she can get."

We sit down, taking in the whole chapel. "I bet this place looks a lot different in daylight."

Oliver shifts around, pulling his arm around my shoulders as he gets a better view. "I think so. Those windows are going to look out on the ocean, and we'll get a lot more open light. Not that it isn't nice now, but tomorrow, it should look fantastic. The sort of place . . ."

Oliver goes quiet, turning back around, and I lean in. "What?"

"Nothing," he says, giving me a nervous smile. "Just fantasy running away from me."

Before I can push the issue, Roxy walks up, sliding over to find her seat next to me. "Hey, you two lovebirds, I wanted to know if y'all will come to Trixie's with me tonight? I'm gonna be singing and it will be fun to have a few drinks. Just a little non-wedding fun, ya know?"

"It's up to Mindy," Oliver says diplomatically, giving me a look. He wants to, I can tell, although I'm not sure why.

I don't know. I'd love to hear Roxy sing, but what would being out with Oliver outside the fantasy be like? Going with him to Trixie's isn't part of the wedding charade.

"Come on, Mindy, it will be our last night of fun together. What can it hurt?" Roxy asks. "Be a big sis."

"All right," I agree, worried.

❄

THE BASS OF THE MUSIC IS BUMPING AS WE WALK UP TO THE CLUB doors. The line's long, but as soon as the bouncer sees us with Roxy, he waves us through no problem at all. "Hey, Roxy Rox."

"Thanks, Enrique," Roxy says, giving me and Oliver a wink. We go inside, and I have to say, Trixie's is a nice place. The lights are dim, so I can't tell too much about the decorations, but there's lots of mellow blue under-lighting that gives the tiles on the floor a shiny tint. There are flashing lights and lasers, but they're restricted to the stage area in the back of the room and dance floor. It's about three-quarters filled right now, a couple of gay couples but mostly pairs of men and women dancing, grinding on each other as the house DJ spins some sexy club tunes. "So what do you all think?"

I nod, looking at Roxy, who's dressed in a sparkling red halter dress that makes her look cute and sexy. She's totally ready to perform. Oliver is easily the hottest man in here in his fitted black jeans, gray t-shirt, and blazer. I feel sexy myself, dressed in a tight black dress that Roxy said made me look hot.

A guy with blonde hair and the bluest eyes I've ever seen approaches us. He's a handsome guy, about six feet tall. He's dressed in some dark pants and a dark vest over top of his skintight white shirt, but he's clearly not interested in women. Not with the way his eyes crawl over Oliver before he turns his attention to Roxy.

"Hey, Roxy-girl!" he says with a totally put-on lisp, pulling her in for a hug and air-kissing noisily around her face. "You singing tonight?"

"You bet your ass I am. Hey, Brad," she says, gesturing at us both, "this is my sister, Mindy, and her fiancé, Oliver."

"Oh, my gawd!" he says, bringing his hands to his lips, his eyes passing over me and going wide as he takes in Oliver again. "Have I met you before?"

Oliver chuckles, shaking his head no. "Not that I know of."

"Honey, you look like Brad Pitt, with a mix of Chris Pratt and a little bit of Henry Cavill with a side of whip cream and a cherry on top."

We all three laugh, even Oliver, who looks surprisingly relaxed after just being hit on by a man. He just takes it in stride. "Well, Mindy seems to like me."

Brad looks at me, nodding in approval. "Congratulations."

"Thank you . . . I think," I say with a laugh. "So, how long have you known Roxy?"

Right then, the music changes and *Freekaleek* comes on, Petey Pablo's classic earning a cheer throughout the club.

"Oh, hell-o, bitch, this is my song!" Brad yells, bobbing his head and raising his hand while moving his body like an eel. "Sorry. Gotta go!"

He grabs the nearest guy and moves into the crowd and starts twerking. He's dropping it low to the floor and jumping back up again with surprising quickness for a man his size.

"Yaaas, bitch! You better work it!" Roxy yells. "Shake dat ass, bitch!"

Looking at him, I can't help but laugh. "This place is fun."

Roxy smiles, turning her attention back to Oliver and me. "See? I told you. You guys needed to get out. You've been cooped up with us crazy people for five days. It's just not healthy. You needed some relaxing fun."

"Thanks, Roxy," Oliver says, grinning. "Been a long time since I've been in a place like this."

"Come on, I have a table reserved," Roxy says. We go over and sit down, and the music cranks up another notch, making it hard to be heard.

"So when do you go on?" Oliver yells, and Roxy checks her watch.

"About thirty minutes!" she yells back. "You gonna dance?" she asks me.

"Dance?" I ask, shocked. "You've seen me dance!"

"Yeah, but Oli here hasn't!" Roxy teases. "He hasn't seen your Spaz Special yet!"

"I bet she's a great dancer!" Oliver retorts. "I know she can move!"

"Yeah, well, let me see you two tear up the floor," Roxy says. She checks her watch again, shaking her head. "Okay, I've got to prepare. Y'all have fun."

She slides out of her chair, gives me a kiss on the cheek, and leaves. My eyes are immediately drawn to Oliver, who's looking back at me with intensity in his eyes. "Well, let's get some drinks."

The music quiets down for a moment, and he calls a waitress over. "Grey Goose martini for me, and Mindy . . .?"

"Stoli and soda," I order. "Twist of lemon?"

The drinks come quickly, and *Freekaleek* is still playing when I take my first sip. Off in the crowd, I still see Brad getting his groove on. Filled with excitement, the bass of the music is pumping my blood, and I throw back the rest of my drink quickly, deciding to run with it.

"Can you dance?" I ask Oliver suddenly. "I might be bad, but I'm not as bad as Roxy makes it sound."

I think he's gonna tell me no, but then a grin comes on his face. "I might have a few moves."

"Wanna go?" I ask.

He climbs to his feet and my heart soars. "Sure, why not? It'll be a warmup before Roxy gets on stage."

We make our way to the now crowded dance floor, moving into the hot undulating bodies, the bass of the music bumping us as much as the people we're weaving around. *Freekaleek* is still thumping, the extended club mix obviously a Trixie's favorite.

I'm glad. With all this tension in me, I need to let it all out. I've been holding on too tightly, and Oliver notices it as we start dancing. "Relax," he says, grinding against me. "Just have fun."

He places his hands on the small of my back, gyrating against me like he's Channing Tatum and we're in *Magic Mike*. The heat inside my body only rises as he uses it like it's his personal playground, his hands moving down to grip my ass, his intense gaze burning into me.

Watching him, feeling him, I'm fucking shocked. He can move. What can this man not do? He can turn me on with a wink of an eye, fucks like a bull, can tame wild dogs, and now I find out he can move that incredibly hot body of his like nobody's business. *And work mine like it is his business.*

I'm hot and wet between my legs, and it has nothing to do with the temperature in the club.

If I could get him to fetch me Funyuns and make a macchiato, he'd be perfect.

"Wow!" I say, wiping sweat off my brow once the song is over. The way he worked me was fucking hot, and I'm glad the song wasn't longer or else I might not have my skirt on anymore. Seriously, I'm so fucking hot I almost feel like having him take me down the hallway and fuck me. "You can really move!"

He grins. "I'm glad you liked it."

Another song comes on and we dance. Not as hot, but that's mostly because of the song, and then we have to go sit down. The music ratchets down a notch too, and I can see the stage crew getting a mic in place for Roxy.

"Shoot, you wore me out," I say. We sit down, and Oliver orders another round. "Next round is no alcohol for me, okay?"

Oliver nods and sips at his martini. "Just wait until after Roxy's done and we get back to John's."

His words warm my cheeks, and I down about half of my Stoli and soda, needing to cool off.

Brad comes over to the table with his friend just as Roxy climbs up on stage, grabbing the mic out of the stand and waving to the applauding crowd. "What's up, Trixie's?"

"Go, Roxy!" I yell, supporting her. "Work it!"

Roxy laughs, and she begins singing several songs, all pop. Taylor Swift, some Selena Gomez, and a few other pop standards. I cheer through each one. Even Oliver gives her a shout out.

"She can really sing," he says, impressed. "There's no way she can give up on this."

"Yeah, that's my baby sister," I say proudly. I haven't heard her sing in a long time and it's really great. I love hearing her. She was right. I needed this."

After her third song, she takes a moment to pause to address the crowd.

"Hey, everybody. I'm glad y'all are enjoying my set, but I'd like to share something with you. Tonight, I have two very special guests . . . my sister, Mindy, and her fiancé, Oliver. Can y'all give them a round of applause?"

A spotlight opens on us, and everyone is suddenly looking at us and applauding us, and my cheeks burn. *Roxy, I'm gonna fucking kill you!* I say In my head while I bow my head stupidly. Meanwhile, Oliver looks less disturbed, and he just smiles and nods his head at people, giving a little wave.

Up on stage, Roxy laughs. "Ain't her man the best? The past week, we've spent time together, and I've been so inspired by their love. I want something like that one day. So I'm gonna mix it up a bit and dedicate my next song, *I Wanna Love You Forever* by Jessica Simpson, to them both. Because they make me want to have my own forever love."

She clears her throat and a serious expression goes over her face. *No, Roxy. Not this. I can't handle this.* I glance over at Oliver, who also looks uncomfortable, but then he looks at me, and I can see pain in his eyes. A pain that mirrors mine.

You set my soul . . .

Each word is like a stab in my heart as I force myself to listen. The emotion in Roxy's voice rings out. It's so strong. So real. So raw. She really cares about me and my relationship. How in the hell am I supposed to tell her that it's a lie?

I'm gonna love . . .

She hits the high note, and tears come to my eyes as Brad jumps out of his seat while the crowd goes wild. "YASSS, honey!" he yells, leading the cheers. "SING, BITCH, SAAAAAANG!"

I climb to my feet, clapping as Oliver rises as well, and we both exchange awkward glances.

Tears are streaming down my face and I'm unable to speak over the lump in my throat. I'm crying, but not for the reason I should be. Even Oliver's looking choked up, and I wish I could feel worthy of what Roxy just gave me.

"How'd I do?" Roxy says to me after she gets off stage, dabbing at the tears in her eyes with a napkin. "I hope I didn't fuck it up too much."

The tender, vulnerable look in her eyes just adds to the tears streaming down my face. But it isn't because of happiness or gratitude. It's because I feel like an absolute fucking fraud.

As I take her in for a hug, I can only tell her the truth.

"Baby, you were absolutely amazing."

CHAPTER 20

OLIVER

"Woo, that was so much fun!" Roxy says as we walk through the doors of the mansion at one in the morning. After her set, we stayed another couple of hours, and she's feeling pretty tipsy. "I'm so glad you guys came."

"We're glad we did too," Mindy says quietly, exchanging a glance with me. I know what she's feeling and thinking. The raw emotion Roxy displayed for us set us both on edge. I feel worse for Mindy. She wanted to please her family too much and didn't think of the consequences. Now we're mired in a web of lies. Even if she did want this to last past this week, the amount of lies and bullshit is so deep that it could poison any chance of our having peace.

We can keep it up for a week, but for longer? Hell, I can barely keep the stories straight now, and I've been the ones telling them. No matter what, for Mindy, it has to end after we go home.

Nothing can be done about it now, I say to myself. *Only two nights left.*

I don't know if I could go back to my life though. Knowing that

Mindy's literally around the corner? I'll never be able to have a minute's peace.

"You guys looked really good together," Roxy continues. "I saw you dancing on the floor. Y'all were tearing it up."

"Yeah," Mindy says quietly without much enthusiasm. "Listen, Rox, I'm kinda tired, and with the ceremony tomorrow . . . well, I'm gonna head up to bed."

"Sure," Roxy says, giving me a big wink. "You too, Oli?"

"Yeah," I agree. "Roxy . . . you've got real talent. Don't stop singing, okay?"

My words pierce some of the fog of alcohol around her, and she nods. "Sure, Oli." She gives me a big hug, squeezing my neck hard. "I'm gonna love having you as a brother-in-law. Thank you."

We all three head upstairs, Roxy in front since she's down the hall from us and her balance isn't quite what it needs to be. As Mindy and I make sure she doesn't fall and break her neck, she rambles on. "I can't wait for your wedding. It will be something truly special. Mindy, you gonna let me walk you down the aisle?
"

Mindy hesitates, glancing at me. I place a hand on her arm, giving her a nod. Even if we're a lie, Roxy can walk her down when Mindy does get married. "Of course," she says weakly. "That would be great, Roxy."

"What's wrong?" Roxy asks, turning on the riser. I guess she could hear it in her sister's voice. She weaves a bit, and I steady her shoulders as she peers at her closely. "This ain't the time to be gettin' sappy!"

"Just tired. The dancing, ya know," Mindy says quietly. "Takes it out of you."

"Girl, you act as if you're as old as Grandma." Roxy giggles. "Y'all go on. I'm good to get to my room. Good night, sis, I love you both."

"Night, love you," Mindy says. "Thank you for the song."

"Goodnight, Roxy," I echo, feeling like I just got punched in the chest. Roxy loves me too? Fuck me, what am I supposed to do now? No matter what, we're going to break her damn heart.

We go into the room. Neither of us says anything, although I can tell she's having the same thoughts I am.

Mindy walks over and sits down on the bed, sliding off her shoes before she leans forward, putting her elbows on her knees. "I had fun tonight. Until . . ." Her voice trails off. She shakes her head, her eyes clouded as I come over and sit down next to her. "It never really hit me how far we've gone with this thing until I heard the emotion in Roxy's voice. How much she feels for us."

I'm silent. I'm not sure what to say. I want to tell her that maybe Roxy's convinced our love is genuine because it *is* real. Maybe the silly girl sees something we're too stupid to see. But I don't know if I'm ready for that yet. As much as I love being with Mindy, we've only been with each other for five days. Everything I've ever been told tells me it's impossible to know if you love a person that fast.

But at the same time, no one has ever made me feel the way she makes me feel. I never believed in storybook love before, the sort of all-consuming, all-encompassing love that hits like a bolt of lightning and changes your life forever.

"I just wish I'd never done this," she says.

"Don't say that," I say, more emotionally than I intended.

"But I can't help it," Mindy softly wails, tears coming down her face. "I lied to everyone. My family. I'm just a fraud. A big, fat, terrible fraud. I'm a horrible person!"

I put my arm around her, comforting her as best I can. "You're not. You just want them not to judge you and to please your mom. It's totally understandable."

"Yeah? Then why can't I just tell them the truth then? Even now, I know if I had to tell her, I'd still lie to save face. And I don't know why I fucking care. I'm always brushing things off and don't take things seriously . . . but this . . . I just can't."

I pull her closer, sliding around so that I'm holding her from behind, just giving her comfort. "Mindy, we all lie to please others. When my parents divorced, I went with my father while Tony went with Mom."

"You don't talk much about your father, really. I mean, beyond him making your life like boot camp."

I nod my head and bury my nose in her hair. Even after a night at the club and tinged with sweat, she smells good. "After college, majoring in business, of course, my father brought me into the family business as his right-hand man. Oh, I was being groomed for success, given a nice chunk of stock, a Vice President's position right off the bat . . ."

"But you gave it up. Why?"

I nod, holding her more tightly. "Because I never wanted to be in pharmaceuticals. Steele Pharma started off generations ago doing good stuff. We developed treatments for yellow fever, for bacterial infections, all of that. When my father took over, though, that started to change."

"Why?" Mindy asks.

"Because you make more money selling skin tighteners, tooth whiteners, or wrinkle removers than you do curing diseases anymore. My father shifted all the R&D into cosmetic areas, and now the only real medicines Steele makes are generics on stuff that's a generation old or more. That's not the sort of life I wanted to lead."

"So you quit?" Mindy asks.

I shake my head. "No. Not for years. I was like you are now, living a lie and hating every minute of it. My father and I started fighting, and it got worse and worse until I had to walk away. I had to, or else I'd never be able to speak to him again. So I know what it's like, and I'm here for you."

Her body trembles, and I hold her closer. She starts to cry, and I turn her to me, holding her in my lap and letting her bury her head in my shoulder. I murmur in her ear, stroking her hair and back, letting her know I'm there for her. "Mindy, if it counts for anything, I wouldn't want to lose this week."

"Why?" she asks, sniffing and looking up into my eyes. I stroke her cheek with my thumb and give her a little smile.

"Because if it hadn't been for this week, I might never have met you."

Mindy cuts me off by pulling me close and kissing me, her mouth hot on mine. She's desperate for reassurance and lost in the fantasy that's not really a fantasy anymore. I have to have this moment too, a chance to reassure her and to show her, even if it's just once, what she really means to me.

We tumble to the bed, and I'm careful not to crush her underneath me, her hands tugging at my shirt to stroke my back, not with the rough urgency of our earlier passions but tenderly, searching for something we can't put into words yet. She mewls, moaning like a kitten as I lift her top up to her armpits and explore the silky soft skin of her body. "Oliver . . ."

I stop and look into her eyes, swallowing back the feelings that are threatening to overwhelm me. "I'll be very careful, Princess."

I sit back, unbuttoning the rest of my shirt and shrugging it off, before I scoot back off the bed and unbutton my pants, her eyes drinking me in the whole time. "Mindy, I know tonight's maybe our last chance. I want this time to be special."

She nods and sits up, pulling off the rest of her clothes and dropping them over the side of the bed. Mindy's smile fades as she looks at me in amazement, blinking silently until my eyes meet hers, and I swallow, pulling her to her feet. "You truly are the most beautiful woman I've ever known."

"You make me feel beautiful," she tells me, stepping closer.

Mindy smiles and puts her arms around my neck, mashing my cock between us as she kisses me again. She's just short enough without her shoes on that I have to bend my head more than what's comfortable, but it's okay, and she leads me back to the bed, stretching out beside me as we keep kissing.

I've never felt my heart filled with such pleasure and pain as we just kiss and let our hands stroke over each other's skin. I never touch her breasts or between her legs. Not yet. I want to explore everything else, goosebumps of pleasure breaking out on her skin as I pour myself into her. Mindy's touch is just as electric, my brain frizzing out again and again as she finds another spot on my skin that leaves me gasping and moaning. I've never let myself be this vulnerable, this open before, and I know that no matter what, tonight's going to change me forever.

"Oliver," she whispers in my ear, even the tickle of the warm air causing me to tremble in anticipation, "I want to taste you."

Mindy kisses down my body, her eyes beseeching as she looks up at me, smiling. I nod, and she reaches out with her tongue.

I don't know how to describe what happens to me the instant her tongue touches the tip of my cock. It's like a rifle shot goes through me, my nerves all lit up at once, pleasure beyond anything I've ever thought possible. She licks softly, my body shaken by the sensations each time, and I'm awakened to new heights of ecstasy. After teasing my head with long, loving sucks, she buries my cock in her throat, bobbing up and down until I'm on the edge, and she pulls back, looking me in the eyes with deep emotion.

Love, my mind insists on saying. Is that what this is? This feeling inside me, or is it just that I'm caught up in a fantasy that I hadn't even planned? Am I going insane, or is Mindy looking at me with a feeling that I never expected? We were supposed to be buddies, friends with benefits as I help her out of a jam. This was never supposed to grow beyond that.

Maybe I faze out a little, because the next thing I'm aware of is the sound of a foil packet being opened, and Mindy's kneeling between my legs, rolling a condom down my cock. She rolls over, spreading her legs and giving me a beseeching look.

I nod, climbing on top of her and lifting her hips, her eyes still fixed on my face as I line myself up. I push in, the feeling of her pussy again mind-blowing, and I feel something inside me as Mindy opens up doors to my heart and soul.

It's not her body, as perfect as it is. It's in the way she looks at me, her eyes full of meaning. I bring my hands up to caress her breasts in gentle strokes. We move slowly, wanting this instant to last forever. The world outside doesn't exist as I bend down and kiss her and begin to thrust in and out slowly.

Before, I've been aggressive, powerful, blurring the line between having sex and being greedy with her body. Part of it was the game—Mindy's got a freaky side to her too, and we both enjoy it that way. But this isn't the time for that. Instead, I'm gentle, trying to show her through my body the feelings that I'm too afraid to say. I see it reflected in Mindy as my fears are replaced with a warmth that builds in my chest as we kiss and look into each other's eyes. I kiss her deeply as our bodies move together, my cock rubbing over the places deep inside her with every thrust.

"Oliver . . ." Mindy whispers before words fail her and she moans incoherently. My hips speed up to give her what she needs. She wraps her legs around my waist, giving herself fully to me as we build, faster and harder. Our hips start to slap together, and I feel myself building toward a huge orgasm, my back flexing as her fingers claw at my skin. I want to give her everything I have, everything I am, but I can't make words either, and all I can do is make sure she's given everything I can give her.

My body is trembling, her pussy sending vibrations through me as we build higher and higher. Mindy's shaking, and I squeeze her ass, on the edge myself. Suddenly, her eyes open wide, and she's there, crying out softly in a choked wail. With a final hard thrust, I come, filling the condom as I try to soothe the pain deep in my heart. She's an angel, a fantasy, and I give all I can to her.

My body trembles as I hold Mindy afterward, sweat drying on my forehead as we lie looking into each other's eyes. She's still in so much pain, and I wish I could take it all away from her. "What is it?"

"Oliver . . . I love you," she whispers, cupping my cheek.

I'm shocked, and my heart leaps in my chest. Is she for real? I want her to be, but how can we really feel this way? Finally, stuck, I tell her the truth. "Mindy, I love you too."

She nods and gives me a little smile. I can see the question in her eyes, the same one I have. Is she caught up in an emotional moment, or are her words the truth? I know what I feel.

"Thank you," she whispers and snuggles against me. Her breathing calms, and in minutes, I can feel her nod off. After she's asleep, I give her a kiss on the forehead, still troubled.

I was telling her the truth. Crazy as it sounds, I was.

Was she?

CHAPTER 21

MINDY

I can't help but feel my pulse quicken as I hear the violins and flutes start up, the pre-ceremony music just as beautiful as I thought it would be. In fact, everything is as beautiful as I could have ever dreamed of. Everyone is dressed to perfection, all the women looking gorgeous in nice dresses and all the men in their suits or tuxedos. The flowers are perfect, the weather is perfect, everything is amazing. Even the sun and clouds are cooperating, with just enough puffy cotton balls in the sky to break up all the eye-watering blue without taking away from the impact of the sky and the ocean.

The procession music starts, and the priest comes down the aisle, his plump, cherubic face smiling over the top of his vestments and his Bible held to his chest reverently. After him comes John, who looks dashing and proud in his tuxedo, his face beaming as he looks forward to the next thirty minutes that will change the rest of his life.

Behind him are the flower girls, each of them looking innocent and joyful as they sprinkle white rose petals down the aisle. Their dresses fit just right, and their gold-trimmed baskets twinkle merrily as the musicians swing into the pause, building toward Mom's big entrance.

"This is so beautiful," Roxy whispers next to me on my left. She's the prettiest I've ever seen her, and I almost can't believe the angel sitting next to me is my little sister. "I can hardly wait!"

I nod, unable to form words, and I turn my head the other way to get a better view of the back of the church. As I do, I see Oliver, sitting on my right. He looks so handsome in his own tux, his bright eyes taking it all in, his jaw set, and he's whispering something to himself as he takes it all in.

It's the only flaw in this perfect day. Every time I look at him today, I feel sick. I know it's drawing to a close. After tonight, what we have will be no longer. We don't even have much time today. It's Mom's day. We'll have the reception and party that'll last to at least one in the morning, and we'll spend all day with the family tomorrow. Both days, we're going to go to sleep exhausted, and then Monday morning, we board the plane to go back to the real world again.

Who knows what's going to happen then? I guess we could continue dating, and a part of me is hopeful we will. But there is no guarantee.

All day, I've had another image running in my head though. We go back to town, and I go back to work at the Beangal's Den. He calls a few times, and maybe stops by the shop, but as we look at each other, we just know that the fantasy was just that, and our time is over. I found myself crying in the bathroom as I took a shower this morning because the image was so strong in my head.

Why couldn't he see that I was serious last night when I said I love him? Was he just giving me a last little bit of fantasy? I gave him time to say more, but he didn't. All I wanted was for him to say that he wants to see me at home, that we can make it work somehow. But he didn't, and now . . .

"You okay?" Roxy asks, seeing the tears forming in my eyes. "It's a lot, I know."

"Yeah," I agree quietly. "What's taking Mom so long?"

"I dunno. I wonder if . . ."

"Hush, you two!" Grandma whispers. "I am not going to have this tarnished because my granddaughters can't stop jabberjawing!"

Roxy gives me a smirk and I can't help but smile a little. Grandma looks like she's about to burst because she's so happy. The musicians swing into *The Wedding March*, and we all stand as the doors in the back of the church open and Mom steps in with Aunt Rita.

"My goodness," Roxy whispers, truly stunned, and I have to agree. Sure, we saw Mom in the dress just last night, but today, with her hair and makeup done, the lighting just right, and all the buildup . . . she's more beautiful than I've ever seen her in my life.

Aunt Rita looks proud enough to burst herself in her dress, a pale apricot color that makes her look young and beautiful. They reach the altar, where Rita passes Mom over to John and steps back to her position on the side.

The preacher starts his speech, but to be honest, I stop paying attention. Instead, I think about Mom. She's beaming, looking at John with her eyes lit up, the perfect bride. Despite whatever turmoil I'm feeling inside over my own life, I couldn't be happier for her. She truly looks happy.

After Daddy's death, she never crumbled. Even as Roxy and I mourned, even as the insurance money ran out and the costs mounted, she was our rock. She was the one who made sure enough of Daddy's life insurance was set aside to pay for college for Roxy and me. She was the one who worked hard raising two daughters who were, in reality, not that easy to deal with. She sacrificed a lot for us, and though we may have never actually said it, we appreciate what she did for us and never want to disappoint her.

I was a bit worried when she met John as I saw her become what I thought was too comfortable with her new lifestyle. But over the past week, she's reassured me. And now, I'm nothing but happy for her.

"And now," the minister says, turning to John, "John, do you take Mary Jo to be your wife, to love and honor, to cherish and protect, in good times and bad, as long as you both shall live?"

"I do," John says, sliding Mom's ring on her finger, and my heart catches in my throat. We're at the ultimate moment, and I can barely breathe.

The minister turns to Mom. "And do you, Mary Jo, take John to be your husband, to have and to hold, to love and cherish through sickness and in health, in good times and in bad, as long as you both shall live?"

"I do," Mom replies, sliding the ring onto John's finger.

"The veil, please," the minister says, and John lifts Mom's veil. The world doubles, then trebles for a moment before I realize that I'm crying, and I hurriedly wipe at my eyes. I have to see this clearly. "You may kiss the bride."

John and Mom kiss, and as they step back, I glance at Oliver. He's beaming, and a thought runs through my head.

If only . . . if only.

※

"LET THE PARTY BEGIN!"

Leave it to Roxy to kick the reception off right. She bursts through the doors of the reception hall already thrusting her hands up in the air, ready to turn the reception into her own personal rave if she has to.

I can't help it, I'm caught up in her enthusiasm—everyone is—and pretty soon, I'm laughing and joking along with everyone else.

"Well, hello, there!" Brad yells as he crosses the floor. Of all the guests at the wedding or the reception, he's easily the loudest, both in the way he talks and in the way he's dressed. Then again, anyone wearing a bright lilac suit and pink bowtie to a wedding is going to stand out. "I was hoping to see you!"

"I think he's talking to you," Roxy laughs, poking Oliver, who's just returned with some wine from the open bar. I take a sip and it's good wine, that's for sure. "I mean, I'm pretty sure I'm hot as hell right now. But I know he doesn't have eyes for me."

Oliver hands me my drink, chuckling. "Hello, Brad. Enjoy the wedding?"

Brad grabs the wine from Oliver's hand before tossing it back, grinning. "Honey, I'm just looking forward to the day I get to be up there. I'm gonna be one sexy bitch!"

"I bet you are," I retort, laughing. "You got the lucky guy all picked out yet?"

"Hmmm . . ." Brad says melodramatically as he looks around the room before rolling his eyes back to Oliver. "The best is already taken."

I blush, but Oliver handles it with a smirk and a laugh. I think he realizes Brad's just messing with him. Or at least I hope he is.

"Mind if I show your woman what she's missing?" Brad asks, grabbing my wrist. "Come on, Mindy, let me show you what you're going to be missing."

I hand Oliver my wine, and he gives me a smile and a toast as Brad and I head out to the floor. Mom and John aren't here yet, so the floor is still mostly empty. I'm shocked when *Look Back At Me* comes on, but Grandma doesn't look upset as Trina and Killer Mike drop some of the raunchiest twerk anthems of all time.

"Come on, now, work it!" Brad says as he starts, and there's no way in hell I can pass it up. I start dancing right next to him, dropping it as low as I can in my party dress.

I pop my hips from side to side as Brad tries to keep up. By the time the four and half minutes are up, my legs are burning but I'm laughing my ass off, Brad's antics and dancing leaving me breathless. When the song ends and the DJ takes back over, we make our way off the floor, and just in time. The DJ starts some jazzy music, and the doors open for John and Mom to make their grand entrance.

"Well, that was good timing." Roxy giggles as she hands me a glass. "By the way, Oliver's eyes never left your ass the entire time you were out there."

I don't really have a reply, and when Oliver sits down, I try my best to keep up with everything. But I can't—my attention keeps getting pulled back to Oliver, and I see him giving me looks too. Is that longing I see in his eyes? But if it is, why can't he just say this isn't over when we leave?

Up front, it's time for the toasts, and after a hilarious one from Grandma, it's my turn. I make my way to the front of the room where the mic is set up, trying to remember what I worked up this morning when I had a few minutes. I clear my throat, and look out at the crowd, at the cousins and second cousins and John's family with all their kids, and my mind goes blank. "Ahh . . ."

There's a nervous titter in the crowd and then silence, and I'm about to break down when Oliver stands up. "I know I've only known Mary Jo and John a week," he says, making his way to the front of the room and putting his arm around my shoulder. His blue eyes find mine, and I feel both strength and longing flood my heart. Oliver smiles and gives me a kiss on the cheek before continuing. "I know that's not a long time to get to know someone, but I don't need a week. I don't even need another minute to know that John is one of the luckiest men in the whole damn world.

"Some of you are probably thinking I'm saying this because I want a better wedding gift when Mindy and I tie the knot," he says, earning a few laughs. "And I'll admit, the thought did cross my mind. John, I happen to think that Monaco is a great place to take a honeymoon, don't you?"

His joke earns more laughs, and even I have to smile, putting an arm around Oliver's waist and holding him tight. He hugs me, then continues. "But seriously, I know that you're a lucky man, because so am I. Because any woman who was able to raise two daughters as wonderful, as beautiful, and as special as Mindy and Roxy . . . that's a woman you want to have by your side for the rest of your life. The apple doesn't fall far from the tree, they say. Well, the reverse is true. To the luckiest man in the room and to his lovely bride. May your lives be filled with happiness and joy."

There are tears in Mom's eyes as Oliver raises his glass, and as we make our way back to our seat, I give his hand a squeeze. "Thank you."

"I meant it," he says quietly, giving me that same heart aching look. The toasts continue, with Roxy going last, dedicating her singing instead of a normal toast. As Mom and John dance on the floor to Roxy's version of *Wonderful Tonight*, I can't help but feel my throat grow tight for what feels like the thousandth time today. Oliver sounds moved, too. "They're going to have a good life."

"I hope so," I whisper, choked up. I look at Oliver and reach over, taking his hand. "Will you dance with me, next song?"

He nods, taking my hand in his, and as Roxy finishes up, we stand and go to the floor. I'm hoping for something faster, something that won't tear my heart out anymore, but Roxy sees us, and we're trapped as she starts up. *A Thousand Years*.

"Just dance," Oliver says quietly, sensing what I'm thinking. He pulls me into his arms, and I let myself move, losing myself in his eyes as we dance. I'm scared, I'm hurting, but I let myself go, putting my arms around his neck and dancing with him. Christina Perri's lyrics might be a total lie. I haven't even known Oliver for a thousand hours, let alone a thousand years . . . but the heart's the same.

And I'll give him a thousand more, if he'll have me. I'm just too scared to tell him, to tell him that as I look at him here on the dance floor, I want the lie to be real. That he's better than the fictional *Harold* I created as a lie. That I want him, that I need him. That I *love* him.

"Oliver . . ." I say, trying to form the words, but before I do, there's a tap on my shoulder, and I see Mom giving me a smile.

"May I have this dance with my daughter?" Mom asks, and Oliver nods, moving off to dance with Grandma. For the rest of the reception, we have fun, but Oliver and I never get a chance to talk until dinner arrives and we sit down. The tables have been rearranged, and Oliver and I have joined Mom, John, Roxy, and Grandma at the head table.

"You know, Oliver, you're full of it," Grandma says as the filet mignon is brought out. "I heard you tell Mindy that you can't dance. You move like a cat."

"Well, what I said was I can't twerk as well as Brad," Oliver says with a grin. "That's not a lie. I didn't say I couldn't dance."

"Yeah, well, you keep it up, and I'm going to have to drag you out there to see if you're lying about that," Roxy jokes, sipping her wine. "What a great reception."

"This wedding has been wonderful," Mom says. "Best night of my life . . . or second best . . . or hell, I'm just going to say it's tied, and this one doesn't involve me giving birth!"

"Yeah, well, after this, I can't wait until Mindy's and Oliver's," Roxy says. "I so wanna see that ceremony."

There's a clatter of silverware, and I look up from my plate to see Mom staring at Oliver and me, her eyes wide. She suddenly snaps her fingers, grinning ear to ear. "That's it!"

"What?" Roxy asks, and I feel a wave of despair sweep over me.

"Mindy and Oliver! What if you got married tomorrow? This place is so wonderful!"

"What?" I ask, hoping to nip this in the bud. I can't do this, I just can't. "Mom, that's not what we planned. Besides, you need to get packing after this. You've got a honeymoon to get ready for."

"Nonsense!" Mom says, and I feel nauseous. I glance at Oliver, but I can see the same desperation in his eyes. We're trapped, and I don't know how we're supposed to get out of this without hurting someone. "The whole family is here. It'll be Sunday. Instead of us gathering for some stuffy lunch, we can have the wedding here. John, you can get that handled, right?"

Grandma doesn't say a word, but the way she's looking at me, I can see the hope in her eyes. She's not as forward as Mom is, but she's hoping we say yes, I can see it.

"But Oliver's family—," I began to protest, but Mom cuts me off, holding up her hand.

"Can have their own ceremony for you two. You've already told me you both wanted to have a wedding some place like here. John is more than willing to take care of it. I mean, you've already been engaged for a year. Wouldn't it be wonderful?"

I open my mouth to say no, but I freeze when I see the weight of everyone's eyes on me. I hate that Mom put me in this position, but I know she's just being Mom and she means well. I look uneasily at Oliver. He's quiet and tight-lipped. This isn't a game now. I can tell he's as flustered as I am. All I can do is look in his eyes, and as I do, I keep thinking about the way he said he loved me last night and the way he looked at me while we danced today.

What am I supposed to do? In a perfect world, I'd have met Oliver a year ago, he'd have walked into the Beangal's Den, and he'd be my actual fiancé. I wouldn't be lying. I wouldn't be trying to decide which is worse, a sham marriage or breaking my family's heart.

I lick my lips, looking around the table at everyone as they all stare at me. Even though there's conversation at the other tables, at ours, it's quiet. I can hear my heart pounding in my chest.

Now would be the time to tell them the fucking truth. I can't keep mounting lies on top of lies.

But looking at everyone, I feel my heart squeeze. I can just imagine the look on their faces when I fess up. God, I might actually kill Grandma by breaking her heart. Congratulations on the wedding, Mom. Your daughter's been lying and killed Grandma because of it the same night. Sorry.

Oliver starts to try to say something. "John, Mary Jo, this place is amazing, but this is your time. You guys should have the spotlight."

John waves it off, wiping his lips with his napkin. "If that's what you're worried about, forget it. Mary Jo wants to see her daughter happy. Mary Jo and I are far too old to be worried about this day being special just for us. If you want to make it special, let us give you this gift. Let me do this for you."

I look around at the hope in their eyes. The pressure is enormous, more than anything I've ever felt in my life. Any thought of telling them the truth dies in that moment as I look in Mom's hopeful eyes.

"Okay," I say, ignoring the shock that flashes in Oliver's eyes. "We're getting married here."

CHAPTER 22

"*H*ow could you do something like that?" I ask, pacing back and forth in the middle of the room. "I mean, I know this, all of this, is because you've dug yourself a big ass hole, but . . . fuck!"

It's hours after the reception, and we're back in our room. I think almost everyone else is asleep, but I'm still dressed in my wedding outfit. I've at least taken the time to strip off my bow tie and jacket, half unbuttoning my shirt to try and be able to breathe because I'm so pissed.

Mindy's found the time to get out of her dress, pulling on a sexy little pair of sleep shorts and a large V-neck t-shirt that does nothing to hide the fact that she's gorgeous. In fact, if I weren't so mad, I'd be obsessed with showing her just how gorgeous I think she is.

She looks sad and conflicted. "They were all looking at me and depending on me. I knew I should have said no, but I couldn't do it."

"It's pretty easy. No. *Nyet. Nein. Non*," I bite back, forcing myself to take a deep breath when I see her lip tremble. I hate how angry I sound. But this came completely out of left field. I know I've been lying the whole time by saying I'm Mindy's fiancé, but this was something that didn't have to be. But on another hand, I don't know why I'm so worked up. "You could have at least said you'd think about it, that you don't want to answer without having a private conversation with me. Played it off or something. Not get us deeper into some shit . . ."

"I'm usually strong and independent, but when it comes to family ––" she says softly, her voice cracking. She stops and starts again. "You don't *really* want to marry me, I know. You hate me now."

"I—" I try to reply, but I choke up. I can't speak over the lump in my throat. Is that what she wants? A real wedding? Is that why she's looking so miserable right this moment? Does she really think I hate her? "I don't hate you. And I don't know what I want, not while I'm this angry. Not while . . ."

Mindy nods, and I see the hurt in her eyes. But after a week of lies, of half-hidden comments and games back and forth, I can't lie anymore. I'm too pissed off to really respond to that.

Still, I feel like shit because I can't assuage her pain. I know she's trying to please her family. It's noble from a certain point of view. And she isn't the only one who's guilty of lying. I know we're both in too deep. But this seems like she stepped over the line. Save your mom's feelings? Sure, I get it. Sham marriage? No, there's got to be a line somewhere.

When she speaks again, her voice is small and filled with shame. "I'm sorry. I know I'm a terrible person, Oliver. I swear I'm normally not such a coward. It's okay if you hate me. If you don't want to talk to me ever again after this is over, I'll understand."

Not talk to her ever again? It hurts to even hear the words. And I don't know why I can't just tell her it's okay, we'll do it and just get through it. I guess I'm just still raw over everyone's emotions, seeing them hope for Mindy, wanting us to consummate our love. Love that they don't know is supposed to be fake.

"Don't say that," I say more harshly than I should.

"Don't say what?" she asks, her voice raw and choked with half held-back tears. "That you hate me? Go ahead and say it. At least someone this week knows the truth about me!"

"That's not true—" I start, stopping when my thoughts start to tumble over each other. I hate the lies, but I can't hate Mindy. And the truth about how I feel about her is so enormous, so insane, it scares me to even think about it, let alone say something about it.

"You're so mad right now you can't even talk. You think I'm weak!" Mindy continues before I can get my head right, emotions sweeping her away and taking me with her like a lake that's broken through a dam. We're helpless in the rush, and all I can try to do is hold on for dear life.

She's definitely not weak. She's one of the strongest women I've ever known, and that's what I love about her. She just puts others before herself a lot of times. I've seen it in everything Mindy's done this week. From this whole charade to the stories she's told me about her life back home, even the ways we've had sex, everything this woman does is to please others. Her deepest desire is the desire to see other people happy. She drinks it, survives on it like it's her daily bread.

196

I'm unable to offer anything, not trusting myself to speak. I don't really know what I can say. I'm angry, so angry that my fingers are trembling as I hold them behind my back just to give them something to do. I'm hurt. And worst of all, I think I'm madly in—

"I'll just go fucking tell them," she says, jumping to her feet. "Get this over with like I should have in the beginning. I don't know why I did this."

I step In her way. "Don't," I growl. As much as I wanted her to say no at the time, I don't want to see her hurt more by telling her family and upsetting everyone. "We just need to carry this thing through at this point."

She tries to step past me but I grab her by the arm. "Don't," I repeat, staring into her beautiful eyes that are now blazing in anger. "You're not going out that door."

She tries to twist out of my grasp, but my hand is like iron, and while I'm not squeezing her, I'm not releasing her either. "Let go of me!"

"No." I step closer until we're almost touching foreheads, my own anger growing. "You're not going anywhere, Princess. You committed us to it, and we're going to fucking do it."

"But you don't want to," she hisses. "And you have that right. I shouldn't have said yes. I'll just tell another lie," she says, lowering her head in shame. "I'll tell them we changed our minds, that your mom said she didn't want you to have it without her."

"No!" I repeat, pulling her back from the door. "We're doing it, and that's final. We'll get an annulment as soon as we get back."

She goes lax in my arms. The anger evaporates, leaving just a wounded hurt in her eyes. It's like she's upset that I'm going to annul our fake marriage. It's what she wanted, wasn't it? And how could I get married and stay married to someone I've only known for five days?

"What do you really owe Gavin?" she asks quietly out of nowhere after a long pause. "Why would you do this for him? And don't try to tell me it's nothing. I've been trying to figure out this whole time why a man like you would go through all of this, even for a friend, when I know you can't be that close to him. Brianna and I are besties, and she knew nothing about you until that first day. So what is it? I haven't been able to come up with a damn thing."

My first reaction is to play it off, be evasive. She goes over to the bed and sits down, pulling her legs up to her chest and looking at me with a wide, trembling gaze.

I want to lie, but the way she's looking at me is like a mute, desperate plea for some sort of truth, some way to understand in this world of lies. She's drowning. I'm telling her that I demand to go through with a sham marriage after a sham week. As much as we've gotten to know each other, as much time as we've spent over the past week, I know she'll know if I'm lying.

I can't do it. I won't lie. "I lost to him in a game of poker."

"A game of poker?" She furrows her brow. "You're doing this over a game of poker? Are you fucking nuts?"

I lick my lips. I hate to say this. "I wish it were that simple, that I'm insane. But it's more than that. He beat me out of a little more than half a million dollars."

The breath escapes her in surprise. "No wonder you agreed to do this," she says when she regains her voice. She shakes her head angrily, then looks at me with venom in her smile.

"Gavin fucking owns your soul, doesn't he? So this whole week, you've been just trying to do what he asked, and I know what he asked of you. He said to show me a good time, be everything I could dream of. Be the perfect fiancé, and by God, you did it!"

"I agreed to be your fiancé," I agree. "But since then—"

"So you telling me you loved me the other night, that was just part of you trying to get your half mil back, wasn't it? I was such a fool. I even started to get lost in the whole damn thing. I was beginning to believe it. But now I know. This whole thing has been fucking fake. How much was that I love you worth, huh? A hundred thousand? Two?"

Anger tightens my chest. It's like she's accusing me being some sort of gigolo, a whore doing this for money, when she was the one who wanted and needed someone. "Isn't that what this is supposed to be? Fake. Why are you acting like it was supposed to be anything else?"

I know my words are angry and hurtful, but I speak before I think. I'm out of control, the pain too damn much. "I did my job, Princess."

She hangs her head, tears streaming down her cheeks to drip onto her thighs like diamonds on caramel. "You heartless son of a bitch."

"You're going to call me names now? I'll let you fucking know that I have more than enough money. Losing that much is never fun, but I didn't need that money, Mindy. And I told Gavin to kiss my ass with his request and was just going to pay up until I saw . . ." my voice trails off, my voice blocked again.

199

"Saw what?" she asks, getting off the bed to look in my face. She's hopeful, I can see it, but I'm too afraid of what I'm trying to say.

Instead, I swallow it all back, forcing it into the depths of my stomach where it sits like a sour pill, roiling and churning at my gut. "Nothing. You have no right to be mad. Yeah, at first I was doing this because of money, but all of that changed when I got to know you. I've had a good time, regardless of the fact that it wasn't supposed to be real at first."

She crosses her arms, scowling at me.

"It's the truth. I don't make up lies to save my ass." Fuck. I regret the words as soon as they leave my mouth. I wish like hell I could take them back. "I didn't mean—"

Mindy's hand lashes out, unthinking and fueled by the hurt and shame that's boiling inside her. She hits me with every ounce of fury in her tiny body, probably even before she knows she's doing it, whipping my face to the side.

"I hate you!" she hisses, spit flying from her curled lips to splatter on my cheeks. Her manicured nails, shaped and done just for the wedding today, slide down my face as she pulls away, and I feel red hot fire as they almost break my skin. "Fuck you!"

It doesn't really hurt . . . stings a little, but not truly painful. What hurts more are the words, and anger boils up within my stomach. She hates me? She thinks I don't fucking care about her? When I'm willing to go through this whole charade for her and even do this sham wedding?

"Fuck me, Princess?" I hiss, grabbing her by the arms. "Whatever you might think, that wasn't part of the deal. I could have slept on the fucking floor this past week. So if anyone wants to talk about fucking, it should be you, because you've loved every damn minute of it!"

"You fucking . . ." Mindy rasps furiously, but I cut her off by pulling her into me and smashing my lips into hers in an angry kiss. For a moment, she resists, but then she seems to melt into me.

"Fucking?" I growl when we pull back, my hand wrapped in her hair. Her green eyes are blazing in want and fury as I push her onto the bed, grabbing her t-shirt and pulling. It tears like tissue paper, and her lithe, sexy body tenses as she pants. "I'm going to show you fucking."

"Asshole." Mindy hisses like a cat as I pounce on her. I pin her arms above her head in one powerful hand, giving her another bruising, battling kiss before I use my free hand to maul her breasts, squeezing and pinching her nipples until she's moaning and whining at the same time as her tongue duels with mine. I kiss down her neck to her left breast, sucking hard as I let go of her wrists. My tongue runs over and around her stiff nipple as I reach down, yanking her panties to the side and slamming two fingers deep inside her in one vicious thrust, wiggling them up and down inside her wet pussy.

Mindy claws and yanks at my hair while I relentlessly finger fuck her, pumping my fingers in and out of her pussy while I rub her clit with my thumb, but I barely feel it. The sting of her fingernails on my skin just makes me thrust harder and harder, adding a third finger. Soon, most of my hand is pounding her soaking wet pussy as I bite and chew on her nipples, and she's not fighting anymore. Instead, I feel her hips thrust into my hand even as I push harder, and she's clawing at me, wanting more.

I bite down hard on Mindy's right nipple, pulling back as she howls, her back arching as she coats my fingers in her wetness, coming hard on my hand and her feet beating into the bed over and over.

I'm merciless, rubbing my thumb roughly over her clit even as she comes, pulling away from her breast to stare in her eyes. "I've given a lot to you," I growl into her face, yanking my fingers out and shoving them in her mouth. "But it's my time to take."

Mindy sucks on my fingers, tears in her eyes as my words sink in, but I'm too angry, too driven as I pull them out and lift her leg, getting between her legs and staring in her eyes as she sneers at me in anticipation of what's going to happen. "Take? Is that all you've got?"

I growl, tearing my shirt off before pushing my pants down, freeing my cock and grinding myself against her. "You've been cock drunk on me since before you ever saw this fucking thing," I taunt back. "I'm the best you've ever had, and I'm the best you ever will have."

"Then prove it," Mindy says, clawing at my back again. I grab her hair and pin her to the pillow as I wet the head of my cock with her juices before thrusting in hard. She howls in pain and pleasure as I go all the way in with one deep stroke, slamming into her pussy and driving the breath out of her.

"Like that?" I hiss as I pull back and thrust deep into her again, grinding my cock into her. I thrust in again, her pussy squeezing me even as she sneers at me. "Tell me you love it."

"No . . ." Mindy whispers, her eyes brimming with tears. They pierce my fog of rage enough that I let go of her hair enough to plant my hands on each side of her head, staring into her eyes. I kiss her hard, our tongues fighting as she claws at my neck and back, my cock hammering her pussy hard. The only sounds in the room are our moans and the harsh smack of our hips as I fuck her hard and deep.

Mindy gasps in pain but at the same time pushes up into me, challenging me. "You've gotta earn it, you son of a bitch."

Mindy mewls, pulling her knees up as I push her up harder, staring her in the eyes still. "Say it! Tell me you love it!"

I pull back, thrusting in hard again, and as I speed up a little, I growl, my anger pouring out through my cock and my voice as I fuck her. My cock drives deep into her body again and again, pounding her with everything I have as I grab her around the throat lightly. She moans, staring right into my eyes.

"I never hated you," I pause and whisper before I start thrusting into her again. My hips slap against hers hard as she scratches down my back, the pain making me speed up. "I wanted the impossible, to have you after this too. Even if you are ungrateful."

"I'm sorry," Mindy manages, her fingers not letting up on my back, and I wonder if she's drawing blood

I growl, squeezing tighter as I speed up, hammering her into the bed until my cock is throbbing deep inside her. Mindy's squirming, and I speed up until she screams, her pussy clamping tightly around my cock as she comes again. I keep going, ignoring her moans until my cock is ready, and I pull out, groaning as I come and spray her chest with my seed, crying out as the last of my anger is gone and all that's left is . . . I don't know.

I sag, sitting on the bed and shaking my head, saying nothing. I lie down and stare at the ceiling, both guilty and totally shaken to my core. I've never been that rough before, and I certainly have never come that hard before. My heart aches in my chest, my thighs tremble, and I don't know what to say.

Tell her you love her, you damn idiot! Tell her that somewhere along the line, maybe Tuesday or so, you fell in love with her for real! Tell her that she's worth more than all that money, she's worth the entire fucking world!

I roll to the side, but before I can say anything, Mindy gets up. Reaching down, she finds the shredded remains of her shirt and wipes herself off before balling it up and tossing it uncaringly in the chair. "Mindy . . ."

She looks at me, and in her eyes, I see something that chills me all the way to the depths of my soul. She looks dead. Her doll's eyes have no emotion left in them. "I'm sorry for lashing out at you," she says almost robotically. "I know this was all supposed to be fake. But somewhere along the line, I started to feel like it was real. It was a mistake, and though we just had sex, I know it was just sex. But . . . I just don't want to fight anymore. So please, no more words tonight, Oliver. No more pain."

I open my mouth to tell her that I do truly love her and that if she loves me too, maybe we can make something out of this fucking mess. But before I can, she turns away. "After the wedding, you're free to never speak to me again. Actually . . . after we get back home, I don't want to see you again. It'll hurt too goddamn much."

She walks into the bathroom and closes the door, leaving me feeling like I just got punched in the chest, and I roll onto my back, covering my eyes. I lie there for a moment before getting up, pulling on my boxers, and going out to the balcony to stare up at the moon, which doesn't have any answers either.

CHAPTER 23

MINDY

"I never thought I'd live to see the day," Mom says, tears shining in her eyes as she looks at me in the mirror. We're in the dressing room at the reception hall, putting the final touches on what I'm wearing. The wedding begins in fewer than thirty minutes, and Mom's been fluttering around me all morning. I know she means well, but all she's doing is making it worse. I've been so nervous all morning and so guilt-ridden that I refused breakfast and haven't been able to talk in anything more than grunts and one-word answers.

My chest is tight as I gaze at myself in the full length mirror. I look beautiful—even I have to admit it. My hair is pulled to the side and hangs over my right shoulder, letting my back remain bare in my body-hugging lacy white gown. My shoulders are bare, and it's just a little risqué, with a deep curving V-cut that drops deep between my breasts.

When I was a lonely teenager who didn't have a boyfriend, I'd stay up and look at bridal magazines. I'd dream about my wedding, how I'd look, and what sort of gown I'd wear. I had it all planned out, the perfect fairytale wedding. And suddenly, so fast I'm still reeling, it's here. Well, sort of. My eyes filled with tears when I first saw the gown in the bridal shop. I wanted it right away, and I couldn't stop myself despite my guilt. The perfect gown for the perfect fraud.

"Ha," Grandma says to Mom, "you never thought *you'd* see the day? Well how about my old crusty ass?"

"Momma, please," Mom says, smiling into the mirror. "Don't make Mindy laugh in the dress. She's barely got room to breathe as it is. I can see why you skipped breakfast."

Anxiety is twisting my stomach tighter. I want to say something, but instead, I just turn away from the mirror and put on my high heels. Mom need not worry about me laughing. I haven't been able to so much as crack a smile since I woke up this morning from a fitful hour of sleep. Since last night, my emotions have been running rampant. The hot, angry sex with Oliver last night was amazing. I came deeper and harder than I could have ever imagined. If just a few things would have been different, I'd be smiling and joking just as much as my family is.

But now I know that for Oliver, it meant nothing. He was repaying a debt, and the sex was just his little way to put his own twist on the whole thing. The kind words, the cuddles, the laughter. All of it was just him getting into his role. He never loved me. Hell, last night, he probably fucked me so hard because he wanted it to hurt, to show me just how angry he was.

This whole thing is one big fucking fraud. And Oliver's right—I'm just a liar.

"Are you okay?" Mom asks me, seeing the tears that are threatening to fall from my eyes.

I flash her a weak smile, forcing at least my lips to turn upward some. "Yeah. Just nervous, Mom."

"Oh, baby," she says, giving me a hug. "I understand. I was so nervous yesterday. And the day that your father and I got married, I was so worked up I got sick. But there's nothing to be nervous about. This is your special day. Be happy. Rejoice in it. All of your family is here to see you except for Grandpa Johnny."

"But he's watching from heaven," Grandma says. "You can be sure of it."

Their words are supposed to make me feel better. I know that, but they only succeed in making me feel worse. Grandpa was old school, one of those men who always talked straight. He never told a lie that I knew of, even when it might have saved him a lot of pain. He never would have done what I've done, and if he's looking down on me, he's not proud of me.

"Thank you both," I reply, forcing the words out. "I'm so glad you're both here to see my special day."

I try to make conviction ring true in my words, but they sound false even to me. Still, they chalk it up to my pre-wedding jitters and come over, giving me a kiss.

"We're both so proud of you!" Mom says, patting me on the cheek.

I do my best not to break down into tears as they leave the room to find their seats in the chapel hall, and I take a minute to try and compose myself before I leave. Outside in the hallway, I see Roxy waiting for me. She's my maid of honor, and I don't think I've ever seen a maid of honor so giddy that she's hopping from side to side like a boxer getting ready for a fight.

"Girl, you look so beautiful," Roxy says with a smile. She's wearing the same gown from yesterday because it compliments my gown just right. She's added a few flowers in her hair, weaving them into the curls the hairdresser did. She's a vision.

"Thank you. You look gorgeous too," I reply, trying to just keep myself from breaking down. My sister is more beautiful than she's ever looked in her entire life . . . and it's for a lie. How is she supposed to ever believe in love after this?

"What's wrong, bae? You don't look happy like you should be," Roxy says, stopping her bouncing and stepping close, putting a hand on my shoulder. "Are you feeling all right?"

I flash another weak smile. By the time the day is over, my cheeks are gonna be sore from flashing fake smiles all the time. Each one feels like I'm lifting a half ton with hooks driven through my cheeks. I'm exhausted already, and I've got hours of this to still look forward to.

"Just nervous," I tell her. "You know how it is."

"Yeah, right. Honey, if I had a man like Oliver, I'd be like let's get this shit over with and bring on the consummation!" She giggles.

I fidget with my gown. Even Roxy's normal humor isn't enough to get a laugh out of me, and Roxy notices. She takes my other shoulder, squaring up and looking me in the eyes. "I know. Every wedding is a performance. And if I know anything, I know how it is to be nervous before performing. And I know you're doing this as much for Mom, Grandma, and me as for you. So thank you. It will be okay though. I don't say it enough, but you kick ass."

"Thanks," I say, though I feel dead inside. Kick ass? I can't even man up about a fake wedding. I don't kick ass. I suck it. "It really means a lot to me that you're here."

"I wouldn't miss it for all the world," Roxy says before stopping. "Oh, wait!"

"What?" I ask, and Roxy smiles, rooting around in the cups of her gown for something before pulling out a small packet. "What's that?"

"An old button, a blue Tic-tac, and a penny I borrowed from Aunt Rita. All wrapped in a new handkerchief," Roxy says, tucking it inside the left cup of my gown. "There, all the bases covered. Time to do your damn thing."

We walk to the back of the chapel, waiting for my moment. We're doing it a little different than Mom's yesterday, and Oliver's going to meet me by the altar. I'm the only one getting the big entrance, the total star of the show. It makes me want to puke, and as I hear the warmup music and then the minister's opening remarks, I'm nearly shitting bricks.

"It's time," Roxy says softly as *The Wedding March* starts. "Ready?"

Ready? No chance in hell. My anxiety is through the roof, my heart is hammering in my chest like a Dubstep concert, and I feel like I'm sweating this damn gown through. I'm far from ready. But I have no choice. "Let's go."

The doors open, and for a moment, I feel stalled. Dread is a force field, keeping me from taking the first step through the doorway. I feel myself start to lean back, ready to run, but Roxy gives me a gentle push and we walk into the room.

As the sound system plays, we begin our slow walk down the aisle. The room is filled with almost as much family as yesterday. Familiar faces are all around, cousins and family friends. All those damn eyes staring at me above wide smiles. Fraud! they seem to scream. I tear my eyes away from them, staring straight ahead. My legs feel weak, and I'm glad Roxy's walking me down. I think I'd stumble otherwise.

Even in my frazzled state, I see how beautiful the place is. They even put more decorations up than Mom had and changed the theme. Instead of being a sort of airy elegance, it's almost totally over the top. There's finery everywhere, gilt-edged curtains and bunting all around the hall. There are flowers all over. I don't even want to know just how many flower shops John emptied out on this. They even redid the altar, making it sparkle and shine even more than before.

It's a wedding chapel worthy of a Disney movie. It's a room that a real Princess would walk down the aisle in. Except it's not fucking real.

I blink to clear my vision, and my breath catches in my throat when I see Oliver. He's waiting up ahead at the altar. Standing by himself except for the priest, he's the perfect groom. He's wearing a tailed waistcoat, his hair slicked and styled just right, his hands in front of him respectfully. Every inch of him screams poise and strength, and he's fucking gorgeous. But my heart does a weird twist, and with each step, the blackness that's threatened to over-whelm me all day grows.

I should've known someone like him was too good to be true. I should've known that getting involved too deeply would end in heartbreak.

I should have . . . and now it's too late.

By the time we reach the altar, I'm a mess. My breathing is ragged and I'm trying to do my best to control my arms from shaking.

Roxy even has to help me up the first step before she lets go and peels off to take her seat.

Oliver's eyes are on mine, but they are carefully neutral, his emotions hidden behind a mask. I can't read what he's thinking.

The priest clears his throat and begins. "Dearly beloved . . ."

Just like yesterday, I lose track of what he's saying. I hear noise, music once, but mostly just noise. Instead, I think about my misery.

It's not going to end today. What, is Oliver going to go on a fake honeymoon with me, pose so we can Photoshop ourselves on the beach in Cabo? When is enough, enough?

"If you'd face each other," the minister says quietly, and I'm jerked back to reality as Oliver takes my hand and turns toward me. Through my veil, I look at him again, his face a mask, the joy on his face not reaching his eyes. "Oliver Steele, do you take this woman to be your . . ."

I don't hear anything, I stare at Oliver as he listens, and I see a glimmer of something in his eyes when the minister finishes. It's pain. Still, he nods before clearing his throat. "I do"

"And Mindy Isabella Price, do you take this man to be your . . ."

I open my mouth to say I do, but the words die on my lips. There's so much pain in Oliver's eyes. I'm ruining this, not just for myself and not just for my family, even if they don't know it, but for him too.

I tear my eyes away from Oliver to look around the chapel. Beside me, I can see Roxy in tears, hungrily awaiting my answer. I see Mom staring at me, her face shining with so much emotion and pride. Beside her are Aunt Rita, Grandma, and cousin Layla. Behind them are John, Uncle Charles, and everyone else, all of them waiting for these two simple words. The heavy weight of guilt becomes almost unbearable.

I'm a liar. A big fucking liar.

The priest clears his throat again as the silence stretches on. I look back at Oliver, and something inside me breaks. No more of this, no more lies. "Oliver . . . I'm sorry."

I throw off my veil as I hike my dress and jump off the altar, stumbling on the thick carpet for a moment. There's an audible gasp in the audience as I book it for the back doors, and I hear a sharp wail of dismay from someone—I think it's Roxy.

Suddenly, Mom grabs my arm, trying to pull me to her. She pulls me around, and I see confusion and pain in her eyes now, too. Everywhere I look, there's pain. "Mindy, stop! What are you doing?"

I jerk my arms free, stumbling backward. I can feel the tears start to flow, but I don't care. Let them all see. Let everyone see the fraud that I am, not the fairytale princess that they came here to see. "Leave me alone! Why can't you just leave me alone!"

"Honey, please," she says, still not understanding. "You're just scared and overreacting—"

"It's all fake!" I yell at the top of my lungs. Mom stops, and everything freezes. I'm not even sure if they're breathing or if they know what I mean. "Don't you understand? Everything! Oliver, my engagement, all of it! Everything is fucking fake!"

Sobbing uncontrollably, I hike up my dress and run from the chapel, leaving everyone too shocked to even try and stop me.

CHAPTER 24

OLIVER

I pause in the hallway, my hand on the knob. It's early afternoon now, hours after the service was supposed to happen, and I can't think of another time in my life that's been more difficult. The image of her stricken face still dominates my mind, the way she looked at me as she apologized and then ran from the chapel.

Yeah, it was fake. Yeah, we were going to get the damn thing annulled by Friday next week. But it still stings because of how I really feel about her.

I don't know how, I don't know when, but standing at that altar today, I let myself start to wonder. I wondered if we could lie our way to reality. If there were a way to keep digging deeper and deeper and end up on the other side free and clean.

Her running away felt like she abandoned me. Just when I was beginning to work past the doubt and pain of her words last night, she just abandoned me at the altar. She left me out there, all alone, to face all those people by myself.

It was hard dealing with that. For a few minutes there, I wasn't sure I was going to be able to get out of the chapel alive, surrounded by accusatory glares and shouted questions from her family. But I didn't say anything. I didn't betray her.

But I can't let this stand without doing something. I have to tell her I'll help make it right . . . I have to tell her that I want . . . something. Something I didn't even have a chance to fully figure out before the whole day exploded into chaos like a party favor from hell.

I open the door to see her lying across the bed, her shoulders shaking from giant sobs. She jerks upright almost immediately when she hears me step in the room, and I see that she's stripped out of her gown at least, wearing just a long nightshirt that makes my chest ache with conflicting emotions. I want to hug her, I want to kiss her, and I want to choke her. In the end, I stand right where I am.

"What are you doing here?" she says, her voice a soft croak. "Come to yell at me?"

"I came to see how you were doing," I say softly, taking a step into the bedroom. "You left before anyone could even react."

She sniffs, wiping at her nose with her forearm. Not sexy, but totally understandable. "I'm obviously not fine. But I'll live."

"I'm sorry," I say quietly, sticking my hands in the pockets of my tux. "I should have done more."

"Why? All of this is my fault. I deserve all of it. You only did what you were asked to do."

"You don't have to face it alone." I step closer, but she scoots back, and I freeze, knowing that if I get closer, I'm going to spook her even more. "Your family is waiting to hear an explanation. Listen, I was thinking as I walked back here that I'll tell them I made you do it. That I'm the one who had a marker on you, and that I'm the bad guy."

I walk closer and sit on the far edge of the bed, reaching out slowly until I take her hand, that soft, warm hand that I didn't get a chance to put a ring on today. The hand I regret leaving empty. "Come on. Get up, get changed, and let's go out there and—"

Mindy pulls her hand back and snorts, shaking her head. "I'm done with everything but the truth. I deluded myself thinking this would just be some casual little white lie."

"But I can still help . . ." I start, but Mindy holds up her hand, getting off the bed and stopping me cold.

"And we're done too."

I shake my head, trying to negate what she's saying. No, it can't be over. "Mindy, think about it. You're just upset right now. Please, think about what you're saying."

She cocks her head, giving me a sad little half-smile. "No. For the first time all week, Oliver, I am thinking about what I'm saying. Your debt is paid."

I try to speak, but she spins on a heel, going to the big doors to the balcony and hugging herself, her voice hardening.

"It's fine with me. I totally understand. And I'm not mad. I can't imagine any man not doing the same in your position. The problem I have is more with myself. I'm angry for putting myself in this position. I don't blame you for any of it. Hell, you wanna know what really pushed me over the tipping point to telling the truth? I suppose I should thank you, because you did. Seeing that pain in your eyes, I realized that I was going to ruin it for you too. It was just one too many people I've hurt. And while you never loved me . . . I did fall in love with you. And I can't keep going on hurting the people I love. So, I just want to free you. Let me face my problem on my own."

I stand up and walk over to the window on shaky legs. She really loves me? She said it before, but I wasn't sure if she really meant it. "Mindy, don't be so hard on yourself. I know you didn't mean to do this with malicious intent. I see the good in you. You're so special, so funny, and you've made me think. You've made me laugh. If you're guilty of anything, it's caring too damn much. You are a good person. I've seen your heart. You only wanted to please your mother."

She's quiet for a long time, and I'm beginning to think that she's listening, that I'll be able to bring her to me, that we can handle this together. But when she speaks next, her words hurt even more. "Please leave, Oliver. I don't need you to try to save my feelings. I'm so very sorry, but I want to be alone right now. I'll tell the truth, that it was my idea and I didn't intend for it to go this far. And I'll tell Gavin you did your part."

Gavin and the money? I can't believe that she still thinks this is about money. "Listen to me—"

"Just go!" she shouts, turning to me, furious and in pain. "Just forget this all happened."

Her words tear at my heart. She's being unreasonable, but I can see that she's so emotional right now that I can't get through to her. "Mindy, come on. Our plane leaves in the morning, I have one more night to stay in this town, you know."

"I think you should go now."

"Excuse me?" I ask, surprised. "Mindy, what are you saying?"

She shakes her head, pointing at the door. "I think it would be best if you don't stay here tonight. I just can't see you right now, and it's going to make things even harder."

I stiffen. As much as I hate it, I have to leave her alone or this could get worse. "If that's what you want."

"It is. Please leave, Oliver."

I don't want to I want to defy her. But I know it's pointless. She's too overwhelmed with emotion.

"Very well," I say quietly. I walk to the door and stop, turning to look back at her standing at the balcony door, staring out into the backyard again. "I know you don't believe me. Maybe I deserve that, but I don't think so. I enjoyed the time we spent together. Despite what you may think, it wasn't about the money. I hope you work things out with your family."

She doesn't say anything as I walk out. I close the door and realize that I've got two suitcases worth of things in there. "Fuck it," I mutter. Besides my tablet, there's nothing that was all that personal. Instead, I start down the hallway. Maybe Sam can give me a ride to the airport or I'll just call a cab.

I'm at the head of the stairs when I see Roxy coming up, heart break etched into her young and previously innocent face. "Oliver? What're you doing?"

"Leaving," I say softly. I can't be angry at Roxy, no matter if she was part of the pressure that Mindy was feeling. I like the girl too much, and I know she would have made a great sister-in-law. "Mindy's asked me to go."

Her face goes white with shock. "What? Why? Oliver, if you think the rest of the family . . ."

I look at her face, seeing the tears in her eyes. My heart twists for Mindy at what she has to do and how her family is going to react. "I've enjoyed getting to know you over this past week, Roxy. And don't ever give up on your singing. You've got a gift."

"Oliver, please stop," Roxy says as I start down the stairs. I don't, and when I'm about halfway down, she calls out to me, wailing. "Dammit, please tell me what's going on!"

I stop and look up at Roxy, promising myself that when I think about this week, it's not going to be this Roxy I remember, but the Roxy who was a vision behind the microphone, the Roxy who made me laugh. "That's not my place to say, Roxy. Give my regards to everyone . . . and take care of Mindy for me, okay?"

I turn and walk out, leaving the mansion for good. I can call for a cab while walking down the road.

CHAPTER 25

"It was all fake."

The words hang in the air. They're the first thing I say to my immediate family after what has to be several long minutes of silence. It's just Grandma, Mom, Roxy, and me. John wanted to join us, but Mom asked that he stay at the wedding hall to take care of things there.

After throwing Oliver out of my room, I ignored Roxy's pleas for me to come out for hours, sobbing into my pillow. I couldn't imagine facing anyone, and I felt like doing nothing more than hiding under my bed. Eventually, though, I calmed down, and I found myself putting on a t-shirt and pants. I felt like it was my duty to talk to them, to face them. So I dragged myself out here.

"All of it?" Roxy asks, and I can see the tears in her eyes. She genuinely liked Oliver and me together. I've always known that Roxy was a lot deeper than the image she puts out. There's no way someone who wasn't could sing the way she does.

"The whole thing."

I lower my eyes, tears threatening to spill over my lashes and down my face. I don't want to see their faces. I don't want to see the many questions in their eyes.

It hurts down deep inside, where you're supposed to carry your guts and instead, I just carried my fear. I can't believe I thought I could joke my way through something like this. That I thought being silly could solve something so serious. How wrong I was, and now what started as a silly little white lie over a year ago has come to this.

"Why?" Roxy says softly. "I sang for you guys, Mindy."

I swallow the lump in my throat and let the burning pain in my chest try and fuel me. I can't lie to them any longer, so I might as well be totally honest. "I just wanted to avoid any relationship questions. You can be a little hard to deal with sometimes, Mom. But that's no excuse. It was stupid. And after a point, I didn't want everyone to think I was a liar, and I just dug myself deeper. So . . . enter Oliver. I didn't even know him before this."

"Oh, honey," Mom says, and I look up for a second to see tears in her eyes. "I know it must feel like I put pressure on you with my expectations, but I wouldn't have loved you any less had you shown up without a fiancé."

"You do put pressure on us, Mom," Roxy says quietly. "All of us. With me, you don't like my singing."

Mom stops, wiping at her cheeks. "I just . . . I want what's best for my girls."

"How is being miserable and jumped on best for us?" I ask her. "Mom, you bugged me even in college about whether I was going to find a guy. You made it seem like I was going to school for a wedding ring and not a degree!"

"I just . . . being young, it's the time for love," Mom says, defending herself. "I wasn't trying to say you had to marry some guy right out of school."

"You made it feel that way sometimes." I look over at Roxy, who looks miserable as she twists her hair around her finger. "I can't even imagine what you've been through!"

"Me?" Roxy asks, getting up. "Really, Mindy? You ask about me? I really liked Oliver and was invested in you both! I thought your love was real. It sure did seem like it. But anyway, I'm your sister. We used to share everything!"

"Yeah, well, I'm sorry!" I yell before taking a deep breath. I look at them. "I'm really ashamed about all of it. You know me—carefree. I didn't think it was a big deal when I started. I just didn't want to disappoint anyone. I wanted to make you proud."

Roxy comes over and puts her hands on my shoulders. "Please, you know you're the favorite. Everyone's proud of how you did things on your own. I love you, and you know I'm going to be on your side no matter what."

I swallow back tears and look around to everyone. "I'm sorry to all three of you. I took it too far."

"I knew I should have said something earlier," Grandma says, and everyone turns to look at her. Reading the question in my eyes, she waves it off. "Oh, I don't mean about Oliver. That's one fine hunk of a man. He had me pretty well fooled. I mean about you, Mary Jo."

"Me?" Mom asks, and Grandma nods.

"Honey, after Jacob's death, you got a little off kilter. The girls are right, you kept nosing in where you don't belong. But I hoped that with John, and this past week . . . well, I kept seeing y'all grow closer again, that you were fixin' what needed to be fixed. So I figured it would all work itself out. Guess I was wrong."

"I'm sorry," Mom says, looking at Roxy and me. "I don't mean to put pressure on you girls. I really don't. Neither of you ever has to worry about disappointing me. I could never feel that way about either of you. You're two beautiful, strong women, and I couldn't be more proud of you."

Her heartfelt words help, and I come over, kneeling in front of Mom and hugging her. I'm shocked a moment later when Roxy grabs the two of us and hugs Mom too, the tears flowing hard and fast. "I love you both," Roxy cries before sitting back and wiping at her eyes. "But Mindy . . . if you ever, and I mean ever, pull some shit like that again . . ."

"Don't worry, I won't," I promise her before suddenly laughing and squeezing her tight. "You too, okay?"

"I won't," Roxy promises me. "Still . . . I had my hopes pinned on you guys. You looked so good together."

"You weren't the only one, Roxy," Grandma says. "I swear, Mindy, either there was real feeling between you two or you need to look into acting."

Grandma's and Roxy's words shake me, and I'm on the verge of tears again. The hard part is, I think they're right, and my chest aches. Roxy puts an arm around me, stroking my hair as I start crying. "Roxy . . . I feel lost."

"I know, honey," Roxy says as Mom hugs me too. "I know."

"I was a fool," I blubber. "I should have never done it."

Grandma laughs. "If I had a nickel for every damn fool thing I'd done when I was younger, I'd be rich," Grandma says. "The big thing is, Mindy, what are you going to do about it now that you've made your mistake?"

I cry more until I feel the tears start to dry up. "I'm going to make it up to you guys. I'm so sorry."

"You do what you can when you feel your heart broken," Grandma says, standing up painfully and coming over, stroking my hair. "You move on as best you can."

"Move on?" I whisper, fresh tears coursing down my cheeks. Move on means moving on from Oliver. "What if I don't want to move on? What if . . . what if I really love him? And what if I told him I hate him?"

"Then have faith that he loves you too, and trust in fate," Grandma says. "Love finds a way."

I nod miserably. Love finds a way.

What do you do when you can't see the way?

CHAPTER 26

OLIVER

I feel like hell, and Anthony gives me a double-take as he gets out of my Audi. At least he listened when I sent him the text last night telling him to skip getting the driver.

"Damn, was it really that fucking bad?" he asks, looking at the cheap discount jeans and t-shirt that I bought after walking to the hotel last night. "I mean, what the hell are you wearing?"

I don't say a damn thing, and Anthony presses the issue. "Oli, come on, man. Your face looks like you're sniffing shit."

Fresh off my flight, I'm not in the mood to hear anything right now. I'm still smarting over Mindy pushing me away. I feel like so much is unresolved. I've been kicking myself for hours, cursing myself for being a coward for not dealing with Mindy's pain and instead walking out on her.

"Hey. You gonna talk? What happened while you were there?"

"Just shut up and drive."

I look over and see the look on his face. I didn't mean to snap at him, but I haven't slept since walking out of the mansion, and I'm going on fifty-five hours awake with only an hour and a half of sleep a day and a half ago.

I just haven't been able to get her out of my head ever since I left. I kept hoping that she would show up on the flight, that she'd sit down next to me in the first-class seat and we'd have a chance to talk. That maybe I'd get her to listen to what I told her, make her believe me when I said that I do care about her. That I love her.

I look over, shaking my head. "Sorry. I didn't mean to snap at you. I just don't want to talk about it right now, Tony."

"All right," he says, surprising me. Usually, when he knows I don't want to talk about something, he pushes the issue even more. The thought makes my throat tighten again, and I turn away, looking out the passenger window as Tony pulls out. He gets to the airport exit and hangs a left, heading toward the highway back home.

"Mom has been a lot better," he says, changing the subject. "Her ankle's all healed up, and she's already told her boss she's going to go back to work tomorrow."

"Well, that's good," I reply, glad to have at least some good news.

Anthony laughs. "Yeah, well, my social life is going to enjoy it too. I'm ready to handle my business. Oh, speaking about business, Martha and I found the perfect property for you."

"Oh yeah?" I ask, being pulled into the conversation. "What property is that?"

"Remember the ones she was supposed to look at? She's been holding down the fort really well, I think. She spent all week going around, then she put down a retainer deposit on two of

225

them. She took me to both of them, and I've gotta say, you've got to see the one down by the university. It's awesome. We have an appointment to see it in two days."

"What was it?" I ask, leaning back. "University's a crowded area. It can't be cheap."

"Yeah, but it's a steal, man. I ran the numbers, and it's good. Used to be a Chinese restaurant."

"Chinese, huh?" I reply. "Too many of those around."

"Yeah, well, the place might smell a lot like moo goo gai pan, but hey, I've got a lot of good memories of moo goo gai pan," he says with a lift of his eyebrow, trying unsuccessfully to lighten my mood.

Good memories. I'd like to have good memories again.

❄

"Everything's good," Gavin says, leaning back in the deck chair. I really should have checked in with him a few days ago, but I had to spend the last two days just getting some rest.

"That's good," I reply, leaning back in my own chair and sipping at an iced coffee. "You look like a man who's having a good streak."

"Yeah, well, I'm not gonna risk the money again," Gavin says with a chuckle. "You know, it's a shame things didn't work out between you and Mindy. I had hopes."

"She's a remarkable woman," I say, "but sometimes, stuff happens. You know how it is. I had fun, at least."

"That's a shame," Gavin replies with a sigh. "She's back in town at the coffee shop, by the way."

"Oh, yeah?" I ask, surprised. "I feel like six feet of warmed over leftovers. How in the hell did she do that?"

"Good question. Bri and I tried to insist that she take a few more days off, but she walked into the shop Wednesday and went right to work. She's not having much fun, I hear. She and Brianna have been talking every day. She's even been taking Rafe with her, hoping that Rafe would cheer Mindy up. Trust me, that could totally boomerang on us. Mindy sometimes doesn't have much of a filter, and Rafe is . . ."

"A tape recorder?" I ask, and Gavin nods. Even though I'm still depressed, I have to laugh at that. "Yeah, I bet. And I know what you mean. Most of her family's that way. It was surprising, but I liked it. They're real."

Gavin laughs. "Yeah, I can imagine. So the rest of her family's the same?"

I nod, laughing for a moment. "You should meet her little sister. Roxy's a total trip. The time she took us to the club and . . ."

Memories flood me, not only of the fun times but the way Roxy sang for us, and I clam up, draining the rest of my coffee and looking out at Gavin's backyard. "Anyway, it was what it was."

"I can imagine," Gavin says quietly. "You know, Oliver, sometimes things get weird. If you asked me three years ago, I'd have told you that I'd be riding out the biggest contract of my career. I wouldn't have guessed I'd be retired and a family man."

"Why'd you do it?" I ask him, turning and looking him in the eye. "Not giving up football and all that. I get that. Why'd you put that money on the line for Mindy? Hell, until the last card, I had your ass."

Gavin looks back at me, and I know he's measuring something in me. Finally, he answers. "If it hadn't been for Mindy, I'd have never had a chance with Brianna. She's a wiseass, but she's also totally amazing, and I was hoping . . . well, I was kinda hoping that she'd find the same happiness that she gave me and Bri."

I nod, getting up and grabbing my empty cup. "I hope so too, Gavin. I really do. Thanks for the coffee."

"No problem," Gavin says, getting up. We shake hands, and he walks me around the house to my car. Just as I'm about to get in, he stops me. "Oli, one more thing."

"Yeah?"

"Don't walk away."

❄

"Looks like the property is yours," the agent says, shaking hands with me. "I mean, I still need to run this by City Hall to get the title transfer registered, but I'll have that to you by Monday afternoon."

"No rush," I say, looking around the huge space. Two floors and a basement, with the upper floor being the former owner's apartment and storage area. And Anthony was right, it was a steal. "I'll get the contractors in here starting tomorrow though."

"Of course, Mr. Steele," the agent says. "If you want, I can give you the number of a guy I know who does good work."

"I'd appreciate it. Martha, what do you think?"

Martha looks around. "It's a great property, Oliver. If anything, it's overkill for what you need."

"About that," I say, then look at the agent. "If you don't mind?"

"Of course not," the real estate agent says, taking my contracts and putting them in his briefcase. He takes out two sets of keys and hands them to me. "I had the locksmith make a backup set, just in case. Enjoy your new place, Mr. Steele."

He leaves, and Martha gives me an inquisitive look. "What's up?"

"I've got a change of plans," I tell her. "I'm not using the first floor or the basement."

Martha lifts an eyebrow. "What do you mean?"

"Follow me," I say, walking down the stairs to the basement where the kitchen is. "Look at all that. What do you see?"

"About ten thousand dollars in renovations. Unless you want to make fried rice," Martha says. "Why, what do you see?"

"I see a working kitchen, and I see people working here," I reply, walking around. "Look at this, a working walk-in fridge, plenty of storage space, and lots of room to expand. And upstairs, that can be converted into your office."

"My office? What about yours?" she asks. "You're confusing the hell out of me."

"Change of plans," I repeat. "I'll fill you in on the details, but I'm going to need you busting your ass for me over the next week. Then, Steele Security Solutions isn't going to happen. Instead, I've got a new job for you."

"What? And what are you going to be doing?" Martha asks.

"You've got the world in your palm, Oliver. Steele Security Solutions has at least a half-dozen clients lined up. What're you doing?"

The world in my palm. She's right, I could have everything in the world. But the one thing I want isn't here.

Yet.

"I'm not walking away," I tell her, smiling. "Come on, I'll tell you the details on the way to dinner. I'm buying."

CHAPTER 27

MINDY

"I had to leave paradise to come back to this shit," I mutter under my breath, looking around at the chaos of the Beangal's Den. Two weeks back, and I'm missing the mansion already.

It's not any busier or more chaotic than normal, the logical side of my mind insists. In fact, for a Saturday mid-morning, it's slightly less insane than normal. The line's not out the door, and if someone wanted a table, they could get one.

Still, the customers are driving me up a wall. Cassie's doing better, but Sarah's off today. I've got a new part-timer, a college girl named Nancy. She's learning, but I'm too frustrated to be a very good mentor, manager, or leader to her right now. Hell, I can barely believe I'm keeping myself together.

"Hey! Where the hell is my coffee?" someone yells, and I look up to see the same lady from before. Great. Why's she even coming back if she always seems to have a problem?

"Cassie, can you please?" I order, pointing in the customer's direction. If I have to deal with her, I'm going to have to make sure the sharp knives are as far from me as humanly possible.

"On it, boss," Cassie says, and I'm somewhat glad. She's improving. Unfortunately for her, though, the bitch seems to be in a particularly foul mood.

"I just want my fucking coffee, not more excuses."

That's enough. I look up from the latte that I'm mixing and step over to the customer, patting Cassie on the shoulder. "Go finish that. Let me handle this, Cass."

"Sure, boss."

Cassie leaves, and I stare at the customer, who's wearing the same faux fur trimming from last time. "Look, I told you last time that we don't tolerate that sort of behavior here. Please stop with the swearing or you can leave."

Sticking her nose in the air, she sniffs at me, not backing down. "This is three weeks in a row I've had a problem here. Last week, they couldn't even get my order right after writing it on the damn cup. Besides, I know who runs this place, and I'm tired of your bullshit. They serve better coffee on the other side of town."

"You said that last time too," I half growl, just holding onto my temper. "If you're so dissatisfied with the service here, please give the owner a call."

She shakes her head. "Yeah, you can't say shit because you know you're horrible."

"Listen. Please leave now. If you don't, I'm going to have to call security," I say as calmly as I can, barely keeping my thoughts about her fake fur and bitchy attitude to myself.

"Whatever, you guys fucking suck!" she yells loudly, grabbing her Louis Vuitton knockoff purse and storming out the door. "Bitch!"

I let out a sigh. I never in my life thought I'd say this, but I'm sick of working here. I know it's not just because of the customers. It's because . . .

I hate to admit it, but I hurt. Every morning, I wake up and my body aches, my arms are empty, and my eyes burn from crying in my sleep. I haven't been exercising, although I've still lost weight because I'm barely eating.

I keep telling myself to not think about him. Whenever Brianna tries to tell me anything about him, I tell her to shut up. She's pretty much given up on the whole thing, which just makes it hurt more.

I feel a buzz at my side, and I step into the back, checking my phone. I've got a text message . . . Roxy.

Mindy-girl, I just had a feeling that you needed a hug from home. I hope you're feeling better today. I know you left feeling like shit, and I know I got on your case again. I'm sorry. You're my sister. I love you. Gimme a call?

A sad smile touches my lips. Last Wednesday, after I left the mansion and came home, she called me. There were a few tense words in there, but the bond we have is maybe the strongest thing in the world, and soon, we were telling each other how sorry we were as we cried over the phone. Roxy admitted that she'd been pressuring me too and apologized, saying that she'd get over it and that she was coming out to visit me as soon as she got free time away from her singing gigs. She said she wanted to see if there are more Olivers out here. I didn't have the heart to tell her that Oliver's one of a kind and that I doubt even I'm going to find him again.

"What's happening?"

I look toward the employee entrance, sticking my phone back in my apron pocket as I see Brianna with a tired but still awake Rafe on her hip. Seeing him brightens me a little, but he can't push it all away.

"Nothing much, just slaving away as usual. Hey, thanks for covering a few shifts when I was gone. How's my little Rafey doing?"

"Firsty," Rafe says, perking up a little as I tickle his ribs. I walk with them back out into the cafe area and start mixing Rafe an iced chocolate milk while Bri checks out the menu.

Brianna looks over the menu. "So why don't I see you serving the unicorn frappe yet?"

I laugh. I know she's just joking. "Do I look like a freakin' leprechaun? Besides, that's the guys across town."

Brianna bursts into laughter, and I'm grateful I caught my tongue just in time as Rafe starts chanting. "Lep-a-chan! Lep-a-chan!"

"Aye, top o' the mornin' to you," I reply in the fakest accent ever, handing Rafe his chocolate milk while Bri chuckles. "What? I'm not Irish enough?"

Bri shakes her head. "You're a lot of things, but no. Thank you, though. That was good. First joke I've heard you crack in a week."

I shrug, rinsing the milk blender while Rafe finds a stool and Bri hangs out where we can talk. She knows everything, and I need someone to help me process all that happened. Being my best friend, she's been positive. She's even gone so far as to suggest there's still a chance for us.

Of course, she's out of her mind. I haven't seen the man in two weeks. If he wanted to get in contact with me, he could've. Despite telling him to go away, I started missing him even as he walked out the door, and that hasn't let up at all. But I get it. If I were in his shoes, the way I treated him at the end there, I'd swear off coffee forever and switch to smoothies.

But I've waited, hoping to hear something, anything, Even if it was from Brianna that he'd given Gavin a call and said something about me. For the past two weeks, I've spent almost every hour by my phone, hoping to hear something. I never have.

Bri gives me a soft smile. "You sleeping yet?"

"What do you mean?" I ask. "I got a whole three hours last night!"

Brianna rolls her eyes and looks over her shoulder at Rafe. "If you don't get seven hours of sleep tonight, I'm sending Gavin in to cover your shift tomorrow and getting your ass falling down, sleep the morning away on my sofa drunk. Got it?"

"I'll slam espressos all night just to see Gavin in one of the shirts and aprons," I joke, and Brianna grins. I go back to work, Bri stepping behind the counter to help out a little with the wash-ups as the crowd rolls in and Rafe finishes his tiny little drink. We small talk the whole time, nothing important, and when Rafe's done, I take his glass and give him a hug. "You take care of your Mommy, okay?"

He smiles, waving his hands around.

"Love you, kiddo," I say, standing up to give Bri a hug. "I promise you, ten espressos tonight."

"Girl, bye," Bri says with a chuckle. "I'll have Gavin ready. See you tomorrow."

Bri leaves, and I watch her go for a moment before I get caught up in work again. It's so busy, and I jump in to help Cassie with clearing tables as the lunch crowd settles in. I'm tired and not watching where I'm going when I turn with a blender cup and bump into Nancy, who's got a tray full of empties. "Oh!"

Thankfully, she doesn't drop her tray. I jerk back enough that I bounce my hip off the counter and drop my blender cup. The polycarbonate cup hits the floor, making a hell of a racket but not breaking into a million pieces, and I give a deep sigh of thanks. "You okay, Nancy?"

"Yes, Miss Price," she says, probably afraid I'll bite her damn head off. Instead, I take a deep breath, calming myself. I squat down, checking the blender cup. It's okay.

"So . . . got the new unicorn frappe yet?" says a deep recognizable voice, and I rocket to my feet, staring in shock. My heart jumps in my chest when I see him leaning against the counter in a light blue dress shirt, his eyes twinkling and his smile warming my chest. Where the hell did he come from?

"Hey," I say awkwardly. "Oliver."

His familiar grin nearly melts my heart, and he leans a little bit more over the counter, dropping his voice to that sexy purring growl that I've dreamed about for two weeks. "Miss me, Princess?"

Did I ever. Not that I'm going to tell him about the number of times I've typed him texts and emails and then deleted them over the past two weeks. "A little."

"A little?" he asks with a raised eyebrow.

"Listen, about sending you—" I start, but Oliver reaches across the counter and puts a single finger on my lips, stopping me as my body thrills at just the single touch of his skin on mine again.

"Shh, you don't have to explain. I know it all. I only left to give you time to reflect. I always intended to come back to show you that I truly cared."

His words fill my heart with something that I haven't felt since coming home, flowing from him like cooling waters on the agonizing burn within me. It's unbelievable after how I pushed him away, but he's here, and his eyes are calm, amused . . . and loving. They also tell me the truth. Everything isn't going to be sunshine and lollipops right away. There's a lot to work on, but I take joy from a very simple fact—he didn't give up on me.

"Why'd you wait so long?" I ask him directly, back in my element.

Oliver chuckles, and I swear he looks a little bashful. "Would you believe I intended to come by last week, but then . . . well, I got caught up in something?"

"Better be something good." I say, putting my hands on my hips.

"Just some business stuff. I wouldn't want to bore you with the details. I know how much you hate when I go on and on about myself and my business."

I smile, biting my lip. "Mmmhmm. But that's not good enough. Spill it."

He winks, giving me that patented Oliver smirk. "Trust me, Princess. Got time for a ride?"

❄

"When can I open my eyes?" I ask, my shoulders getting stiff. "I'm getting carsick."

"Just a moment," Oliver says, chuckling. He stops his car, and I hear him come around the car to open my door and help me out. Taking me by the hand, he has me walk a few steps, then stop. "Okay, open them."

I open my eyes, and I'm totally confused. "Why'd you bring me to The Flaming Dragon? This place closed down two years ago."

"It's not The Flaming Dragon," Oliver says with a laugh. "Come a little closer and you'll see."

Oliver takes my hand and leads me to the door, producing a key from his pocket and opening it. "Oliver, what's going on?"

He opens the door, and I look in shock at the big letters that have been penned on the grease board next to the door. *FUTURE LOCATION OF MINDY'S PLACE (Steele & Assoc. 2nd Floor).*

"Welcome to the location of your new business," Oliver says. "Ours, to be exact. If you want."

"Huh?" I comment, reading the sign again and again. It still doesn't make any sense. "Oliver, what—"

Shock rolls through me as my brain finally kicks into gear, and I put my hand over my mouth, speechless. Oliver leads me over to one of the stools that still line the big counter, sitting down next to me. "I'd asked my assistant to look for a few places where I could base my security business. She had this place on the list, mainly because of the location, and, well . . ."

Oliver takes a deep breath and puts the key to the place on the counter. "It's yours. You own the place outright, Mindy. I told Martha I'm splitting my money in half. One half is to be used by her for real estate deals, other investments, whatever. She's going to run it out of the office upstairs, close enough that I can help her out if she needs it."

"What are you going to do?" I ask, feeling the teeth of the key. "And what about the Den? Gavin and Brianna are my friends. I can't just abandon them."

"Who do you think told me about the unicorn frappe?" Oliver asks quietly. "As for me, well, I don't know a lot about running a restaurant, but I do know business, and if you don't need a business manager . . . I can be Johnny on the spot wherever you need me, boss."

I hold up my hand, concerned. "Oliver, before we go any further, why are you doing this?"

"Mindy, I've spent every minute since I walked out of the Wentworth mansion regretting one thing."

"What's that?"

"Not being honest about how I feel about you. Sure, I started this as a way to get out of a debt, but from the moment I first saw your picture, I was drawn to you. When you challenged me—"

"I challenged you?" I ask, amused. "I seem to remember you sitting there like a living sex god, telling me that you weren't going to do a damn thing I said. And you proceeded to do just that."

"I think we sort of liked toying with each other," Oliver says with a chuckle before growing serious again. "But I'm not joking now. I need you. I need you in my life, and when I told you I loved you that first time, I meant it. So I regret not staying, not doing my best to take care of you."

I swallow, emotion choking my words for a moment before I can answer. "And if I still say I don't want you in my life?"

"Then the building is still yours," he says softly, "but you'd be lying. I can see it in your eyes, and well . . . let's just say I've gotten a little bit of inside help."

Gavin and Brianna. I look at the open raw emotion in his face, and I know that he's telling the truth. There's only one answer I can give him.

"So I get to be the boss, huh?" I ask, smiling as I look at him. "And if I tell my new bus boy to kiss me, will he do as he's told?"

Oliver pretends to think for a minute, then he stands up, pulling me into his arms and lowering his lips to mine. "I'll have to demand at least minimum wage," he teases, and then he's kissing me, his strong hands pulling me against him, our bodies hungry for each other. I moan into his mouth as his tongue finds mine, his hands stroking my hair before running down to cup my ass. Our lips part, and he looks into my eyes again, touching his forehead to mine. "I love you, Mindy."

"I love you too," I moan in reply. "Oliver, can we start over?"

He shakes his head, giving me a smile. "No, but we can move forward."

"Then let's move forward."

Oliver smiles and picks me up, setting me on one of the empty tables, dust puffing up as he does. "Hmm, we're going to have to clean that," he jokes as he pulls my shirt out of the waistband of my pants. He kisses my neck until I'm trembling before kissing back to my earlobe, licking it before whispering in my ear. "I love you."

"I love you too," I moan in happiness as I reach for the buttons on his shirt, undoing them quickly and peeling his shirt off, swinging it around my head like a lasso for a moment before flinging it across the room. I laugh, joy in my heart. "I've always wanted to do that."

"You'll get to do anything you want from now on," Oliver reassures me, his voice catching as I pull him close and bite his neck. Our night of rough passion has taught me a few things, and one of them is that I like it a little rougher with Oli than I did with other partners. "Mmmhmm."

"Anything, huh?," I growl playfully as he reaches for my pants and yanks them down along with my panties. "Well then, first things first—no more condoms."

"That I can do," Oliver says as he undoes his pants. His cock emerges and my mouth goes dry as I see it again in the dim, dusty light filtering through the soaped over windows. "What's wrong?"

"Nothing," I say as I wrap my legs around him and pull him closer. "I've just missed you. And that mind-blowing cock of yours. Speaking of blowing . . ."

"Later," Oliver says as he crushes my lips in another soul-searing kiss. I moan in agreement as I feel him line up naturally with me and slide in, stretching me open. My heart thrills as he fills me, body and soul, and I clutch at his powerful shoulders as we start moving as one, his cock sliding into me over and over. I squeeze my pussy around him as we look into each other's eyes, opening up fully.

How did I miss this? How, when from the first time he looked in my eyes as we had sex, I saw this same gleam, the same tenderness, the love in his eyes?

It doesn't matter now as we move, our souls joining even as his cock speeds up. Our lips meet in another kiss, and we share breath, my heart hammering in my chest as we push together. His cock lights up my body as he drives into me harder and faster. Claiming me? No, he claimed me weeks ago. Now, we're completing each other.

"Oliver . . ." I moan as he speeds up again, his cock hammering me and his balls slapping against my ass. I claw at his neck, passion overwhelming tenderness as we kiss hard, biting his lip as he growls, his cock swelling. I feel him tremble, and with a deep groan, he comes, filling me with his warm seed.

My body reacts, and I'm coming too, squeezing and milking his cock of every last precious drop of his essence as I hold him, sobbing in joy as he stays deep inside me, holding me close as we ride out our orgasms. When I finally come down, he's holding me tenderly, and I hear the vulnerability in his voice. "Mindy, I'm so . . ."

"I know," I whisper in his ear, wrapping my arms around him and holding him close. "Like we said, let's move forward."

Now the hard work starts, but I'm not afraid of hard work.

CHAPTER 28

MINDY

I look up at the sign, pride swelling in my heart as the workers make the final adjustments to the sign. *Mindy's Corner.*

"Wow, they work fast," Brianna says, coming out of the cafe. She looks up, nodding in approval. "I'm glad you named the place after yourself."

"Well, Oli gets to name the second floor, so I get to name the first," I say with a smile. "And besides, I get to have the bigger sign."

"It's not the size of the sign that counts," Brianna jokes. "Although it certainly doesn't hurt."

"We talking about signage or sausage?" I tease, and in a move that reassures me I haven't totally lost my damn mind this past month, Brianna blushes. "Oh, come on, I'm woman enough to admit that Gavin's probably got Oliver beat."

"And you're not jealous?" Brianna asks. I shake my head, and she grins. "Why's that?"

"Simple," I say, slinging an arm around her shoulder. "My man has a tongue that can tie and untie my apron blindfolded, and he's definitely not lacking downstairs. Also, the fact that he can make my toes curl without making me walk like a cowboy after he takes me from behind is a plus."

"Hey!" Brianna says, blushing. "I don't walk like a cowboy!"

"Well, let's just mosey on inside again then . . . *cowgirl*. See how the boys are doing."

We go inside, where I see Oliver and Gavin working together on the back wall of the restaurant, and I have to laugh watching the two undeniably manly men getting salmon pink paint splattered on themselves.

"Keep that up, and I'm going to make you take off that T-shirt!" I tease Oliver, who turns and gives me a cocky grin before peeling his shirt over his head. Not to be outdone, Gavin pulls his shirt off too, and while I make Brianna a Pina colada iced frappe, we get to watch our men work. By the time the frappe's done, I need a drink myself.

I whip myself up an iced mocha with all the shiny new equipment. Best of all is the grill downstairs. We're going to be able to expand to a full restaurant setup when we want. In the meantime, downstairs is going to be our bakery. I've already taught Oliver how to make cinnamon rolls. "Hey, can I ask you a question?"

"Sure," Brianna says, not even pausing her eye-fuck of Gavin. "If you really wanna know, yes, we did, and yes, I loved it."

"Please," I laugh, shaking my head before growing serious again. "Not that. Although we're coming back to that story in a minute. Actually, I wanted to know . . . are you and Gavin really okay with my leaving the Beangal's Den? I mean, he bought that place for me to manage."

"Oh, don't worry there," Bri says, smiling. "It was really complicated, but basically, we sold the Den back to The Grand Waterways, and as payment, Gavin took an equal amount of stock value in the hotel corporation. We know you wanted your own place without worrying about complying with hotel rules."

"Really?" I ask, and Brianna nods. "Thank you, Bri."

"Oh, it gets better," Oliver says, turning around. "Gavin has decided to work with me on investing. Now, he's nowhere as rich and powerful as I am . . ."

"Unless you keep playing poker with me," Gavin mock-growls, and I have to laugh.

Oliver laughs before turning back to me. "Anyway, Gavin's pooling some investment money with Steele and Associates, seeing as how I know how to turn rich into super-rich. Trust me, Princess, these two are going to be sitting pretty while I'm elbow deep in flour."

"Sounds good to me—I'll just have to wash you up more often."

"I knew there was a reason you decided to keep the shower in the apartment upstairs."

Turning back to Bri with a smirk, I tell her, "Now, about that 'yes, we did, and yes, I loved it.' Tell me all about it." Just as I expected, she blushes and ducks her head. Yep, still got it.

❄

The line outside the cafe is buzzing, and I'm moved. Sure, it took a little bit of shameless self-promotion. And yes, Gavin has agreed to lend his bit of star power to the whole affair, but to see fifty people lined up when this isn't even the official grand opening?

"Whoa," Oliver says, looking as handsome as ever in his white dress shirt, sexy black jeans, and his apron with *Mindy's Corner* stenciled over his heart. "Hope we've got enough cinnamon rolls."

"I'm sure if you don't, I've got something that'll keep them entertained," a voice from behind me says, and I turn, nearly squealing in delight as I see Roxy come up from the basement. "Hey, Sis."

"Roxy? What the hell are you doing here?" I ask, running over and giving her a big hug. "How'd you get there?"

"Ask Mr. Sexy Pants over there," she says, grinning. "He invited me. Said he had something I just had to see."

I turn to Oliver, who's grinning. "Just in time too. Where's Brianna and Gavin?"

"Just a moment!" a muffled Bri yells from downstairs. "Dammit, you know I can't resist these rolls, especially since I'm pregnant again!"

I chuckle, a little jealous but knowing that Bri's earned it. Since finding out she's pregnant again just two weeks ago, we've both been giddy planning for her new baby. I'm hoping for a little girl. Bri and Gavin appear a moment later up the back stairs, Gavin wearing one of his old jerseys which I'll admit he still fills out well, while Bri's wearing a Mindy's Corner apron. For one day only, they're working together again under the same roof. "Yeah, well, don't eat all the damn profits!"

"Oh, I wouldn't worry about that," Roxy says guiltily. "I ate one, too. Damn, if I knew you were this good, I'd never have let you leave home."

"That was Oliver, actually," I concede, and Roxy looks at him in amazement.

"No shit?"

"No shit," Oliver replies. "Ruins the texture of the dough."

"Is there anything you can't do?"

"Well, there's one thing," Oliver says, "but I can fix that right now."

I turn and my heart stops as I see Oliver get down on his knee, reaching for my hand. "Mindy, I know it's a little fast, and it's a hell of a lot shorter than the year you were engaged to that loser Harold, but . . . I can't imagine a better couple of months than I've had right by your side, and I want to keep it going. I've called you Princess ever since we first met, and it was a joke at first because you acted like you were a queen. It's not a joke anymore. Princess . . . will you let me be your prince? Will you marry me?"

He reaches into his apron pocket and pulls out the same ring that he'd given me for our fake engagement, and I gawk. "Where did you get that?"

"I had a talk with your stepfather," Gavin says with a chuckle. "He mailed it to me. Now answer the man!"

"Yes! Of course I'm saying yes!" I gush, tears coming to my eyes as Oliver slides it back on my finger. "Oh, Oliver . . ."

Oliver stands, and I jump into his arms just as the line of people outside, attracted by what they saw through the windows, erupts into cheers. Oliver holds me tight, kissing me hard after he sets me down with a grin. "So, Princess . . ."

Roxy wipes away the tears from her eyes. "Oh, I'm so jealous of you. I mean . . . not trying to move in on yours, but I need a man!"

"It'll happen. Probably when you least expect it," I tell Roxy, hugging her before exchanging hugs with Bri and Gavin. "You're going to find a man just as awesome as these two men," I say, gesturing at Oliver and Gavin.

"Nah, luck never runs in threes. I'm gonna be lucky if I don't end up with a loser who stalks me and tries to count my pussy hairs."

Brianna gawks at Roxy for a second before turning to look at me. "You're right, she is worse than you. How am I ever supposed to let my Rafe near you two?"

"Ear plugs. Good ear plugs."

❄

"Mom, it's me!" Oliver hollers as we get out of his Audi. After a five-hour "sneak preview opening," I'm not sure if I'm ready for any more today, but I insisted on this after Oliver's proposal. There's no way in hell I'm meeting my soon-to-be mother-in-law at the wedding. I'm assuming I'm already going to have to meet his father that way.

"You know, she's gonna be pissed about this," I whisper under my breath.

"You'll be okay," he reassures me. "My mom is a sweetheart. Just ignore my brother and you'll be okay."

"You know, you didn't have to do this," I say as I see the front door open. "I mean, we could have taken her to dinner or something."

"I got to meet your family right in their home. Now you get to meet mine," Oliver says with a smirk. "Or is my princess afraid?"

"Oh, hell no," I growl, punching him lightly in the shoulder as the screen opens and a woman who's a little older than Mom comes out. She's got Oliver's hair, and while she's not as energetic as Mom, the love in her eyes as she comes out and hugs Oliver is evident.

"Mom, you're looking good. I'd like you to meet . . ."

The woman's eyes go wide as she takes me in, smiling. "Is this the girl you left to go see all those weeks back?"

Oliver nods proudly, putting his arms around me. "Yes, Mom. Sorry, I know I've been caught up in getting the cafe open, but . . . well, Mom, this is Mindy Price. We're getting married."

"Oh, my God," his mom says. "She's beautiful. Come in, come in!"

We go inside, where I see a younger version of Oliver coming in from the back yard. "You must be Anthony."

"Yeah," Anthony says, looking a little shocked. "Holy shit. Oliver, you brought in a dime piece."

"And your head is about to be a showpiece if you don't show some respect," Oliver growls, but before the boys can continue, their mother steps between them.

"Now, now, boys, none of that," she says with a chuckle. "Anthony, you know better than that."

I laugh, waving it off. "Don't worry about me. I've heard far worse."

We visit for another two hours. After dinner, the brothers volunteer to wash up the dishes while I talk with their mother. She goes outside, where she lights up for a moment before staring at the cigarette in her hand and crushing it underfoot. "Nope, no more of those. I want to see grandbabies someday, and I won't be doing that with cancer sticks all the time."

"Thanks," I concede. "So Oliver told you almost everything, huh?"

"Almost," she says, chuckling. "Never has told me just why the hell you two took a dog for a walk for all those hours, but I'm sure you had your reasons."

I blush in the deep purple twilight, nodding. "Yeah, well, your son . . . he's good for me."

"You're good for him too," she says, smiling. "When he came to town, he was so bitter at his father, and I can understand that. But he was going down the same path his father did, all business and no heart . . . until he met you. So thank you. And Mindy?"

"Yes?"

Oliver's mom comes over and gives me a hug. "I'm going to love having you as a daughter-in-law."

I hug her back, happy. "I'm going to love having another mother, it seems."

EPILOGUE

OLIVER

"How's it going guys?" I ask, sticking my head in the door. I don't work the line anymore. Mindy's Corner has grown fast enough that we hired a real chef and staff within six months, and now, two years after opening, we're going strong.

"Doing well, Mr. Steele," Jake, the head chef, says. "Hey, when you've got a minute, I want you to try something."

"What?" I ask, curious. "So I can prep my stomach while I unload the van. I know how you are."

Jake laughs. He knows I've had to work doubly hard the past year to keep my body in good shape. The man's a good cook. "Yeah, well, I'm going to put it on the menu starting Monday, so if you don't want to try the Trenton now, I can't be blamed if your son doesn't like it. Where is he, anyway?"

"Hanging out with his godparents," I reply, stepping closer. The pizza looks delicious, and I have to smile as I cut a slice and sample it. "Jesus, this is good. Has Mindy tried any?"

"Of course, the Boss is upstairs being the Boss," Jake says. "So any tweaks for the recipe?"

"Not a one," I say, patting him on the shoulder. "You know, when you said you wanted to start a line of pizzas, I thought you were nuts. I thought you were double nuts when you decided to name them all after famous steels and swords. Thank you, I don't know if this one's going to bump the Valerian from the popularity list, but it's damn good. My son will be proud once he has teeth."

Jake gives me a grin, and I go upstairs, letting the kitchen staff unload the van of tonight's supplies. I find Mindy, looking more radiant than ever, making up a frozen drink. "Okay, the leprechaun rainbow frappe," she tells the two new girls who we just hired to work the coffee bar. In the corner is Sarah, who we snatched from the Beangal's Den and made the front of the house assistant manager, prepping for opening. "Now watch carefully. You don't want to mint-nuke someone."

She's confident and sexy, and I have to admit my cock stirs in my pants watching her at work. She finishes, tucking the shamrock stirrer into the glass and presenting it. "Remember, if you screw it up, just grin, give the customer a little bit of charm, and you'll be cool most of the time. Now practice for me."

"I always thought it was the low-cut blouses that got you out of trouble," I tease her as she comes over and wraps her arms around my neck, giving me a kiss. I reach down to squeeze her ass, growling lightly. "Don't make me spill chocolate on you as an excuse to get you upstairs to the shower again."

Mindy chuckles, wiggling her hips against me until my cock is throbbing in my pants, and I'm glad that I'm wearing my cafe apron. "Yeah, well, maybe we can look at that idea of getting Trent a little sister tonight."

I pat her ass, grinning. "For sure. By the way, Bri says that our Trent and her Alicia are meant for each other."

Mindy laughs, shaking her head. "Remind me again how lucky we are not to have taken Roxy's idea on our son's name?"

"Oh, I don't know," I say, laughing. "Maybe if our next child's a boy, we can go with her idea. After all, Richard's a fine name for a boy."

"I am not naming my son Dick Steele," Mindy says, shaking her head.

I have to agree with that one, both of us turning as there's a crash from the coffee area to see a pile of green slush on the floor. One of the new girls, Rose, looks at us with fear in her eyes. "Mrs. Steele, I'm sorry, I just . . ."

"Did the same damn thing I've done a hundred other times," Mindy says calmly. "Get it cleaned up and try again. Sarah will give you a hand. Remember, you've got afternoon shift tomorrow, and with St. Paddy's Day coming up, those things are flying out the door."

"On pink unicorns," I joke, earning a stuck out tongue from Mindy. "Hey, guess what Martha told me? She found us a house. Or, as she called it, *Step One of the Steele Estate Project.*"

"No way," Mindy says, grinning. "Where?"

"A couple of miles out on the other side of town," I tell her, laughing. "It's not as big as Gavin's ranch, and it's nowhere near the size of John's mansion, but it's got plenty of space and three acres for Trent and however many more we want to play and grow."

Mindy bites her lip, nodding. "When can we go see it?"

"Sunday afternoon," I tell her. "Now, get this . . . you won't believe who the owner is."

"Who?"

"Your favorite banned customer."

Mindy gawks, then grins at me, shaking her head. It's been a running joke between us, one that's crept to the whole staff, really. "No freakin' way."

Motherhood's finally found a way to tone down Mindy's foul mouth. At least a little.

"Way. Martha confirmed it herself. Apparently, Miss Fake Fur and Attitude has been banned from every coffee shop in town for the past six months. The last one, she went on an epic rant where she threw an iced pumpkin swirl and swore that they totally sucked and she was coming to Mindy's Corner."

"Too bad we have a very strict no fake fur, no fake bitches allowed policy."

I laugh, pulling my wife in for another hug. "Yep. But her husband's being transferred somewhere for work. I'd hate to be that poor schmuck, but it's not my problem. I'm only worried about two things—my queen and our new castle."

"Castle, huh?" Mindy purrs. "I like the sound of that, my king."

It's good to be the king.

Want the FREE Extended Epilogue? Sign up to my mailing list to receive it as soon as it's ready. If you're already on my list, you'll get this automatically!

Irresistible Bachelor Series (Interconnecting standalones):
Anaconda || Mr. Fiance || Heartstopper
Stud Muffin || Mr. Fixit || Matchmaker
Motorhead || Baby Daddy

PREVIEW: HEARTSTOPPER

BY LAUREN LANDISH

Roxy

"So, how about we go back to my place?" this creep asks for the second time. Is 'no thanks' somehow going to change in three minutes?

I try to hold back my annoyed scowl. Go back to his place? I'm about ready to splash my untouched beer in his fucking face. I've turned him down for a dance. He's not that bad-looking. I'm sure he could find some girl in here, even with his creepy ass vibe. Why the fuck's he still here with me?

I look around and see that my bestie Hannah has deserted me. I can see her over on the dance floor, twerking her ass up against some cute dude. I'm certain he's about five minutes from blowing a load in his slacks with the way she's moving.

I look back over just in time to see Dr. Strangelove pushing the bottle closer to me, like he's trying to remind me that it's there and force me to drink it, but he's gotta learn that there's a lot of scrap in this little body. "Drink up," he says.

That's it. I just can't with this guy.

I open my mouth to finally tell the guy to fuck off. I've been overly polite and have made it perfectly clear that I don't want what he's selling. But before the words can leave my lips, a penetrating voice behind me speaks up. "Everything okay, Angel? Sorry I'm late. I was busy upstairs."

I spin in my seat to get a look at the voice and my heart stops. Seriously, I might need a defibrillator to get it back beating again as the breath leaves my lungs. I take in the purest blue eyes I've ever seen under dark hair that glimmers and sparkles as the lights of the club catch deep within it. His chiseled jawline frames a sensual mouth, and it's hard to pull my eyes away from his gaze and take the rest of him in.

He's tall and broad-shouldered, his custom-tailored suit fitting him perfectly.

Fuck being a heartthrob. He's a heartstopper. That's what this guy is.

My mouth opens like a fish, but Mr. Heartstopper winks at me and I'm able to brush off my momentary shock enough to play along. "No, honey, I was just having him warm your seat for you until you got back from that little curb stomp appointment." I flash a smile, not letting the nervousness I feel flicker through. I turn and give Dr. Strangelove a pointed look. "Does that guy still have all of his front teeth?"

My former creepy-ass suitor scowls, and for a moment, I fear he's about ready to fight for his seat. But when Mr. Heartstopper gives him a hard look, he gets up from his seat, mumbles something, and disappears in the crowd.

Relief flows through me and some of the tension leaves my body when I can't see his face anymore. The music thrums, mixing with my heartbeat as I look at my savior, and I feel like this night's going to change my life. The stage is almost prepared for the main act, a rock band that's hot on the charts and has a fresh sound. I've been looking forward to it, but now I have another sweet distraction.

Trying to shake off my anxiety, I poke the guy playfully in the chest. "You got a blue leotard under there?"

He arches an eyebrow at me, confused but with a grin on his face. Fuck, he's hot. "No, why?"

"The way you showed up and saved me from that creep, you must be Superman," I joke. "I'm wondering where you keep the red cape."

He chuckles, taking the seat next to me. "Nope, not Superman, but I have to admit to being called the man of steel a few times in my life."

I arch an eyebrow. "Modest much?" Looking at him and his cut physique, though, I don't doubt him. That suit can only hide so much of his body.

"You asked what I had under my suit. I was just telling you. Being real, you know?" His eyes twinkle, and something tells me he's biting back a joke. I can't help it, I smile. I like a man who can keep up with my sense of humor.

But the other half of my mind is dirty enough to know what he's talking about. He has balls of steel and a huge, throbbing, steely cock. Fuck, we haven't even introduced ourselves and I'm already getting hot.

"So what's your name then, Superman?" I ask.

He chuckles as if he's unused to a woman being so direct with him. "Jake," he says. "How about you, Angel?"

"Roxy," I say. I love the way he calls me Angel, even though I feel like anything but right now. Angel definitely sounds better than horny succubus. "And before you ask, yes, I rock hard."

He laughs. "Cheeky, aren't you? I like the name. It's cute."

"Why not sexy? Or hot? I like that better than cute."

"I'd say you have all three covered," he growls lightly, sitting next to me. "I can think of a few more words to describe you too."

A flush comes to my cheeks at his compliment and I'm momentarily robbed of speech. This guy's a silver-tongued devil, and he's got a voice that seems to heat my body every time he speaks.

He nods at my beer. "I don't peg you for a Bud Light girl."

I recover and shake my head, making a face. "I'm not—haven't touched it. I don't really like beer."

He grabs the bottle and sets it in front of him and signals one of the waitresses. "Let's get something new for the lady!"

She comes over and gives him a look like she'd love to take him out back and ride him like a cowgirl. I know Jake has to be used to it though. The man's probably a player. Then again, maybe that's what I need tonight—a man who knows what he's got, knows how to use it, and knows how to make me scream to the heavens. "Something in particular?"

He turns to me, giving me a wink. "She'd like a Sex On My Face."

I gawk, shocked at his forwardness, but the waitress doesn't even bat an eye. And in my mind's eye, I can see myself grinding all over those sexy lips of his. My face turns red at the thought and I push it away. For now. "Of course, sir."

"You didn't have to do that," I say, trusting that I was just ordered a drink and not a room at the Holiday Inn.

"Nonsense, you've got to try it," Jake says with a laugh. "It's one of the house specials."

His persuasive charm just wins me over. The waitress brings back the drink, and at first I think it looks like an iced tea. I take a sip, my eyes widening. "This is good!"

He winks at me. "Told you. Take it slow. I've heard that they can hit hard." He takes the beer and sniffs it, then turns it up, drinking about half of it. "So, how'd you hear about the club?"

"My friend Hannah," I say, pointing her out on the floor. "She told me about it. I needed a night out to relax and have some fun."

And I need a man like you to take care of a certain need, I think to myself.

Jake nods. "Well, you picked the right place. Even for opening night, it's not over the top. This place has class."

"You're telling me," I agree. I think it'll be what makes Club Jasmine popular for a long time. They could pack this place and tear the dance floor up, sure. But the building's got enough inherent class and charm that it'll be a chill spot too. "What about you? What brings you here?"

A slight smirk comes to one of his lips. "I'm friends with one of the owners."

I stare at him as I take a sip of the delicious drink. It's something else he's not letting on to, but honestly, I don't give a fuck. I didn't come here to learn his life history. And I damn sure don't care about his friend. I just can't get over how handsome he is. Those lips look like they could do damage between my legs, and the more I see them move, the more I want to feel them pressed against mine.

He asks me more questions about myself, but I can barely hear or find the focus to answer. I can only focus on his perfect smile. The more he talks, the more I feel like I want him. Even if it is only for a night.

I finish my drink in a hungry gulp and lick my lips in the most seductive manner I can. *Damn, I don't know if that drink was seriously that good or if literally anything would taste amazing right now.*

"I was thinking . . ." I say, running my hand along his arm. Shit, I'm playing the seductress to the hilt. I even have my next line planned, something about how I'd like to have a little more sex . . . on *his* face.

He raises a brow at me, and anxiety twists my stomach as I look into his eyes. I'm suddenly uncertain. He has to get more pussy than animal control. My ego can't take a hit right now.

But looking around the room, I realize one thing. He's the only one I want. If I can't have Jake, I'm going home alone.

I suck in a breath. Fuck it—you only live once.

"Look, would you like to go somewhere?" I cringe. I know I must sound so fucking desperate, like some slutty skank. But isn't that what I came here for? I'm hot and heavy and this guy is doing crazy things to my ovaries just by sitting next to me. I *need* him.

He turns, looking me in the eye. "Direct, aren't we? I can't imagine an angel like you . . ."

I'm shocked when he seems to steel himself. He turns the bottle up and in one gulp drinks the rest, smacking it down on the bar, and growls almost ferally. "Let's go."

He gets up from the seat and I jump to my feet. He puts his hand on the small of my back as he leads me to the back of the club. "Where are we going?"

"Told you, I know the owners. There are . . . private places around here," he says, and I dismiss it. Fuck, I don't care if he takes me into the VIP bathroom. I'll take it right now.

The show is about to start for the band. I'm gonna miss it but I don't care. He takes me through a door and into a hallway. We come up to another door, and like magic, he produces a key to get in. Before I can ask him why he has a key, he's on me like a dog in heat, pushing me up against the wall and devouring my mouth in a hungry, fiery kiss.

Our lips crash together, and he's doing crazy things to my body, his hands roaming over my dress and lighting my skin on fire.

"Take me," I moan, my thighs trembling with need. Ten long months. And if that huge, hard cock pressing against my thigh is any indication, I want it right fucking now.

"Not here," he half-moans, half-slurs in lust, stepping back and taking me by the hand. He leads me down the darkened hall to a room. He opens the door and turns on the light. It's a medium-sized room with a bed and some rugs in the center. What the fuck is a bed doing back here?

But I don't care about that. I want him.

He's back on me again, and we're kissing, his hands tugging on my dress. With every inch of my skin that's exposed, the fire in my stomach grows as I feel all the sexual frustration start to boil over.

"I'm gonna give you a night to remember," I growl in his ear as I pull off his shirt. "You'll never forget Roxy."

Damn, call the exorcist. I don't know what's wrong with me. It's like the devil himself has possessed my body.

I rip off his shirt with an animalistic snarl. The air freezes in my lungs when I see the hard abs of his stomach. He wasn't fucking lying about being the man of steel. The rest of him has to be pure perfection.

"Your tits are amaaaazing," he says, his slur growing, his hands squeezing my breast weakly.

What the fuck? Damn, how is he drunk already? He only had that one beer. I pay it no mind. I push him back onto the bed, tugging my skirt up to my waist and mounting his hips, feeling the hard bulge of his groin rub against my panties.

"Fuuuuuck, baby," he moans. His voice is sluggish. "I love how aggressive youuuu are . . ."

"Shh, baby," I tell him, slipping my dress down and showing him my breasts, turning my dress into just a band around my waist. "You ain't seen nothin' yet."

I swear it looks like he's fighting to stay awake. But I don't need long to send him to heaven. I trail my hands down his abs and down to his happy trail. Reaching his belt, I hungrily unbutton his pants.

"Baaaby . . ." he moans, almost like he's gasping for air. I take the gasps as if he can't wait to be inside me. Fuck, I can't either.

I get his pants down and am about to pull his cock out and slide on a condom when he grabs onto my breasts with the force of Zeus. He holds tight and lets out an unearthly gasp, his eyes fluttering.

I stare down at him in shock as he takes one last breath and then seems to go unconscious.

"What the fuck?" I know I was about to give him the most glorious send-off he ever had, but did he really just pass out? "Hello?"

It takes some effort, but I'm able to disengage his death grip from my breasts. They ache, and I wonder if I'm going to have a few bruises on them tomorrow. "Hello?" I repeat, leaning in closer. "Jake?"

I shake him, and when he doesn't respond, I give him a little slap on the face. He doesn't move at all, and fear starts to clench in my belly.

Hands shaking, I place my hand on the side of his neck. I don't feel anything, and I'm getting more worried. What the fuck?

My heart pounds in my chest as I stare down at him in disbelief.

The Man of Steel is dead.

Want to read the rest? Get Heartstopper HERE or visit my website at www.laurenlandish.com

ABOUT THE AUTHOR

Want the FREE Extended Epilogue? Sign up to my mailing list to receive it as soon as it's ready. If you're already on my list, you'll get this automatically :).

Irresistible Bachelor Series (Interconnecting standalones):
Anaconda || Mr. Fiance || Heartstopper
Stud Muffin || Mr. Fixit || Matchmaker
Motorhead || Baby Daddy

Want to connect with Lauren Landish?
www.laurenlandish.com
admin@laurenlandish.com